SAVAGE

Mohinder Singh Sarna (1923–2001) moved to Delhi from Rawalpindi after the tumultuous partition of India, and joined the Indian Audit and Accounts Service in 1950. In a writing career spanning six decades, Sarna produced several volumes of poetry, short stories and novels, many of which have been widely translated into other Indian languages and made into telefilms. Sarna's work has received critical acclaim, and is prescribed in university syllabi in India and abroad. He was the recipient of the Sahitya Akademi Award, the Sahitya Kala Parishad Award, the Balraj Sahni Trust Award, the Nanak Singh Fiction Award on four occasions, the Katha Award, the Bhai Santokh Singh Poetry Award, the Giani Gurmukh Singh Poetry Award, the Sewa Sifti International Award, the Zehne Jadid Award, the Bawa Balwant Trust Award and the Waris Shah Samman. He was recognized as the Shiromani Punjabi Sahitkar by the Government of Punjab in 1989.

He was married to noted Punjabi translator and poetess Surjit Sarna.

Navtej Sarna is an Indian diplomat. He is the author of the novels *The Exile* and *We Weren't Lovers Like That*; the short-story collection *Winter Evenings*; the non-fiction works *The Book of Nanak* and *Folk Tales of Poland*; and a translation of Guru Gobind Singh's *Zafarnama*.

By the same author

IN PUNJABI

SHORT-STORY COLLECTIONS

Pathar de Aadmi
Shagnan Bhari Sver
Vanjali te Vilkani
Supnian di Seema
Kalinga
Chavian di Rut
Sundar Ghati di Saun
Sua Saloo Sua Gulab
Kala Badal Kali Dhup
Nawen Yug de Waris
Aurat Iman
Merian Chaunvian Kahanian
Gatha Gam de Marian di
Katal Panjan Panian da

NOVELS

Peerhan Male Rah
Kangan te Kanden
Neela Gulab
Sua Rang Majeeth da

EPIC POETRY

Chamkaur
Saka Jin Kiya
Paonta
Ab Jujhan ko Dao

AUTOBIOGRAPHY

Meri Sahitik Svaijeevni

SAVAGE HARVEST

STORIES OF PARTITION

MOHINDER SINGH SARNA

translated by Navtej Sarna

RUPA

Published by
Rupa Publications India Pvt. Ltd 2013
7/16, Ansari Road, Daryaganj
New Delhi 110002

Sales centres:
Allahabad Bengaluru Chennai
Hyderabad Jaipur Kathmandu
Kolkata Mumbai

ISBN: 978-81-291-2487-6

10 9 8 7 6 5 4 3 2 1

Printed at Parksons Graphics Pvt. Ltd, Mumbai.

Commentators and critics have appreciated my Partition stories more than my other stories. Perhaps this is because I passed through that cataclysm unprotected. I was an eyewitness to those massacres, those acts of fanaticism and barbarity. The blows of barbarism fell more on my soul than on my body. I saw the blood spurting from the jugular vein of humanity; I saw humanity sobbing as it breathed its last. It shook my faith in mankind and in life. Deep inside, my resolve and direction wavered and my ideals dimmed. The earth had slipped from under my feet, the universe seemed in disarray. Joys and smiles were wrapped up in a shroud and buried in the soul's grave. Stories and verse made no sense. I did not want to do anything, write anything, be anything.

—Mohinder Singh Sarna
Meri Sahitik Svaijeevni (1990)

To the defenders of humanity

Contents

Translator's Introduction

Sometime in the mid-seventies, when he was posted in Dehradun, Mohinder Singh Sarna—my father—received two letters from faraway Poland. The letters extolled some of his short stories that the letter writer had read in a magazine. Amazingly, they were written in Punjabi. Years later, when I was preparing to leave for my posting to Warsaw, we searched all over the house for those letters but without success. And yet I was able to home in on the correspondent within days of my arrival: he was the librarian at the Indology department in Warsaw University. A heart patient and a man of shy and retiring temperament, he was not someone who would come to diplomatic receptions. So I shared a cup of tea with him and his wife in his small Warsaw apartment, staring unbelievingly at the rows of books in Hindi and Punjabi on his bookshelves, including some early editions of my father's books. It was a moving and sentimental meeting, and one that pleased my father greatly when I wrote to him about it.

Chance encounters and conversations with readers, birthday wishes from people who had never met him, researchers dropping in to ask him about his work or letters of admiration from writers whom he respected—these were the kind of things that pleased him, much more than literary awards and honours. He did not move a finger to get any one of them and yet when he was honoured with them, including the Sahitya Akademi award—much later than he deserved—he accepted them with grace and humility. He was not an extrovert; networking, even literary networking, was alien to him. He hardly ever went to seminars or conferences and even less to literary soirées. Readers and critics wondered what kind of person he was, where he lived, what his age was and so on. Small talk did not come easily to him and he admitted that he did not know the first thing about public relations. I remember him looking at me with astonishment once when I mentioned the word 'contact'. I know that he kept no account of his royalties, such as they were, and I very much doubt that he ever signed a contract with a publisher. Yes, when the Sikh Publishing House, which had published his first four books, was shut down in the early fifties, the proprietors gave him, supposedly in lieu of royalties, a large number of hardback English classics, which became a treasured family collection. When I think of him writing, it is always leaning forward in his bed, over a foolscap sheet of paper clipped on to a clipboard that we used to take to our examinations, his small neat black letters progressing across the paper rhythmically and relentlessly: the stories would go straight from that clipboard to the publisher with virtually no revision. He also wrote extensively in his head, while sitting smilingly through conversations or on his long walks. As I grew up, I learnt to recognize these moments.

Writing was his first love and real calling. Even as a schoolboy he had delved deep into Punjabi poetry and prose from the treasure troves that had been collected by his father, who was passionately steeped in Sikh political and historical thought, as well as the cultural renaissance launched by the Singh Sabha movement in the early twentieth century. When the young Sarna joined Gordon College in Rawalpindi, he discovered English literature and began to collect leather-bound editions of the classics. Those beloved books, as well as Sarna's unpublished collection of poems, were all left behind in the panic of Partition. He never went back to Pakistan but yearned for those books; they appear in the short story 'A New Taj Mahal'.

When he got a job at the army headquarters in Delhi in pre-Partition India, this carefree bachelor threw himself into the literary life. Poetry soon led to short stories, which caught the eye of the celebrated Punjabi poet Prof. Mohan Singh, who proceeded to publish a large number of them in his journal *Panj Dariya* (*Five Rivers*) over a period of four or five years. When Sarna stopped over in Lahore to meet Mohan Singh, the poet remarked that the young man had obviously been influenced deeply by Russian writers—his characters had the stamp of Russian peasants. 'I have not read Russian writers,' Sarna told him, 'but now I surely will.' The well-thumbed volumes of Gorky's stories, bound in leather the colour of dried blood, that still lie on our bookshelves, are evidence of his determination.

When the partition of India intervened, accompanied by untold brutality and barbarism, the family was swept up as a helpless molecule in the whirlwind of riots, rape, pillage and killing. Sarna was holed up with his father and younger brother in Rawalpindi. The rest of the family lived from day to day as refugees in Delhi and there would never be word again of a newly-wed sister. He later recalled standing on the balcony of his beloved childhood home in Rawalpindi and watching the Pakistani flag unfurl on government buildings; he was a prisoner in his own house, even when India had achieved independence, unsure whether he would ever reach safety. A fortuitous turn of events got him a seat on a chartered plane and he left, taking only the Guru Granth Sahib with him.

Once in India, he travelled from Delhi to Amritsar in a vain attempt to charter a plane and get his father and brother out; they would manage to come only much later. He saw the same killing and brutality on this side of the border, the misery of refugee caravans going in both directions, the senseless vengeful violence. Faced with the responsibility of bringing up four younger brothers and three sisters, Sarna made a last-ditch effort to join the civil services, studying under a blanket in a crowded hospice near Paharganj. He joined the Indian Audit and Accounts Service in 1950 and spent the next three decades with it, writing during the time he could snatch away from his job in the evenings and on weekends.

He wrote extensively—several volumes of short stories, four novels and four volumes of epic poetry. His early work received instant critical acclaim and was prescribed in university courses. In contrast to his very early stories, everything that he wrote in his maturity contained a powerful social message. Influenced no doubt by the Russian writers as well as progressive Urdu writer Krishan Chander, he firmly believed that literature without a social purpose was worthless: a writer had a duty to decry depraved social practices, to expose the enemies of humanity and to nurture correct social and human values. His short stories in particular throw an uncompromising light on corruption, venality, and social and economic inequity. Employing satire with great dexterity, he exposed the rich and the shallow, the depraved and the greedy. He excoriated the social injustice and materialism that had replaced the idealism of early Independence. Among the most remarkable stories in this genre were 'Do Rotian' ('Two Chapattis'), 'Do Chandigarh' ('Two Chandigarhs'), 'Roti te Ishq' ('Food and Love') and 'Komagata Maru'. In several famous stories, such as 'Phanier' ('Cobra'), 'Heera Mrig' ('My Precious One') and 'Kutte di Zaat' ('The Caste of a Dog'), his satire acquires a biting edge when human behaviour falls far short of that of noble animals.

'Despite all this satire,' he wrote, 'I am not without hope. Hopelessness leads to death and destruction and it has never been my intention to put foot on that path. A writer who is without hope has no right to be satiric. I did not lose faith even when faced by the barbarity of Partition. My Partition stories pass knee-deep through the dark quicksand of blood and crushed bone, but they keep their head, on which they carry their bundle of hope, clearly above the quicksand. This hope is kept intact even in the whirlwinds of barbarity and brutality.'

In the present collection, you will meet many characters—Dina's wife in 'Savage Harvest', Hussain in 'A Defender of Humanity', Ramzan in 'Jathedar Mukand Singh', Abnash in 'The Parade', Sayida in 'A Woman's Integrity' and many others, who do not waver from the path of humanity even when the world around them is dissolving into chaos.

It is something of a miracle that Sarna managed to keep intact his hope in humanity in his treatment of the Partition. His poetic sensibilities had been brutalized by the barbarity that he had seen on both sides of the border. He must have managed to write away some of the pain and horror that he witnessed so close; the rest resulted in his nervous breakdown fifteen years later, partially reflected in the story 'Of One Community'.

When he did put pen to paper again after his recovery, it was to return to his first love—poetry. Deeply impacted in his youth by Kripa Sagar's epic, *Lakshmi Devi* (an adaptation of Walter Scott's *The Lady of the Lake*), and Mohan Singh's *Asia da Channan* (an adaptation of Edwin Arnold's *The Light of Asia*), he had nurtured a subconscious desire to write epic poetry based on Sikh history. As we sat around him in bed in the mid-sixties in cold Dehradun winters, warming our hands over a coal brazier, he began *Chamkaur*, depicting the historic battle between a band of forty Sikhs led by Guru Gobind Singh and a huge Mughal army in ringing ballads. Over the next decade, he wrote three more volumes of epic poetry. Together they make a monumental work, an unmatched depiction of major historic events in page after page of inspired verse.

The present collection of stories is only a small selection from his impressively varied and large oeuvre. But on the theme of Partition, these are his most powerful, most significant and well-known short stories, and those that he would have liked to include in such a collection.

Translating the stories of an author who was particularly well-regarded for the richness of his language and the nuance of his idiom was not an easy task, and I was often tempted to take the easy way out when faced with words and phrases that our generation of Punjabis has lost. One man kept me on the straight and narrow: Dr Jeevan Deol, who went through each story painstakingly and determinedly tried to bring me back to the original intention. I am hugely indebted to him for all his help and acutely aware that even his perseverance may not have been able to fully remove my own inadequacies.

Navtej Sarna
New Delhi

Savage Harvest

As he bent over the furnace stuffed with hard coal, Dina's iron-black body shone with the sheen of bronze; in fact he seemed to be moulded in bronze, resembling some statue of a healthy labourer. The muscles of his well-exercised torso rippled as he swung the hammer around his head, and a great blow fell on the red-hot bits of iron.

The blows continued to fall and echo. Immersed in his work, Dina was lost to the world until the hot sun of late August, streaming in through the open window, began to lick at his very bones. With a start, he looked out. Already the sun was at its height and his work was not even half done. He shut the window to keep out the heat but then found it difficult to breathe. A clammy sweat broke out on his forehead. It had rained furiously all night, as if the skies had opened up, and then continued to drizzle all morning. But now the sun shone brightly and a suffocating humidity had built up. He threw the window open again and bent over the furnace. The sweat was flowing down his ears on to his body in little rivulets. He wiped it off his forehead with his forearm. Thick drops fell on the fire. There was a little hiss and for a split second, a piece of coal found some relief.

He seemed to be on fire with the combined heat from the

sun and the furnace. This fire had dissolved into his blood and was now roasting the marrow of his bones. The sharp, roaring flames made his eyes burn. Every hair on his body had become a wick and it seemed to him that one of these wicks would catch fire any moment and blow up his body like a huge firecracker.

Suddenly he dropped his tools and went to the window. The sky was lit up by the screaming sharp sunshine. His eyes could not adjust to the brightness and he winced. When he could see, he gazed at the fields that spread far before him, and at the sandy path that cut through them and went all the way to the horizon like a straight white line. On the right of the path stood the cotton crop, and the puddles of water in the fields occasionally flashed silver. On the left, the ploughed furrows awaited the seed. The scent of the earth, wet from the recent rain, made him nostalgic and he wanted to jump out of the window. He wanted to roll in the fields and let the pores of his burning body soak in the moisture from the wet earth.

He loved the fields. During the sowing and harvesting, his blood would tingle and a strange freedom would enliven his limbs. He was the village blacksmith, but there wasn't much work for him in the village and he would spend a lot of time helping out the peasants in the fields. There wasn't a man in seven villages that could match him during the harvest or lift a larger load than him. Suddenly his hands yearned for the feel of a sickle.

Sickles, harvests, the sugar cane swaying gently in the moonlight. The call of the golden earth and the lilt in the songs born of this earth... He forgot, for a moment, that a hellish fire raged behind him and that for the last twenty days he had done nothing but mould metal into axes and spears. The season of sickles and scrapes had passed; this was the time of axes and spears. And it had been a strange harvest. Instead of the wheat, those who had planted it had been chopped up.

What kind of a mess had he gotten himself into? It was as if he was shouldering the entire responsibility of arming the warriors of the newly born Pakistan. Pakistan already existed, but to complete that reality it seemed necessary to kill all the Hindus and the Sikhs. He did not understand this fully, but this was what everybody said, from the village heads to the imams of mosques. And this jihad would succeed only if his furnace kept raging and spitting out fierce instruments of death.

He turned again to the fire. The sharp bits of metal in the furnace were brighter than the coals. His head began to swim. A sharp, hot pain rose inside him and he gripped his side. Hunger! He hadn't taken even a drop of water since the morning. Now hunger was ravaging his insides and thirst had turned his lips to wood.

'Oh! Bashir's mother!' he shouted towards the house. 'Give me water, quick.'

A woman of about forty-five brought water in a jug. She wore a nose ring and her silver earrings swayed as she walked. She stared at her husband. He was panting with thirst. She had offered him food and water three times already since the morning, but he hadn't responded and had continued to blow at his fire. What had made him think of food and water now? She looked at the torrid fire, at the bits of iron scattered all over the floor and at the evil pile of axes and spears. Then she stared at her husband's face for a long time, as if she didn't recognize him.

Dina drained the jug at a go.

'More,' he panted.

She brought more water and watched him as he drank.

'That's all,' he said.

The taut veins of his body and forehead relaxed. His breathing eased. And then a shadow of discomfort crossed his face.

'Why are you staring at me like that? Why don't you talk to me? And why do you stand away from me, as if I have the plague?'

She didn't reply. Instead she went into the house and brought him food.

'I'm talking to you,' Dina shouted, shaking her by the shoulders. 'Why don't you speak to me? Have you put rice to boil in your mouth that you can't speak?'

The woman remained silent. Dina tore at a roti and tried to swallow a few large mouthfuls. But the food wouldn't go down his throat. He took a few bitter gulps of water and pushed away the basket of rotis.

'Not talking to me, just staring as if I've been possessed by demons.'

'Allah forbid,' she said, 'but it does appear so to me.'

Dina's mouth fell open in surprise. He had lost all hope that Bashir's mother would ever speak, that she would break the stubborn silence of so many days.

When he recovered somewhat from his surprise, he said, 'I know what's on your mind, but what can I do? Your sons won't let me be. Now Bashir wants fifty axes ready by tomorrow night. He'll be at my neck if they aren't ready. I know you think otherwise but if I don't obey them they'll cut me into pieces.'

'Are they your sons or someone else's?' she asked, a little ashamed of her own question.

'Mine,' he replied, somewhat foolishly.

'Then should they fear you, or should you fear them?'

'You talk as if you don't know your own sons, what savages they are. Can I say anything to them? As if they wouldn't skin me alive...' said Dina.

'They are my sons, too.' His wife's tone was softer now. 'You know they shout at me and curse me. But I don't go making axes for them.'

'I only make the axes,' he replied. 'I don't kill people with them.'

'It's worse than killing,' she said. 'The killer kills one or two or at most, a handful of people. Each axe made by your hands kills dozens.'

A tremor passed through Dina's spine. Then this trembling touched every pore of his body. For a long time he was silent. And then, 'You are blaming *me*! Why don't you talk to your sons, the great warriors who burn two villages every night!'

'Nobody listens to me.' Her tone had grown even softer now. 'How can I tell anyone what to do? Everyone will have to answer for their own sins; why should I say anything to anyone?'

For some time, both of them stared at the floor, silently.

Suddenly the woman said, 'And why don't you eat your food? Do you want to starve?' She slid the basket in front of him.

A soft knock on the front door shook Dina. He stood up in fright. It must be Bashir or his companions. They had come to threaten him. He hesitated with his hand on the latch and looked around. The fire in the furnace was raging; everything was in place. He opened the door. Rusted with the season's rain, it screeched on its hinges.

He jumped back several steps in fear, just missing the furnace. His wife's face drained of blood and a scream escaped her lips. At the door stood the old wife of the Brahmin of the thakurdwar, a net of wrinkles spread across the turmeric powdered on her face. Her head of snow-white hair shook uncontrollably. Their eyes filled with fear, Dina and his wife stared at the old woman. She seemed to be alive, even though she was most certainly a ghost.

At long last, Dina's wife took courage and said, 'Aunt, you are still alive!'

The old woman did not reply. Dina's wife recalled that she had been hard of hearing. Perhaps the affliction had pursued her in death too. She went closer to the old woman and, loudly, repeated her question.

Understanding flashed in the old woman's eyes and she said,

'Can't you see that I am alive? Seven days was I racked with fever. There was no one to give me even a sip of water there. Tulsi has been away for many days. I could've died in his absence... One can go anytime... My fever went down today. I hardly had the strength to get up but somehow I have pushed myself till here. Why are the two of you staring at me so?'

The old woman was drenched in sweat from the effort of speaking and her breath came in uneven bursts. Holding her temples she sat down on the floor on her haunches. The light seemed to be fading in her pupils and every breath came as if it were her last.

Dina and his wife exchanged looks of immense relief. She really was the Brahmin's wife and not a ghost. The fever had saved her from the fate of the rest of the village. Her deafness had prevented her from hearing of the great sorrow that had befallen the village on Thursday night. She hadn't realized that her village was now in Pakistan. She did not know that Pakistan was now in her village. That not one Hindu or Sikh was alive except for a few girls in the hands of the rioters.

Suddenly the old woman asked, 'Dina, have you seen my goat anywhere?'

Goat, thought Dina, her goat! In these days, when the rioters had cooked and eaten even the looted cattle, this old woman was bothered about a goat?

'I don't know where she has run off to,' the old woman continued, 'and she's due. I can't even look after myself now. I can't go looking for her, and how can I catch her anyway? If you see her anywhere, tie her up, God bless you. You know she's due. I hope she doesn't give birth somewhere outside.'

Dina said, 'Old woman, your goat is not there. She has been eaten up and has been digested by now.' But the old woman heard nothing. He was about to repeat himself loudly but a glance from his wife silenced him.

'And look at this,' the old woman said, 'I found this chain near the door of the thakurdwar. I don't know how this goat managed to loosen the chain. This link, where the lock goes, has been eaten through and through. I thought I'll tell you to fix it for me.'

For some time, Dina's wife had been staring at the old woman in a strange manner. She seemed to be wrestling with something. And then, as if everything had suddenly become clear, she said, 'Aunt, why don't you stay here? You will be alone in the thakurdwar. And your fever has just abated. Cook your food here, and bring your own utensils, since you are a Hindu. Let Tulsi return, then you can return.'

The old woman seemed to have grown even more deaf. Maybe it was the effect of the fever. She only caught Tulsi's name.

'I'm telling you, he's gone out of the village. He's gone with Ram Shah's daughter's betrothal party to Nawachak. On the first of next month, Preeto is to be married. I told Shah to gift me a cow. It's not every day that there are celebrations in the houses of the rich. And you know, Tulsi needs the milk and the curds for his health.'

Ignoring the old woman's talk, Dina's wife was trying to catch her husband's eye. She wanted to say something but before she could, Dina was already speaking.

'I know what's on your mind, but we can't do it. I have no objection, but where will we hide her? Soon your sons will be here, their nostrils sniffing out human flesh, and we won't be able to conceal her. They will figure it out instantly, and what will they do to us then?'

'She's old,' beseeched Dina's wife, 'the last of our village's Hindus. A God-fearing old woman. It's only a matter of a few days. Let her son return and then we will send her to some other village.'

'Which village will you send her to?' Dina was almost screaming now. 'Is there a village left where she will be safe? And her son: he'll never return. This time he has been sent to a place from where there is no return. All the Hindus of Nawachak have been killed. Not one of them is left.'

His wife's face fell. She put a trembling finger to her lips, begging him to lower his tone. 'Can't you speak softly? Or won't you be satisfied until she knows that her son has been murdered?'

Except for Dina's outburst, they'd been talking in whispers. But it was unnecessary, for even their loudest tones would not have reached the old woman through her deafness. She stared at them with her fevered eyes.

'What are you two whispering away about? And Dina, why don't you look at me? Just repair this cursed chain. It's not that I'm asking for much.'

'Come tomorrow,' Dina shouted into the old woman's ear. 'I don't have any time today. And go home now.'

'All right,' the old woman croaked, putting her hands on her knees to steady herself as she rose. 'I'll go. If you say tomorrow, then let it be so, but keep an eye out for my goat. I've told you, just tie her up if you see her. Wretched thing. God knows where she has run away to.'

And before Dina's wife could stop her, the old woman had lurched out into the lane.

How much time this old woman had wasted, Dina fumed. He could have made five axes in this much time. And Bashir was not going to listen to any excuses; he would want his fifty.

But he could not put his heart into the work. Something began to gnaw at his heart. He could not dismiss the vision of fever-ridden eyes and snow-white hair. Those eyes were burning holes in his head like two red-hot embers. Most of all, it was her ignorance that bothered him. She knew nothing. That Tulsi was never to return, that Preeto was never to get married, that Bashir had already taken Preeto, along with her rich father's estate.

It was a rotten thing that Bashir had done. Defending the honour of the women of the village was a common burden. Everyone's daughters were just like your own. The loss of any woman's honour was a catastrophe for all.

A horrible scene appeared before his eyes—Preeto, wailing and clutching at her father's corpse; Bashir pulling her away by her hair. Imploring him, wailing and screaming, she had been dragged away. And then she had gone silent, just like a lamb in the moment before its slaughter.

And he, Bashir's father, had watched this evil sight unfold from the threshold. He had not stopped Bashir, or pulled him away by the scruff of his neck and thrown him on the ground. He had done nothing to save the honour of this daughter.

The pale, childlike face of Preeto began to swim before his eyes and her plaintive cries echoed in his ears. He was seized by a shiver, a cold and uncontrollable shiver that seemed a precursor to certain death. The shivering, he felt, could be stopped only if he picked up the red-hot iron from the fire and clasped it against his heart. But why was his head on fire? The entire blazing furnace seemed to have entered his head. He pressed his head with both hands and the fire came on to his palms.

He was going mad. He would end up doing something terrible. He must run away, far away from all this. He opened the window and jumped out.

For a long time he wandered aimlessly in the fields. The afternoon had now become evening. On the horizon, someone had murdered the sun. The blood of innocents had spread across the sky and had dissolved into the waters of the streams and canals. Would anybody eat the sugar cane that had been sprayed with blood? Or wear the cotton which had been irrigated by blood? What kind of wheat would grow in this blood-drenched soil? And what kind of a harvest would it be after this bloody season? The shower of blood that had reddened everything had been caused by the axes he had fashioned. This crop of bones and flesh had been sown by spears made by his hands. And he had just finished making axes for the handful of villages that were still left. Those, too, would be gone by tomorrow night.

He was guilty. Heavily, deeply guilty. Bashir's mother had been right. At least he should not let them lay their hands on the new axes. His sins would not be wiped out even if he prevented that. But what else could he do?

And then he started running, like a man possessed, towards the village. He wanted to reach home before Bashir's men. He wanted to throw the axes in some well or canal from where they would never be found.

When he reached the village, it was dark. The indifferent light of a hazy moon threw faint shadows on to the lane. The previous night's rain had left a muddy slush everywhere. Again and again his feet caught in the thick slush, but he kept walking quickly through the lanes. Suddenly he stopped. He could hear voices coming from a short distance. In fact, they were coming from his house. Had they already come, then? Was he too late? He could clearly hear Bashir's vulgar laughter.

He stumbled against some heavy object near his house and fell on his face. He tried to get up, but couldn't. An icy-cold grip had clasped his feet. He tried to free them but the grip only seemed to get tighter. A terrible fear clutched at his heart and a cold sweat covered his forehead. With a strong jerk, he turned to look back. In the dim moonlight, he saw a thatch of white hair rippling in the wind. The old woman's wrinkled forehead bore a long gash from an axe. And there was a curse in the wide open, frightened eyes. He looked at his feet. They were caught in the chain that was entangled around her forearms.

He screamed once and fainted. That night he was gripped by a high fever. All night he tossed wildly on the bed; all night his delirious shouts echoed in the silence of the village.

'Don't kill me, don't kill me with those axes! Get this chain off my neck! Oh, my daughter! Don't harm my daughter! Don't harm Preeto! Oh, these chains! In Allah's name, don't use those axes! Don't kill me!'

A New Taj Mahal

I ran into the young Englishman again as I stepped out of Rawalpindi station. We had travelled in the same compartment from Amritsar to Lahore and got along very well, despite our differences of age, country and community. Occasionally we had got lost in our separate reveries but whenever we emerged from them, we had begun to talk like old friends.

The Amritsar–Lahore Express on which we'd travelled had restarted the rail connection between India and Pakistan after about eleven years. Much had happened in these eleven years. Two wars had spilt blood needlessly on the soil of the subcontinent, opening up fresh cuts even before the wounds left by the Partition riots had healed. Then the Simla Agreement was signed. Prisoners of war returned home. The taut strings that held our hearts eased a bit and calls for friendship began to be heard on both sides. Then the embassies opened, and one blessed morning the Amritsar–Lahore Express performed its maiden journey as the vanguard of friendship and cooperation.

The young Englishman and I were among the 151 passengers who had boarded that train. With bursting hearts and moist eyes, a large and happy crowd had seen us off at Amritsar station. Another crowd had been waiting at Attari station, laden with good wishes.

There was a crowd outside, and a crowd within: a crowd of yearnings that the handful of passengers had brought with them. There were fathers who were going to meet their sons after years, grandmothers who were going to see grandchildren born in the last fifteen years for the first time and brothers who treasured within their hearts the intense desire to see their sisters, nephews and nieces. America and Canada had become accessible, while this country just across the Ravi may as well have been on another planet.

My eyes had been yearning to see this land across the Ravi. When the train left Attari station, a strange sudden ache rose in my heart. There was a large stretch of uncultivated land between Attari and Wagah that belonged to neither India nor Pakistan. This was what is called 'No Man's Land' in the language of international relations, a place to which no man can lay claim. But what if roses could be planted on this land, roses of a thousand colours and a thousand varieties? Yellow, touched with the first ray of dawn; white, unspoilt virgin white; crimson, like some bride's festive dupatta; and then those roses that can only be seen in dreams. There was a valley of flowers in the Himalayan heights; if only another valley of flowers could bloom between Attari and Wagah, a unique fragrance would spread through the subcontinent.

The young Englishman's question had woken me from my scent-filled reverie. He wanted to know why I was going to Pakistan.

'I'm going to see the city of my dreams,' I replied. 'Rawalpindi, where I was born, in whose lanes I spent my childhood and youth.'

'I, too, am going to Rawalpindi,' he said happily. 'From there I will go to Murree.'

'It's a fine hill station, Murree,' I said, glowing with childhood memories.

'I am going to see my grandfather's grave there. He was Colonel Smith, commandant of the 7th Baloch regiment.'

'It is touching that you have such regard in your heart for your grandfather. Evidently, the new generation in the West has not forgotten to respect its elders.'

'I was only going to see the Taj Mahal. But before I departed my grandmother insisted that I should also visit Pakistan and put flowers at my grandfather's grave.'

'How nice that you should have such regard for your elderly grandmother's wish.'

The welcoming crowd at Lahore had been larger than the crowds at Amritsar and Attari. We were to change trains at Lahore, and in the process we lost each other and the young Englishman ended up in another compartment. But I ran into him again as I stepped out of Rawalpindi station. He waved and smiled as he put his bags into a taxi. He told me that he was going straight from the station to Murree.

I didn't take a taxi but hailed a fine Peshawari tonga instead. I wanted to enjoy the beloved lanes and streets of my city properly from the back of the gently swaying tonga. I asked the driver to stop and wait for me at the last turning in Raja Bazaar, then I stepped into the shoe shop that used to have a board announcing 'Flex Shoe Co.' but was now called 'Frontier Boot House'.

On seeing me, the owner of the shop, who had been sipping his tea, started and stood up. He was wearing a white cotton salwar and a silk kameez with silver buttons. He was fair-complexioned with a full face and thick lips, and his receding hairline made his forehead look unnaturally broad.

'Today I've come to this shop after about twenty-eight or twenty-nine years,' I said as I sat down on the cushioned bench. 'I would like to meet Abdul Rahim sahib.'

A shadow passed over his face as he replied, 'My father has passed away.'

'May Allah grant heaven to his soul,' I said by way of condolence. 'You look like your father. When I saw him last, he must have been about the same age as you are now. When I stepped in here I was almost certain that it was him sitting here, as if these twenty-eight years had not passed, as if time had come to a standstill at this shop.'

'I'm delighted to meet you,' he said. 'My name is Sabir Hussain. And yours?'

I told him my name and began to take my wallet out of my pocket. 'Actually I've come to repay an old debt. In August '47, I bought a pair of shoes from your shop and promised to pay on the first of the following month. But before that date, I had to leave the city.'

His mouth fell open and he glanced disapprovingly, first at me and then at the money in my hand. When he was able to speak again, his voice betrayed his emotion.

'You're no stranger to this shop. I would be highly obliged if you put the money back in your wallet.'

'How can that be? I've carried the burden of this debt on my conscience for so many years. I want to be free of it.'

'But I cannot take this money. If my father had been alive, he too would not have accepted it.'

Somewhat embarrassed, I put the money back into the wallet.

His face eased and he said, 'Now tell me how I can serve you.' Glancing at the worn-out shoes on my feet, he continued, 'Size eight, I'd say. I've got a fine Italian shoe in kid leather in size eight.'

Despite my remonstrations, he made me wear the shoes. They were such a marvellous pair, gripping my feet so perfectly that I couldn't have taken them off even if I had tried. I had been searching for such a pair for many years, but had been unable to find it anywhere in Delhi.

'These I will pay for. You'll have to accept money for these.'

'Certainly, but not in money. With love. This pair was not intended for sale. It was meant to be a gift for a loving customer like you.'

I saw that an assistant had brought in a tray with tea, a cake and pastries.

'If you want to pay for the shoes, then you can do so by accepting this tea, which Shafiq has already brought without my asking,' said Sabir Hussain.

After finishing tea, I hugged Sabir Hussain and Shafiq in farewell and invited them to visit Delhi. I told the waiting tonga-driver to take me straight to Teli Mohalla, where my childhood friend Abdul Sattar used to live.

Rawalpindi's Teli Mohalla was famous not for its oil-dealers, as its name would suggest, but because of its spinning tops. What wondrous things these were can only be realized by those who have spun them in their childhood. To others it may seem an exaggeration that those spinning tops, the round ones and the flat ones, would spin for at least fifteen or twenty minutes with a single pull of the string. They would appear to be perfectly still for ten minutes or more, almost as if they had fallen asleep, when in fact they would be spinning at their fastest. There were five or six families of Muslim artisans in Teli Mohalla who would fashion these tops out of rosewood blocks on their lathes, fix steel needles in them and decorate them with German colours.

I had loved these tops since my childhood and, though I hadn't played with them after my schooldays, I had always praised them sky-high to my children. One major reason behind my close friendship with Abdul Sattar had been the fact that his father and grandfather were master artisans whose spinning tops were impossible to beat. I would often stop in Teli Mohalla on my way back from school and spend hours watching Abdul's father and grandfather create their colourful marvels at the lathe.

When I reached Abdul Sattar's house, I saw his grandfather busy at the lathe where a beautiful round spinning top was taking shape.

'*Salaam aleikum*, Grandfather.'

The old man lifted his head from his lathe and I realized my mistake. It was not Abdul Sattar's grandfather but rather his father, who had grown as old as his own father in the last thirty years.

'Do you recognize me?'

The old man stared at me through his thick spectacles. From the glassy look in his eye I could make out that he'd probably had surgery for cataract.

'No,' he said softly, shaking his head.

'I am Sattar's classmate. I used to come to your house as a child.'

I saw darkness descend over the old man's eyes. He switched off the lathe and motioned me to sit down on a cane stool with his trembling hand.

'Where is Sattar?' I asked.

The old man looked at me once. Then his eyes began to wander in all directions. His eyes fell on the half-finished spinning top and he started the lathe again. It was as if he had forgotten all about my question and, in fact, my existence.

Finally the spinning top popped out of the lathe like a seashell from the mouth of a serpent. He hammered a brass nail into its smooth body and placed the shiny red top in my hands.

'Where is Sattar?' I repeated my question.

He shook his hand as if to say, 'He isn't here any more,' and looked down at the ground. Something broke inside me, and I got up from the stool and sat in front of him.

'What are you saying?' I asked, putting a hand on his shoulder. 'Doesn't he live with you? Has he abandoned you at this age?'

The old man raised his finger towards the roof. An abyss opened up inside me.

'Sattar has gone to Allah. In the battle of Chhamb in '71. People say he became a martyr. Whatever, as long as it pleases God.'

I sat stock-still for a long time holding his trembling hands in mine. I couldn't say a word in the face of his bottomless grief.

Then the bamboo screen over the back door moved and a boy of about fourteen came in. He had wide innocent eyes and curly hair. For a moment I felt I was a child again and Abdul Sattar was standing in front of me.

'All he's left me as a legacy is this boy,' the old man said. 'May Allah grant him a long life.'

I got up and hugged the boy and kissed him on the forehead. On my asking, he told me that his name was Sayadat and he was studying in class nine.

That night I ate at the house of Abdul Sattar and slept there.

The flat roof was bathed in moonlight. Staring at the faint stars I was lost for a long time in memories of the old days. I must have fallen asleep sometime after midnight. As soon as that happened, Abdul Sattar came and stood next to me. Both pockets of his jacket were stuffed with spinning tops. We roamed around Paharganj bazaar and bummed around Khari Baoli and Chandni Chowk, but there was no place for us to spin our tops. Finally we began to spin them on the platform of Delhi railway station. A crowd of coolies and passengers formed a circle around us. Abdul Sattar tried all his tops, the flat ones and the round ones, but my shining red top beat them all. Soundly defeated, Abdul Sattar said, 'Never mind! Even a dog behaves like a lion in his own lane. Come some day to Teli Mohalla in 'Pindi, and I will take your measure.'

I had come today to Teli Mohalla in 'Pindi, but the man who was to take my measure had himself vanished many years ago.

The next morning I took Sayadat with me and roamed around the bazaars and lanes, the gardens and walkways of the city. It was late afternoon when I found myself outside the house where I'd been born, and where I'd spent the first twenty years of my life. Knocking on the door, I experienced a strange feeling, as if at that moment someone was knocking on the door of my heart.

An elderly man opened the door, and I was struck at first sight. The prayer beads in his hand, his white beard, his dress and his personality all pointed to his decent and God-fearing nature.

'You!'

He couldn't say anything more than that, so startled was he to see a turbaned and bearded man standing at his door.

'Yes. I've come from Delhi to meet you.'

He kept looking at me in silence.

'Yes, I have come to meet you,' I repeated in a hesitant tone, 'and to see this house of yours where I have spent my childhood, teenage years, college days and my youth.'

'Your name?' he asked.

I told him my name.

'You are a poet,' he said.

'No,' I replied. 'I mean, yes. In a way. But how do you know?'

A mysterious smile appeared on his lips as he continued, 'You're welcome. Please do come in. This is your own house.'

A grey-haired woman peeped in from the bedroom and then vanished behind the door.

'Shabir's mother!' the old man called out. 'Come see! A poet has come to visit us from Delhi.'

'What are you saying?' I pleaded, nearly frantic. 'I'm not a poet or anything. Not of any standing. Nobody knows me as a poet.'

The mysterious smile appeared again on his lips, and he said, 'We know.'

By this time the lady had tidied her loose hair and covered her head with a thick muslin dupatta. I joined my hands in greeting and bowed towards her as she stepped out into the courtyard.

'May you live a long life, son,' she said, both her hands raised in blessing.

I don't know what magic there was in her blessing that my eyes filled with tears.

A young man of about twenty and an innocent-looking girl of sixteen or seventeen emerged from the other room. The young man stepped forward and shook my hand. He was a fair and good-looking youth, with an air of clean freshness about him.

'That's my youngest son, Naeem,' the old man said. 'He is studying for his MA. And this is my granddaughter Naheed, the daughter of my eldest son Shabir. He has a business in Chakwal, but she stays with us. She is doing her Senior Cambridge at the Convent School in the cantonment. And meet him,' he said to them. 'He is a poet from Delhi and the real owner of this house.'

I was slowly realizing that the elderly man was bent on dragging me through the thorns that day.

Naheed was greeting me. I saw that her face was like a bright lotus and her eyes had the glow of a narcissus. She looked towards me and smiled in a manner that reminded me of my daughter.

'On seeing them,' I said, 'this house seems doubly lit up.'

'There, you see, you have spoken like a true poet,' the old man said, 'even as you remonstrate against being called one.'

I stayed silent. If he was happy in calling me a poet, I didn't want to snatch that joy away from him.

'Come then.' He led me by the hand to what had once been my bedroom. 'Let's put the evidence of your poetry into your own hands. We have guarded your possessions for many years. Today God has given us a chance to return it.'

What I saw upon entering the room was nothing short of a miracle. The books I had bought thirty years ago were arranged in a very orderly fashion in my bookcase. Their firm bindings and golden titles showed that someone had taken care of them lovingly and not let even a speck of the dust of negligence settle on them.

Shabir's mother picked out a key from the bunch hanging from the corner of her dupatta and opened the bookcase. On the bottom two shelves lay a treasure trove of Punjabi books, tracts, magazines and newspapers. These contained the writings of Bhai Vir Singh, old issues of *Khalsa Samachar* and *Phulwari*, and editions of Bhai Charan Singh's newspaper *Mauji*. My father had gathered together this literary and cultural storehouse, and it was from poring over it that I had developed an interest in writing in Punjabi.

The old man was speaking. 'When we came ravaged from Amritsar to this house, we found it ravaged too. Only these books remained, and they too were strewn, upside down, half-open all over the floor. The looters might have gone through each book in the hope of finding hidden currency notes. Whether they found them or not I don't know, but they left the books behind. These books held no value for them.'

Naheed said, 'Grandfather, those who value books aren't capable of looting another's house.'

My lips were silent, but my hand spoke to bless Naheed.

Shabir's mother took a notebook with a brown plastic cover from the middle shelf and started wiping it with her dupatta even though it was already spotless. Then, handing me the notebook she said, 'Here, son, here's your poetry.'

I began to cry. This was the manuscript of my first poetry collection. Most of the poems were from my college days.

The old man patted my back and said, 'Now let's have some tea.'

When we went into the other room to have tea, I saw an even bigger miracle. Our family photographs were still on the wall—just as they were hanging when we had fled the house. We had missed these photographs so much over the past thirty years. Among them was one of my grandfather in a golden frame, which had been especially dear to my father.

My eyes were going from wall to wall, and my head was spinning. I couldn't get a hold on myself for a long time. All I wanted was to be alone somewhere and cry to my heart's content.

In the evening when I went to Abdul Sattar's house to pick up my baggage, his father handed me a heavy khaki cloth bag. I saw that it was full of spinning tops in every colour.

'What's this?'

'For your son, a gift from 'Pindi.'

'I only have one son. What will he do with so many tops?'

'Never mind. May God give him a long life.'

I was to catch the night train. Sayadat saw me off at the station. When I changed trains at Lahore station and boarded the Lahore–Amritsar Express, the young Englishman was sitting in the same compartment as before.

I asked after his grandfather's grave. When he had finished telling me about it I said, 'It just so happens that I visited a grave too.'

'Which grave?' he asked with some surprise.

'The grave of India–Pakistan enmity.'

Seeing disbelief in his eyes I continued, 'Yes, yes, I'm telling the truth. I have seen this enmity buried with my own eyes. And that day is not far when we will construct a new Taj Mahal on the grave of this enmity in the valley of flowers between Wagah and Attari.'

❧

A Village called Laddewala Varaich

The village square was desolate. The approaching twilight drew a sheet of mourning over it. The trees beyond the village stood sad and bereft, as if the life had been drained out of them. From the dungheap near the pond, a dog raised a howl that went around the village like a loud, long dirge and then sank back on to the dungheap. A vulture rose from the trees and, barely able to carry its heavy, well-fed body, slowly wheeled away into the darkness. From the direction of the mosque, the ill-omened owl hooted its invitation to the night. In another instant, the twilight deepened into night and fell over the village like the canopy of death. A weak, pale moon began to lurch across the sky like some woman possessed by a wayward spirit.

A shadow moved under the banyan tree. It peeled itself away from the darkness of the square and slowly took on a human form as it moved into the moonlit open. A hoary head lifted from hunched shoulders and looked up into the sky. The sickly moonlight picked up the tears in the henna-dyed beard and the web of wrinkles that covered the pallid face. Then the head fell back on the man's chest, as if his neck had suddenly snapped.

The old man cast a yearning look at the village. He brushed away the tears that filled his eyes and sighed.

Yes, it was true that it was all over. But he, Khuda Bakhsh Varaich, the old choudhry of the village, its guardian, was still alive. How well had he guarded the village! How well had he lived up to the responsibilities of a headman! His village, the village settled by his forefathers on the paved road from Hafizabad to Pindi Bhatian, the village called Laddewala Varaich, had become a cremation ground and he was still alive like a stubborn stump of wood that refuses to burn.

He held his head in both hands and heaved another sigh.

All his desperate efforts had failed. He had dragged himself through the neighbouring Muslim villages, begged and beseeched the headmen to listen to him for the sake of his white beard, for the sake of the Prophet. He had put the honour of his ancestors at their feet. But they had all turned him away—the Qazis of Qazi da Kot, the Maans of Maani, the Gujjars of Qila Mian Singh, the Dogars of Kotli, the Gondals of Gondlanwala... They had called him an enemy of Pakistan and a murderer of believers.

A young man of Gondlanwala had grabbed his beard.

'Why are you bent on dying, old man? Come to your senses and be on your way, or else...' the young man had threateningly raised his axe.

'Finish him off,' another man had shouted.

'Get rid of him. Why are you dragging this on?'

'That's right,' an old Gondal had screamed. 'If he doesn't feel for his brothers, what are we saving him up for? The Khatris of Amritsar are chewing up Muslims like bits of sugar cane. Our sisters and daughters who were never seen out of purdah are being raped in the bazaars and this man is going around behaving like the infidels are born of his sister.'

He hadn't understood all that they said, but his head had been seized by a sudden trembling and his few remaining dark hairs had turned white instantly. Dragging his weary legs, he had returned to his village. In all his years, never had he felt so worn out.

He had got wind of the plan. They would come on Thursday night. The Baths, Chimnis, Maans, Gondals and Dogars had all got together. They had mopped off the smaller villages and, coming Thursday, after the late afternoon prayers, they would beat the drum and descend on this village from all directions.

Desperately he had rushed from house to house, telling everyone he could of the planned attack. He had explained his helplessness to the villagers and begged them to leave the village before Thursday evening. He had helped them tie up their bundles, dismantle their cots and pack them, and stitch up sacks full of kitchen utensils. He had negotiated with the potters to sell donkeys at reasonable prices to those who did not have horses to carry their things. Then he had blessed the women of the families, bolstered up the spirits of the young men and, holding back his tears, bidden farewell to the old men, apologizing for not being able to do anything to help them.

But one of his own people, a Varaich of his village, had let the word out and it had all come to nought.

Now the whole wretched thing was over. Vultures were circling over his village, and he was still alive.

The dog got up from the dungheap and, walking up to him, began to roll at his feet. The choudhry ignored him. Letting out another long howl, the dog ran away towards the fields.

The old man turned his head away and sighed again.

Yes, even the dog knew. Even the dog was scared of going towards the village where happy homes had been burnt to ashes; where painted cots, spinning wheels and carved stools were still smouldering; where half-burnt human bodies lay rotting; where in the corners of houses and in ditches in the lanes lay pathetic piles of old bones; and where, in the doorway of the thakurdwar, a handsome young man lay on his side, his intestines pulled out by some sharp, hooked weapon.

It seemed to the old man that the shrieks and wails of the dying had merged into the slogans of 'Pakistan Zindabad'. By Allah's grace, Pakistan had been formed in his village too. Here, too, the believers and the Qaid-e-Azam had taken over.

Gripped by a deep fear, he began to follow the dog towards the fields. His beard trembled under the pale, sickly moon and fresh tears stained his cheeks. He did not know where he was going.

At the edge of the first field, he stumbled against a heavy object and fell forward on his face. It was a corpse lying face down. He turned it over and, pressing down on the elbows and knees, straightened the rigid limbs. It was the body of a young boy, no more than ten or eleven. He peered closely at the face. It was the son of Chanda Singh Jat. With his fair skin, round face and light hair that now shone like gold in the moonlight, the boy used to be called 'Sahib' by the villagers, as if he were an Englishman. To celebrate his birth, the father had arranged dances in the village and gifted everyone twenty-one rupees and a pot of halwa. And now, the only son of that proud father was lying dead at the edge of a field. His turban lay where it had fallen, covered with grime, and across his forehead was a long cut from an axe. Dried blood had glued his light hair to his temples.

The choudhry tied the boy's turban around his own waist. Then he locked his hands around the boy's body and, with a strong heave, threw him over his shoulder. He began to walk across the fields, circling the village towards the brick house that Chanda Singh Jat had built behind the madrasa, some way from the village.

For a long while, he stood outside the house. The place was

enveloped in deathly silence. He felt everything die inside him. He had been wrong. Even this isolated house had not escaped the blood-crazed mob. Still, he knocked on the door. A faint whisper could be heard inside the house. A thin hope lit up his face. There was someone still alive in there. He put his lips to the crack in the door and said in a loud whisper, 'Unlatch the door, daughter. It's only me, Khuda Bakhsh.'

There was a long sigh of relief. Someone raised the flame in the lantern. He could sense the light coming nearer to the cracks in the door. But the hand on the latch still hesitated.

'It's only me, daughter. There is no one with me.'

The door opened. The light from the lantern hit him in the face.

A bewildered Nand Kaur, Chanda Singh Jat's widow, quickly latched the door behind him and followed him into the house. Her fifteen-year-old daughter, Jagiro, stood at the kitchen door, her dusky face turned to the wall.

The light fell on the face of the dead boy. Sobs tore through Jagiro. Nand Kaur wailed and beat her breast.

'Courage, my daughters, courage. I feel your pain. Crying and wailing is of no use. You are not alone in your suffering. Not one of our people has survived here. Somehow, you two have escaped their notice. That is why you're still alive. Why was this boy outside anyway?'

'It was I, the wretch, who sent him to the well to bring back the cattle,' sobbed Nand Kaur. 'If only I had known, my son. I felt it in my guts yesterday when I heard the gunshots. Curse me, my son, damn me. Why did I ever send you?'

The old man bit his lip and swallowed his tears.

'Now, don't make too much noise,' he said roughly, 'or they'll come rushing here, and you know them well. Even these walls have ears. We have nurtured snakes among us; otherwise, we would not have come to such a pass.'

The old man's tears had taken the edge off his voice.

'Look, I'm telling you that it's no use wailing and crying. No good is going to come of it. You must leave this house now, before someone remembers you and they come here, slithering and hissing. I would gladly take you to my house, but they'll definitely find out and then you will meet the same fate as the others.'

The old man fell silent, thinking. He could hear his heart beating loudly in his chest. He opened the door and peeped out. The night was dark and desolate. From somewhere near the mosque, the owl's hoots still pierced the silence.

Relieved, he latched the door and returned to the room. The woman was looking at him, wide-eyed. Her daughter was still sobbing uncontrollably, her head bent over her knees. The choudhry put a trembling hand on Jagiro's head and raised her face. Then quickly blinking back his tears, he sat down.

His tone turned rough again when he spoke.

'Why don't you listen instead of just staring at me? Listen to me, pack up whatever you need. I'll take you to a Sikh village during the night. Let's not waste any more time.'

He continued to speak, as if he were talking to himself in a dream, his eyes fixed on the floor.

'That's it, what else? I can't think of anything else. I'm just an old man and they are running all over me. The riff-raff of my own clan, those whom I've brought up with my own hands now stare at me with murder in their eyes. See, one of them went and squealed to the Gondals... As I was saying, from there you can join a refugee caravan. You'll be able to cross the border. You'll find room in a camp in Amritsar. And who knows, by then these people may have come to their senses and you could return and live in your own house again.'

He stopped. The woman was staring at her dead son, as if she had heard nothing. Khuda Bakhsh sat silently, his head hunched over his shoulder, until she turned to him. Then he spoke again. 'We'll take the boy with us. We won't leave him here. On the way there is a well that belongs to the Varaichs. There's no one there; they're all away, killing and looting. We'll cremate him there.'

His tone was sleepy now, and the same drowsiness seemed to envelop his entire being as they left the village. His unsteady steps seemed to sway across the path. Every few minutes Nand Kaur would start, fearing that her dead son would fall to the ground.

But the old man's grip on the dead boy was firm and he walked slowly and cautiously. At the slightest sound, he would freeze and they would move into the shadow of a tree, holding their breath like frightened fledglings. And then they would move hurriedly from the shadow of one tree to another, always trying to escape the moon.

Khuda Bakhsh stopped suddenly near the grave of the Bonga Pir. Not more than ten steps from them, against the side of the grave, some men were lying on the ground. They were facing the other way and had not yet seen them. The three of them sat down right there, at the edge of the field. Their path passed by the side of the grave; the levelled fields, prepared for seeding, glistened under the moon and offered no cover. A cold sweat broke out on the choudhry's brow. He could feel the eyes of the woman and her daughter searching his face for an answer.

Then his face relaxed and he felt he could breathe again. Wiping his forehead he said, 'They are our own people and they are dead. See, they don't move, they don't speak or turn.'

As they passed the corpses, Jagiro screamed and clung to her mother.

'Save your screams, girl!' the old man said sharply. 'There are enough ears to hear you. Just follow me quietly and don't look left or right.'

They had left the village behind and even passed the well of the Cheema clan. The orphaned fields around them, meticulously prepared and ploughed, waited for the seed but their owners had forgotten all about them. Here and there patches of water shone like silver amid the first green shoots of paddy. The sugar cane stood knee-high. In another month or so it would be ready for harvesting. Then the air would be sweet with the fragrance of fresh jaggery, and on every hearth, pots of rice would be cooked in sugar cane juice and eaten joyously. The occasional cotton bud had already started flowering. The following month, groups of young girls would be there, carrying baskets and bags. They would compete with each other to pick the cotton. At night there would be gatherings in every house. The girls, themselves slim as young branches, would card and spin the cotton. And all the time the sweetness of their songs would entice and enchant, and play havoc with the hearts of men.

But this year the month of 'sawan' had been a strange one. It had frightened life into silence. And now, in 'bhadon', someone had gone and murdered all the songs with axes.

The sound of loud laughter rose from the well of the Varaich clan. Then someone began to sing tunelessly in a wavering voice. A few men were drinking and gossiping around the well. The old man and his companions left the path and stepped down, bending low.

The singing stopped.

'Stop staring. There isn't a soul out there.'

'No, brother. I saw the sugar cane move. I think I glimpsed a violet dupatta too.'

'Ha! You see dupattas even in your dreams! Hand me the pan. This is what I call Pakistan brand. I swear by the Qaid-e-Azam, you'll forget all your foreign bottles.'

'I'll be back, brother. Just let me check out these girls first. They may be of use to us and help us pass the night well.'

Their lives hung by the thinnest of threads as they lay down amidst the sugar cane. The approaching heavy footsteps fell like hammer blows on their hearts. Someone caught Jagiro's dupatta and dragged her out. Old Khuda Bakhsh leapt to his feet.

'Old man, you too? And who are these girls?'

'They are ours, young man. My daughters.'

'Well done, old geezer! Trying to fool me? This fair, soft girl is certainly a daughter of Khatris; that old crone may well be yours. Why don't you speak, sweetie? What's your name? And you, old man, what are you doing fooling around with young girls in the fields at night?'

Choudhry Khuda Bakhsh took off his turban and put it at the young man's feet. The sight of his white hair seemed to touch off some memory in the young man's mind.

'Aren't you the one who came to our village? I should have finished you off then. You haven't mended your ways, I see.'

Khuda Bakhsh recognized the young Gondal who had grabbed him by the beard and threatened him with his axe.

'Let's be on our way, little lamb. If your mother wants to mess around with this old man, let her. You're crying? No, no, my darling, come with me. I'll buy you some candy.'

Jagiro screamed and shrunk back in terror.

'I'm with you, my young thing. Move on now.' With that, the young man shoved his knee into Jagiro's waist. Nand Kaur was at his throat in an instant.

'You want to come along too, old woman? I'm not in the business for old nags. I think I should finish you off right here, or you could become a problem.'

He pushed the woman to the ground and raised his axe with both hands. Khuda Bakhsh ran towards him. The axe caught the old man at the hip and he fell.

When he came to his senses, a faint light had just touched the sky in the east. A cool breeze caressed his bare head. The soft fragrance of the sugar cane comforted him. If only he didn't have this red-hot iron stuck in his side... And why was he lying face down in the cane? Was that a thick keekar branch hanging low over him or was it the arm of Death itself?

He was burning with thirst, dying for a sip of water. The well was not far away. It was his own well. Only last month, he had fixed a new wheel and changed all the cans that brought up the water. Where were his servants now? He, the owner of the well, was lying thirsty and they could not even get him a cupful of water. Lazy, ungrateful wretches.

And on that pole was hanging the salwar of his granddaughter, little Salma... How many times had he told the stubborn girl not to wash her clothes at the well but the wretch just wouldn't stop... No, but this was the salwar of Jagiro, the daughter of Chanda Singh Jat... Yes, of course, Jagiro was Salma. They looked so damned alike; it was difficult to tell them apart.

The little salwar, the salwar of a fifteen-year-old, was beginning to grow in his vision. The little green plants embroidered on it became huge, brooding trees. Countless salwars were hanging all around him. In the fields, on the parapets, on the hedges and even on the keekar above his head. They swayed in the wind; they caught in the thorns and were torn to shreds.

His own children had destroyed him. They had trampled on his old bones and rubbed his white beard into the dust. His disgrace was visible everywhere. There was a time when people didn't dare to look him in the eye. And now his sons and grandsons had raised their axes against him. There was no point in living any more.

Barely conscious, he held his waist and staggered to his feet. He tossed one end of his turban over the keekar branch. With tight knots he fashioned a noose and, jumping up, put it around his neck.

The sun came up. The birds began to chirp in the trees. A corpse hung from the keekar tree in the sugar cane field. Its still pupils were fixed on a village in the distance, which the dead man's forefathers had built on the paved road that ran from Hafizabad to Pindi Bhatian. A village called Laddewala Varaich.

Basant the Fool

As I sat down to eat langar at Gurdwara Bangla Sahib, a face in the next row caught my attention. A sad, tragic face, with a soiled, threadbare dupatta wrapped around it. Pain had carved deep cracks into the forehead, the eyes were worn out from too much crying and grief had settled deep into the parched lips. It was a familiar, troubling face but I could not place it. However much I tried to chase the image of that face out of my mind, I couldn't help but feel that I had heard, or perhaps read, the tragic tale etched out in its desolate features somewhere.

I had to be wrong, surely. Where could I have seen this poor woman before? All sad faces look alike, I told myself; all sorrows reflect the same shade. All tragic tales are told in the same voice, the same tone.

And then with the swiftness of lightning, all at once, the face fixed itself in my memory. This was the face of Basant's mother, with its wave of white hair, the mole on the left cheek and the tarnished nose ring. Instantly, my mind flashed back to that September afternoon two months earlier, when I had stood in my aunt's courtyard in Mohalla Chan Chiragh in Rawalpindi, surrounded by a crowd.

I was the deputy director of civil aviation in Delhi. Pakistan had been created; 15 August had passed into history. Pakistani flags had been unfurled that side of Wagah and the tricolour had celebrated freedom this side of Attari. But I had been unable to get any word of the well-being of my aunt and her family. My letters to them were lost in the chaos of Partition and only an occasional one of theirs reached me. One such letter, written by my uncle on 22 August, had arrived only on 11 September. It had spelt hopelessness.

'It is unlikely that we will meet again,' he wrote.

> Rawalpindi has been cut off and there are stabbing incidents all over town. Since 15 August, trains full of refugees have been butchered in Gujrat or Wazirabad, and only a rare one has managed to reach Lahore. And now the Pakistani government has stopped the refugee specials. The road to Srinagar was the other way out, but now even that has been blocked off by tribal bands. Those who left 'Pindi for Patiala after the March riots were wise. We fools did not have the sense to do that. Anyway, let us see what God has in store for us. I feel lost but your aunt has kept her faith. She says that the Guru himself will save us...

That letter stung me like an accusation; it taunted my conscience. Why hadn't I done something? Each passing day had pushed my aunt's family nearer to their deaths, but I had contented myself with sitting in Delhi, reading the newspapers and comforting myself with the thought that, like hundreds of thousands of others, they too would eventually make it across the border. I decided there and then that I would get them out of Rawalpindi or die in the attempt. I owed them at least that much. After I was orphaned as a child, they had taken me in and given me more love and affection than to their own children. They had educated me and made me what I was. Their own son, Parduman, was a laboratory assistant in the Forest Research Institute, Dehradun, and did not have the means to help his parents in these difficult times. But *I* was the deputy director of civil aviation. I could follow the example of the many men of means who had chartered planes from our department and brought back their relatives from Pakistan. Life would not afford me a better chance to square my debts.

I didn't have much time. The government would soon hand over the planes to the director-general of military evacuation in order to rescue army personnel and their families who were still in Pakistan. After that it would be impossible to charter a plane privately. Within a couple of days I had managed to charter a thirty-five-seater Dakota and on 15 September, just four days after I received my uncle's letter, the plane stood at Rawalpindi's Chaklala Airport and I was in my aunt's courtyard, surrounded by a crowd of people from the neighbourhood.

A deathly fear had drained the colour from their faces, as if they could see vultures circling over their heads. They were desperate for seats on that plane. I didn't want to show any favours in handing out the seats. So after my aunt's family and her in-laws had been accommodated, I gave out the remaining nine seats to the people who had asked for them first. I begged forgiveness with folded hands of those who had missed out.

But I was embarrassed by the repeated appeals of Pandit Kirpa Ram and his wife, whom I had known since I was a child. Their young daughter, Kanta, stood behind them, her gaze fixed intently on the floor. Her fiancé and his parents had left 'Pindi in April itself and were now settled in Delhi. The pandit and his wife agonized over their daughter's future now that she belonged to another family, and wished that she should somehow reach Delhi. If that could come to pass, they could even die in peace in Pakistan.

'It's only one seat,' her mother begged. 'Let her not even sit. She can go standing.'

I again pleaded my helplessness. The British pilot of the plane had made it quite clear that if we exceeded the numbers by even one person, he would not take off.

'There is one possibility,' I said.

A dim hope rose in their eyes. 'If someone were to return his ticket, then I could give it to Kanta.'

The glimmer of hope was extinguished in an instant. No one would be prepared to do that. A ticket for the plane meant life. To return it was to step back into death's grasp. It was true that they had been together in that mohalla for generations, sharing in each other's joys and sorrows not like neighbours, but like those bound by ties of blood. But now things were different. The choice now was between life and death. No one was prepared to die in another's place, to step into someone else's pyre.

Kanta's parents cast a hurried, hopeless look over the faces of the crowd in the courtyard and then lowered their darkening gaze to the ground. Placing their hands on their daughter's shoulders, they began to wend their way slowly homewards.

Suddenly someone shouted, 'I will give my ticket... Kanta will go on my ticket.'

I turned in the direction of the voice. It was Basant. Basant, who had always been known as an imbecile and fool. 'Basant the fool', they used to call him in the neighbourhood. Young boys would torment him and even cast stones at him. Paralysis had deformed his face in childhood. His lower lip hung low, and saliva dripped constantly down his face and neck to the handkerchief pinned to his collar by his mother. All day he would limp around the mohalla talking nonsense, a clown in the eyes of everyone.

I looked towards his widowed mother, who had spent her life washing the dirty dishes of the community, and had somehow purchased a ticket to life for her half-crazy son.

'Yes, yes,' Basant struck his chest, damp with his drool, 'take my ticket and give it to Kanta.'

His mother did not say anything. She did not raise any objections or try to stop Basant. Her eyes showed neither joy nor grief, only a mute acquiescence. Seeing this, I returned the fare for the ticket to Basant's mother and took the money for Kanta's ticket from a bewildered Pandit Kirpa Ram's hands. The people of the neighbourhood stared at the angel who had stunned them into silence; his act reminded them that they had never stopped their children from throwing stones at him.

Lost in these thoughts, I kept looking at Basant's mother as I ate. She had taken two chapattis and some cooked potatoes and cauliflower on her plate. She ate one chapatti slowly and then tied up the other along with the remaining vegetables in her dupatta, perhaps for her evening meal. Then she got up and, dragging her feet in a worn-out pair of rubber chappals, went to the tap and washed her hands. When she had finished, I walked up to her, my hands joined in greeting.

'Have you come from 'Pindi?'

She nodded almost imperceptibly in agreement.

'From Mohalla Shah Chan Chiragh?'

She looked at me a bit more intently and then nodded again.

'Are you Basant's mother?'

Pain opened up a crack in her eyes. She seemed to moan in agreement.

'Don't you recognize me?'

'No.'

'I am Narang sahib's nephew. Sardar Nanak Singh Narang who lived in Mohalla Shah Chan Chiragh in Rawalpindi. It was I who brought the plane to 'Pindi two months ago when Basant gave his seat to Kanta. Where is he now?'

She choked. She bunched up her dupatta in front of her mouth and tried to control herself but could not. The tears began to roll down her pain-seared cheeks.

'Basant is no more,' she sobbed. 'He was killed in 'Pindi.'

I wanted to say something to comfort her, to express my condolences, but could not speak.

She wiped away her tears, biting her lower lip. Then she continued, 'One day our neighbour, Mehta Karam Chand, had some pain in his kidney. He had run out of his medicine. Someone had to go to Hakim Abdul Aziz at the Imambara to get some more. He begged all the neighbours desperately, but who would go? People were being stabbed in the streets. In the end, Basant agreed to go. When he was returning from the Imambara, he was stabbed at the Shah Nazar check post.'

Her tears welled up again.

'Don't cry,' I said. 'Not for Basant. We shouldn't cry for people like him. People like Basant don't die, they live on forever.'

She wiped her tears again and folded her hands in farewell.

'Where will you go now?' I asked. 'Do you have any relatives in Delhi?'

'Nobody,' she sighed. 'No one from my side or from my husband's side. His people died in the March riots in Takht Parhi, and mine in Narhali. I am alone today in free India.'

'You are not alone,' I said. 'Not as long as I am alive. I am the one who is alone, really. My aunt and uncle have gone away to Dehradun to live with their son, Parduman. If you come to my house, I won't be alone any more.'

'No, my son, I don't want to be a burden on anyone. I cleaned dirty dishes in 'Pindi. If I get a few houses to work in here, I'll get by.'

'May your enemies wash dirty dishes,' I responded. 'Ramu

cleans our dirty dishes and will keep on cleaning them. You've called me your son. Now come to my house like my mother. Find a wife for me. Find a sweet, pretty daughter-in-law for yourself. I cannot take Basant's place, but I will definitely try.'

Jathedar Mukand Singh

Jathedar Mukand Singh's eyes glowered with rage as soon as he heard the news.

'How did this happen?' he roared at his lieutenant, Nathu the water-carrier.

'Believe you me, the door was locked from the outside. You can still go and see it with your own eyes,' Nathu defended himself. 'These slippery bastards unlatched the window and bent the iron bars.'

'How many tried to escape?'

'Believe you me, three came out. There must have been a long queue behind them, all ready to run. But we nabbed them in time.'

'And where are these bastards now?' Hatred towards all Muslims reared its head like an enraged cobra in the jathedar's heart.

'Believe you me, we have tied them up hand and foot in one corner of the front veranda.'

'You go ahead,' the jathedar ordered, 'and tell the gang to be on their toes. We'll soon put them on the train.'

Nathu knew full well what that meant. Over the last three or four months, the jathedar and his men had put several hundred Muslim refugees on this train. But the train did not go to the Pakistan of Muhammad Ali Jinnah: its destination was the capital city of the Angel of Death.

There was a time when Jathedar Mukand Singh was simply Mukand Singh, a man who wouldn't even step on a dead ant. But now he didn't think twice before killing a man. The desire to avenge the slaughter of his family in West Punjab had made him ruthless. Eighteen members of his family had been massacred in Narhali village during the tempest of violence that had spread through the Sikh villages of Rawalpindi division in March 1947. The mobs, tempted by loot and crazed by religious zeal, had spared neither old nor young. The women of his family had saved their honour by jumping into the village well. The horror had only befallen the Sikh villages, because it was the Sikhs who had snatched away a huge swathe of Jinnah's Pakistan. In Jinnah's dream, Pakistan would have reached the banks of the Jumna River. But the Sikhs had struck aside the hand he had extended in friendship, preventing Pakistan from stretching across the Ravi and thereby saving half of Punjab from going to Pakistan. In one of his speeches, Jinnah had blamed the Sikhs for crippling his Pakistan.

When the massacres took place in the Sikh villages of Pothohar, Mukand Singh had been in the city of Rawalpindi, where he worked in the ordnance depot. His wife and children had gone to his ancestral village, Narhali, after the final school exams. Not one of them came back alive. Such barbarism, such butchery had never been seen or heard of before. Amid his heartbroken sighs, Mukand Singh would say repeatedly, 'There's only one thing that I want in this world: a sword in my hand and a jatha of five hundred Sikhs so I can reduce every last Muslim village to dust.'

His hatred towards Muslims had gone to his head. But he couldn't fulfil his desire in Rawalpindi: every man there was running for his life, and getting together a gang of five hundred was unimaginable.

By the time he crossed over from Pakistan and reached Ludhiana, this desire for revenge had lacerated his innards. His grief had sunk deep into the desert of his soul. His wounds were of the kind that never form scars but just continue to fester. In fact, he never wished for them to heal. He wanted his pain to not ebb but instead keep feeding the furnace of hate raging in his heart. That was how it stayed—the desire for revenge continued to hack away at his innards like a rusted knife.

Even in Ludhiana he did not find his five hundred Sikhs, but he did gather around him fifteen or twenty good-for-nothings, layabouts and thieves. This mob did call itself a 'jatha', though it was actually an insult to the exalted concept of a squad waging war for a holy cause. But the men admired his unrelenting zeal for killing, and he soon became their unquestioned leader. And when he captured a double-barrelled gun and a box of cartridges belonging to a Muslim landlord, he began to call himself the jathedar of this motley gang. Till now, Jathedar Mukand Singh had only raided stray columns of Muslim refugees. But today, he had risen in stature with his attack on the leading Muslim village of Ludhiana district, Theekri Majra.

All the well-to-do families of Theekri Majra, the ones who kept weapons at home, had already reached Lahore and Sialkot. Without them the village was weak and forlorn; its remaining inhabitants, peasants and labourers, were looking for a way to escape to Pakistan. A faint flicker of hope had lit up their fearful faces when they had heard that the next day a large caravan of Muslim refugees would pass by on the main road that ran less than a mile away from the village. They decided to join this caravan. All day they packed their belongings in trunks and little bundles, and loaded them on to carts. Then they began their wait for the next afternoon when the caravan was to pass close to Theekri Majra.

But just when the handful of red that had spread across the western sky had shrunk into a thin line, fate in the form of Jathedar Mukand Singh's gang had charged into the village, shrouded in a whirlwind of dust. The gang looted their belongings, dragged the panic-stricken animals away from their pegs and locked up the villagers in the school building, with its half-baked yellow bricks and rafters. It would have been easy to kill them on the spot but the jathedar didn't want them to have so easy a death. He wanted them to die a thousand little deaths before he killed them. Some remaining vestige of humanity or respect for custom meant that he wouldn't kill women or children, or violate a woman's honour. His mob knew this well and never crossed the line.

The school hall looked like a cattle pen. The terrified prisoners were trembling like captured monkeys.

'Don't you dare try and escape tonight,' the jathedar roared. 'You'll run into our naked swords.' The upturned tips of his moustache shook with anger.

After warning the prisoners, he stepped outside. He put a big lock on the only door of the hall and cautioned his gang to stay alert. One of his companions, a man from the local area, said, 'You get some rest now, brother. In the morning you can count and collect your Muslims.'

A thick darkness had descended in the school hall, unbroken by even a single lamp. The long shadows of fear had deepened the pall. Women, men and children lay packed like animals. They knew that they were under sentence of death without any possibility of appeal. It seemed as if the cold hand of death had already begun to snuff out their lives. Hopelessness had taken the place of sadness in their eyes. All night they started again and again in sudden alarm at the slightest of sounds. All night they prayed for Allah's mercy but Allah, it seemed, was not listening and, unlike them, was fast asleep.

Just before dawn, a few of them bent the iron rods in the window and tried to escape. But only three had managed to squeeze through before the alert guards nabbed them.

The jathedar reached the school veranda, his face covered by his shawl. His shining beady eyes were fixed, with the intensity of a hissing cobra, on the three men who had tried to escape. Guessing his intention, Nathu stepped forward and untied the three men. But they lay unmoving on the veranda floor, as if they lacked the strength to stand up.

'Stand up! Up!' Urged by the shoves of the jathedar's barrel, they staggered to their feet. 'Look up! Why are you looking down?' the jathedar roared. 'You! I am talking to you, you sons of bitches!' Mukand Singh shook them one by one by the collar.

The three unfortunate men raised their heads.

'Why are you shivering? Should I warm up your insides with my gun, then?'

Two of them were young men. The third was a middle-aged man of about fifty or fifty-five. Actually, only the two young men were trembling, their eyes wide with fear, their hands folded, their faces pleading. The middle-aged man stood fearlessly, the fingers of his hands locked together behind his back. The jathedar's brown eyes stared at him from under tightly knitted brows.

'Who gave you permission to run away? You seem to be in a right hurry to reach Pakistan; this gun can send you to Lahore right now without even a ticket. But no, a bullet would be too easy for you. You three should be shredded to pieces.'

A deathly pallor had spread across the faces of the two young men. Their knees and ankles were knocking against each other. Their shattered hopes of escaping turned their panicked breathing into sobs. With folded hands, they pleaded, 'O Sardar, spare us for your Guru's sake. Make us Sikhs. We will serve you all our lives.'

'Sikhism doesn't need the likes of you,' the jathedar barked, his angry face hot and flushed.

The two young men fell at the jathedar's feet, begging, but the barrel of his gun prodded them upright again. The middle-aged man, however, was calmly staring at the gun. His fearless gaze seemed to say, 'Go on, fire away and be done with this drama.'

This fearless and unflinching gaze shocked the jathedar as much as if he had been hit on the forehead by a stone. The man's countenance, unlike those of the two young men, was unmistakably Islamic: his beard was sculpted according to the dictates of the sharia. Mukand Singh bore a deep hatred in his heart for such faces.

He placed the gun's double barrel against the middle-aged man's temple, but the man stood motionless, unblinking, undisturbed. His gaze seemed to be a backhanded slap across Death's face. It was as if he was facing the bullet with the same careless indifference with which Mansur had walked to his crucifixion.

Instead of pressing the trigger, the jathedar shoved him and pulled the barrel away from his head. Blood began to trickle down the man's temple.

'Get the rest of them out,' the jathedar commanded. Nathu turned the key in the lock and flung open the door.

'Get out, all of you!' Nathu roared. But no one stepped out; they knew that death was waiting for them outside. In the end, the members of the jatha pulled, pushed and dragged the women and children out. The men followed their families of their own accord.

'Separate the women and children,' the jathedar commanded again.

The prisoners stood in two lines, one of women and children, the other of men. The children were sobbing and wailing, and the frightened mothers bundled them in their arms as if shielding them from death.

'Silence the children,' the jathedar ordered the women. 'There is no danger to you or them. Your kin in Pakistan did not spare our mothers, our sisters and daughters, our children. But we will take you to join the caravan on the main road this afternoon. But first we'll dispatch your husbands straight to paradise, where beautiful maidens are waiting for them.'

This assurance brought no comfort to anyone. The children continued to wail and the mothers, half-dead with fear, continued to tremble.

'Come,' the jathedar again turned to the three men, 'let us get you your maidens. Don't worry, you three are not going on your journey alone. This whole crowd will go with you. But I have a scheme, which will allow many of your brothers to escape this journey. Each of you will pick one travelling companion from the crowd. Then you three and your three companions can drink from the cup of martyrdom. I swear that the others will not come to any harm. All the remaining men, along with the women and children, will join the caravan this afternoon.'

This strange proposal did not overly surprise the jathedar's motley bunch. They knew that he liked to play new games every once in a while. Once a lame old man, straggling behind a refugee column, had fallen into their hands. Trembling like a leaf, he had stared at inescapable death in the shape of the jathedar. His voice had seemed to desert him along with his senses. Gulping air into his dry throat, he had made a feeble attempt to speak.

'Beat me, whip me, but don't kill me. I plead to you with folded hands. Victory to your Guru, O Sardar, victory to your Guru, victory to your Guru.' The old man had fallen at the jathedar's feet. Mukand Singh had broken out in laughter. He helped the old man to his feet. Then he made him shout 'Death to Pakistan' three times and let him go.

Another time, a middle-aged woman and her young son had fallen into their hands. Part of a refugee caravan, they had wandered off in the grey twilight into the fields of fodder alongside the road, looking to cut some for their animals. There they had been surrounded by the band of men who had been circling the caravan like vultures.

Seeing the raised naked sword in the jathedar's hand, the woman spoke, 'Brother, kill us if you want but just listen to me first.'

'Speak, what is it?' The jathedar's tone was sharp as a dagger.

'All I have to say, brother, is that my parents are from Malerkotla and this son of mine is a grandson of Malerkotla.'

For a moment or two, the jathedar was confused. What was this woman babbling about? Had fear made her go mad? What was this wretched Malerkotla? Then suddenly, Malerkotla lit up in his mind in a flash—it was the nawab of Malerkotla who had protested against the death sentence passed on the younger sons of Guru Gobind Singh. And when the ruler of Sirhind did not heed him, the nawab had walked out of the court in protest.

The jathedar's grip on the sword turned slippery with cold sweat. What terrible sin had he been about to commit? He would not have been able to wipe away the shame of it all his life.

'Hurry up, sister,' he had said, looking down at the ground. 'Run and join the caravan. Don't go around risking your lives looking for fodder for your animals.'

When they recalled all that, the members of his gang were not surprised at his new proposal.

The jathedar knit his brows together and asked, 'So? Do you accept?'

None of the three responded. It seemed that they had not fully understood the proposal.

He repeated the offer he had made.

Again none of the three gave any response.

'Yes or no? Say something!'

A stubborn silence was their only answer.

'Die then, all of you! Go to your heaven together. Take them all behind the school,' the jathedar commanded his lieutenant, Nathu.

'We accept.' It was the middle-aged man, whose fearlessness was badly rankling the jathedar.

'If you accept then choose your travelling companions for hell.' Turning to one of the young men, he barked, 'You first.'

For a moment the young man hesitated. But then the jathedar's double-barrelled gun poked him in the ribs and he stumbled towards the line of men. Each man he passed felt the sting of death; each man he paused by stared intently at the ground as if by doing that he would not be seen. The young man passed by all of them one by one. When he reached the end of the line, he put a tired hand on the shoulder of the last man.

The second young man, too, did the same thing.

'Come along, old man, now it's your turn,' Mukand Singh turned to the middle-aged man.

The man did not hesitate a moment. He took a boy of seventeen or eighteen from the line and, putting his arm around him, came before the jathedar.

Suddenly an old man of about eighty, probably the oldest in the bunch, jumped out of the line, screaming, 'O Ramzan, what madness is this? Nazeer is your only son. How dare you send him to his death?'

Ramzan did not reply. He only tightened his grip around the boy's shoulders.

'Take me instead,' the old man pleaded. 'I've lived my life.'

The old man grabbed Nazeer's hand and tried to drag him away.

'Let it be, Uncle,' Ramzan spoke up. 'The right to choose is mine and I have chosen Nazeer.'

'For the sake of your ancestors, Ramzan, don't let the boy die this needless death. He's the only son in your family. All traces of your family will be wiped out.'

'Let it be wiped out.' There was a deep calm in Ramzan's voice.

'But why don't you choose me instead? I have one foot in the grave anyway.'

'I've only got a right over the life of my son, not over anyone else's.'

The man's moral courage shook Mukand Singh. He tried to put his soul back into the grip of hatred. But everything seemed to have broken inside him. His strength seemed to have ebbed away through his feet into the earth. Ramzan, he felt, was an embodiment of humanity, and was standing at a spiritual height from which Mukand Singh himself had fallen flat on his face. It seemed to the jathedar that his face, his turban, his beard had been badly soiled by the evil-smelling filth of barbarity. Ramzan personified humanity, decency, sacrifice. Truth was on his side, clean, pure truth, just like it had been on the side of the nawab of Malerkotla. It struck Jathedar Mukand Singh that Theekri Majra had become another Malerkotla.

He turned to assure the prisoners, 'Not the slightest harm will come to you. Your belongings and your animals will be given back to you right now. This afternoon my men and I will escort you under our protection to join the caravan.'

Not one of the men in his squad had the courage to challenge his command.

Gul Mohammad Third-Timer

A hijacked Fokker Friendship belonging to Indian Airlines had been blown up with hand grenades at the Lahore Airport, and angry demonstrators had gathered in front of the Pakistan High Commission in Delhi. The demonstrators were mostly college students, but a few political activists were also present. I was also there, in my capacity as a local political leader. We politicians would have been satisfied with shouting slogans and venting our anger, but the hot-blooded students wanted to do something more. They made several attempts to break the police cordon and enter the high commission's compound but were defeated by the strong police presence. But then, in an instant, a powerful group of students did break free and, rushing through the fog of tear gas, jumped over the iron gate of the high commission into its compound. To prevent them from doing something untoward, some of the police and political leaders ran after them, including me.

I was surprised to see a group of Pakistani citizens standing with their baggage on the veranda of the high commission. They had either just come from Pakistan or were on their way back and had turned up at the high commission for some passport- or visa-related matter. Shouting and waving, the group of vengeful students headed towards these travellers when a door opened and a high commission official quickly hustled the Pakistanis inside. Only one fat man got caught by the students, partly because of his own lassitude and partly because of his attachment to his belongings. Something in that fat man's look and the way he moved reminded me of Gul Mohammad Third-Timer, and I screamed... But before I tell you what I said, let me introduce you to Gul Mohammad Third-Timer.

This goes back thirty-two years ago to when I was a class-eight student in Government High School, Rawalpindi. When we cleared our annual exam and entered the class, Gul Mohammad Third-Timer was already there. He wasn't just there: he had been sitting on the same corner bench for the last two years. The previous year he had been known as Gul Mohammad Two-Years, and now he was quickly promoted to the title of Third-Timer since he had remained in class eight for three years running. For reasons known only to themselves, the school authorities had not thought it fit to promote him. It was said that his answers in the examination were so unique and of such high quality that the teachers, with their limited knowledge, were incapable of understanding them.

The English teacher, Master Suchet Singh, had proved to be the most incapable of all. Gul Mohammad had not answered a single question orally over the past two years, and the English he wrote—or what he understood to be English—served only to remind Master Suchet Singh of the saying 'Only God can read what Moses writes.'

I recalled that summer afternoon when Master Suchet Singh entered the classroom and the entire class instantly noticed two changes in him. The first was that the black ruler he used to employ to try and teach English to the likes of Gul Mohammad was not in his hand. The second was that there was a bandage on the fingers of his right hand. The whole class knew that both changes had a single cause: Gul Mohammad Third-Timer.

An incident had taken place the day before when Master Suchet Singh had been making a valiant attempt to teach Gul Mohammad some English with the help of his ruler. It was an event for which the class was not prepared at all, and yet it resulted in what we had been praying for for several months: the breaking of the tyrannical black ruler in two. Half the class thought—and Master Suchet Singh himself agreed—that the reason the ruler broke was the thick layers of fat whose folds encircled Gul Mohammad's body. But other students thought that the carpenter had used inferior wood to make the ruler. No matter the real reason, there was no doubt the entire class was extremely happy that the ruler had broken, though we took care not to express this. Instead we all put on long faces, as if mourning the sudden passing of not just an ordinary black ruler but a ruler made of beautiful smooth ebony instead.

Master Suchet Singh had shot an alert and suspicious look at our faces, but we kept sitting with our heads down, as if we weren't sitting in class but were instead following him in his beloved ruler's funeral procession. He saw the deep mournful shadows on our faces and was mollified. Then he stared with narrowed eyes at the murderer of the ruler and enemy of the English language, Gul Mohammad Third-Timer, who was vigorously massaging his smarting body with both hands. But the very next moment Gul Mohammad completely forgot his smarting body when a tight slap landed on his face. To say the least, our class had never seen nor heard such a slap before. This slap would later be remembered in the class's mythology as the double-action slap: not only did a clear red imprint of five fingers well up on Gul Mohammad's stuffed cheeks but Master Suchet Singh, too, twisted in pain and hurriedly left the room, clutching the fingers of his right hand.

The next day when he entered the classroom, the black ruler was missing and the fingers of his right hand were bandaged. The yellow colour seeping through the bandage showed that he had fried some turmeric in ghee to make a hot compress for his hand. If you looked closely, it was obvious that his fingers were swollen. As always, there were two viewpoints on this in the class. Some thought that Third-Timer had caught the master's hand and bitten it when the slap hit home, but those who knew better were convinced it was all the doing of Gul Mohammad's fat cheeks, which had broken the master's fingers as surely as they had snapped the ruler.

As soon as the master commenced his attempt to teach Gul Mohammad English, he felt the absence of his black ruler keenly. He looked at his bandaged hand and winced. Then he called upon me in my capacity as class monitor.

'Give this scoundrel a slap,' he shouted.

'Sir?' My legs were trembling and I was cursing the fact that I had come to school that day.

'Trying to ignore me? Give him a really tight slap across his fat face.'

His voice was harsh and his face seemed sculpted out of black stone. The entire class had taken the measure of his anger. The absence of his ruler had clearly given his temper a desperate edge. Caught in a fix, I gingerly stepped forward and somehow or the other slapped Gul Mohammad across his face.

'You call that a slap? Or were you trying to give the wretch a caress? Come here and let me show you what a slap is.'

Swinging his left arm, the master hit me hard on the face. Before then, I had clearly never known what a slap is. It felt as if there had been an earthquake, and the earth and sky had exchanged places with each other. The floor, the ceiling, the blackboard, the rows of desks and the students' faces all merged into one another. Stars danced wildly in front of my eyes and it felt like thousands of scorpions were stinging my ear.

'That is what a slap is,' said Master Suchet Singh. 'Now go

and give him a nice hard one like that.

'Ignoring me again?' he barked, seeing that his command had not been obeyed. I stood my ground obstinately.

'Have you gone deaf? Or are you dead?' he snorted and shouted and shouted and snorted, but I did not move.

At last when I opened my stubborn mouth I said, 'I won't hit him. I'll never hit him.'

He growled, 'If you don't hit him, I'll break your bones.'

'Just try and lay a hand on me.'

The master saw open rebellion in my eyes. He said, 'Come with me to the headmaster's office.'

'Let's go.'

Outside the headmaster's office, he hesitated. Then, in a low and embarrassed tone, he said, 'Okay, I'll let you go this time. But don't ever do this again.'

I spent that entire day in school hatching schemes to exact revenge from Master Suchet Singh for that slap. I was still making spiteful plans as I started homewards after school. When I took a quick look behind me near Mai Veero's pond, my feet froze. I saw that Gul Mohammad Third-Timer was walking about twenty paces behind me. I was surprised because he lived in Tarlahi village and returned through the fields every day after school. Perhaps he has some errand in town, I thought and resumed my convoluted plotting again. I looked back again near Saidpuri Gate and was even more astonished. He was still following me. When I passed Bhabris' Market and entered Talwars' Market, I turned and saw that he had just entered Bhabris' Market. I looked back again near the Satkartar Well, and saw Third-Timer near the biscuit bakeries. My legs began to tremble involuntarily. I forgot all my schemes of revenge against Master Suchet Singh, and several unknown fears and doubts entered my mind in their place. I thought I would wait there for Third-Timer and ask him why he hadn't gone off to Tarlahi as usual and was following me instead. But my legs decided not to be part of my plan; they kept trembling. They quickened my walk, almost making me run, taking me across the Trunk Bazaar Chowk and into my home.

As soon as I reached home, I climbed the stairs and went straight to the balcony. My blood ran cold as I looked down. Leaning against a letter box just this side of Trunk Bazaar Chowk, Gul Mohammad Third-Timer was staring at my house, the balcony and me standing on the balcony. Then he turned back on his tracks past the Satkartar Well, Bhabris' Market, Saidpuri Gate, Mai Veero's Pond and the Government High School and set off through the fields to Tarlahi.

My heart sank. I felt that I had been turned into Ali Baba, and the chief of the forty thieves had daubed a mark on my house so that he could come back at night with his thieves, or the residents of Tarlahi village, and attack my house to avenge the slap I had inflicted on him. Even though I had slapped him at the command of the master—and that, too, lightly and unenthusiastically—it was still undeniable that I had slapped him. Gul Mohammad had as much right to exact revenge from me as I had to do the same from Master Suchet Singh.

If only, I wished, my father were at home today. That would have reduced my fear. But my father was on tour. My mother and I were home alone. I said nothing to her, and at dusk began to hide away stones, bricks and old bottles on the balcony while her back was turned.

Well into the night I sat scared stiff in my bed, listening for the slightest sound. More than once the slogan '*Allahu Akbar*' echoed in my ears. But when I strained harder to hear the sounds, they melted into silence every time. It was nearly dawn when I finally fell asleep, my mind gripped by evil dreams. A mob of Muslims from

Tarlahi with spears and flaming torches in their hands had crossed Trunk Bazaar Chowk, urged on by Gul Mohammad Third-Timer, an unsheathed sword in his hand and a martyr's shroud tied around his head. I felt sad that Gul Mohammad had turned a minor slap into such a major communal issue. Left with no choice I rolled up my sleeves, spat on my hands and rained stones, bricks and old bottles over the mob from my balcony, repulsing several of their strong attacks. Finally the marauding mob resorted to extreme methods, sprinkling kerosene oil on our house and setting it afire. The heat of the flames and the noise of the slogans woke me up.

The sunshine from the balcony warmed my bed, and someone was knocking at our door. I got up and opened the latch. An old Muslim with a henna-dyed beard came in, carrying a sack on his back. There were wrinkles under his eyes and the loose end of his turban came down almost to his knees. Pouring melons from the sack on to the floor of the courtyard, he said simply in response to my mother's surprise, 'I am Gul Mohammad's father. I've come from Tarlahi. My child studies with your boy.'

Seeing my mother beginning to mouth a refusal, he continued, 'Don't refuse, Sardarni ji, these melons are from my field. I bless your boy. Yesterday he let the master slap him but didn't let anything happen to my son.'

Then he smothered me in a hug and caressed my head affectionately. 'May Allah grant you a long life. You have made me very happy.' And two tears emerged from his eyes, rolled down his wrinkles and henna-coloured beard, and dropped on to my forehead.

And today when Gul Mohammad Third-Timer was surrounded by the student mob in the compound of the Pakistan High Commision in Delhi, I screamed, 'Friends! Let him be. Our anger is against the Government of Pakistan, not the people of Pakistan.'

They understood what I said and let him go. Gul Mohammad looked at me with grateful eyes. In that instant I realized that I was wrong. He wasn't Gul Mohammad. Maybe Din Mohammad, or Ali Mohammad, or Ali Ahmad. But then, what's in a name?

❧

Of One Community

We were very happy—my mother, wife, son, daughter, my three unmarried sisters and I—when we moved into the government flat on Satya Marg. This flat was smaller than the one we had lived in on Cornwallis Road; it had one bedroom and one bathroom less. That flat had been in the C-II category, because there were too few of the C-I flats to which I was actually entitled. The Satya Marg flat was D-I, which was even lower than the C-II. But, as I said, we were all very happy to move, largely because of the surroundings in Chanakyapuri. This was where most of the foreign embassies were located, along the broad clean avenues, resplendent with gulmohar trees. Chanakyapuri did not look like a part of Delhi; rather, it was as if someone had plucked out a piece of Washington, Paris or Frankfurt and placed it here.

I had asked for the move from Cornwallis Road to Satya Marg. I had been unwell, plagued by restlessness, through the year and a half that we had spent at Cornwallis Road. Though my condition was not new, it had assumed worrisome proportions during this period and the doctors had no clue. At long last, one doctor suggested that a change of place might help, since he had found the Cornwallis Road area depressing. I saw sense in that suggestion. There was an old ruined tomb right across from our flat, which would virtually be the first thing I would set my eyes on every morning. The sight of it at twilight would fill me with dread. And when I went for an evening walk, I was confronted by the ruins of the Old Fort.

So even though the Satya Marg flat had only two bedrooms and two bathrooms, we were happy to have got rid of the ruins. The new flat had an ample study, which could be turned into a bedroom. There was a covered balcony too, that could be converted into another bedroom by enclosing it with windows. So we were not worried about staying in a smaller accommodation. But a slight shadow had fallen on my mother's happiness when she had learnt that our immediate neighbours were a Muslim family. Her mood had visibly darkened the moment she had seen the nameplate on the door across the staircase.

'It doesn't matter, Mother,' I said. 'They will live in their own flat and we in ours. Only the staircase is shared, and if we meet in passing we will greet each other. We are hardly likely to become close to them.'

The riots that had accompanied the partition of the country had left deep wounds on my mother's soul and planted a deep antipathy towards Muslims in her heart. Her younger brother had been killed in Takht Parhi and a cousin of mine in Basali. My mother's newly-wed niece in Thoa Khalsa had jumped into a well to save her honour, while her husband had died fighting the mob of rioters. And we ourselves had barely managed to make it across the border, looted and bereft, after struggling in refugee camps and caravans, witnessing bloodshed and violence, and escaping death by a hair's breadth more than once.

She had convinced herself that Muslims were cruel, merciless and inhuman. I had often tried to remove this deep prejudice from her mind. I told her that the Hindus and Sikhs of East Punjab had behaved as viciously as the Muslims of West Punjab. Those who had committed these atrocities were neither Muslims nor Hindus nor Sikhs; barbarity has no religion. Their faith was merely barbarism, and they were the agents of Satan. My arguments had perhaps managed to take the edge off the hatred in my mother's heart, but it had not been completely wiped away. That was the reason that the presence of Muslim neighbours had cast a shadow over her joy at moving into the clean and pleasant environs of Chanakyapuri.

It was our first afternoon in the new house. We were all busy arranging our belongings. My wife was wiping the pictures and putting them up in the bedrooms. My sisters were setting up the pots, pans and crockery in the kitchen. In the drawing room, my mother was dusting the sofas and chairs, while I was unpacking the large wooden crate of books on the adjoining balcony. Just then there was a gentle knock on the front door. My mother opened it. I peeped in from the balcony to see who it was.

A fair-complexioned woman of about forty-five was standing at the door. She was dressed in a dark green sari and, from the absence of a bindi on the forehead or sindoor in her parting, I surmised that she must be the wife of our neighbour, Shaukat Hussain.

'May I come in?' she asked in a soft, cultured tone.

'Come.' My mother opened the door fully.

I withdrew my head from the balcony door and returned to dusting the books.

The sofas not having been completely cleaned yet, my mother invited the lady to sit down on one of the dining-table chairs, which she had already cleaned, and sat down herself on another across from her.

'We live in the neighbouring flat, Number 17. My husband is a joint secretary in the Ministry of Education. This flat of yours has been vacant for a couple of months. I can't tell you how happy we are that you have moved in.'

I could hear her voice clearly, as the dining table was very near the door behind which I was sitting.

Mother did not respond. She seemed taken aback by this unexpectedly early confrontation with our Muslim neighbours. Perhaps she was unconsciously comparing the visitor to the uneducated, burqa-clad Muslim women she was used to encountering in Rawalpindi.

'You wouldn't have eaten lunch because of your move. I'll send something over.'

'No, no.' Mother's refusal was unnecessarily emphatic and coloured with irritation.

'But why not? It can be ready in half an hour.'

'No, no,' Mother repeated in the same tone. 'There is no need for it. We had lunch before setting off.' She was telling the truth: we had eaten lunch at Cornwallis Road.

'Then you must have dinner at our place tonight.'

'No, no, how can that be? This cannot be.'

The begum seemed to have guessed the real reason for the refusal from my mother's flustered tone and its sharpness. Her enthusiasm flagged a bit and she fell silent. I feared that Mother might say something that would ruin our relations with the neighbours on our very first day. I recalled how one day, while travelling between Gujranwala and Rawalpindi, she had drunk 'Muslim water' instead of 'Hindu water' at the Lala Musa Railway Station. When a fellow-traveller pointed out that she had accepted water from a Muslim, she was overtaken by an urge to throw up. Her bout of nausea had lasted for the rest of the journey.

I sent my wife into the drawing room to save the situation. The begum, who was visibly crestfallen after her conversation with Mother, recovered her spirits upon seeing Simran. She repeated the invitation for dinner.

'I was telling Mother that it would be nice if you had dinner with us tonight.'

'We are very grateful,' Simran replied in a very civil and patient tone, 'but we really won't need to trouble you. The girls and I have set up the kitchen, and the gas is working too. If we happen to have any problems, we will come to you.'

The refusal was the same, but the words and tone were different. Civility had been maintained, and both sides had saved face.

Just five minutes after the begum had left, her soft knock sounded at the front door again. This time I opened the door. She appeared a bit startled on seeing me, but quickly gathered herself. She greeted me with a slight nod of her head, unable to raise her hand in greeting as she was holding two plates, one with bananas and melon slices and the other heaped with dry fruits.

'Come, please come in.'

Simran, too, had come into the drawing room on hearing the door open.

'Oh, there was no need for all this,' she exclaimed. 'Why did you take so much trouble?'

'No trouble at all,' the begum said. 'It's a pleasure. Please don't refuse this time.'

Simran raised no objection and put both plates on the dining table. Happiness and disappointment had begun to play a strange game of hide-and-seek on the begum's face. Happiness that we had accepted the fruits she had brought, and disappointment that we had refused to eat food cooked in her house.

Just then Mother came into the room to see who had come now.

'My husband also wanted to come and meet you,' the begum said, 'but he is not too well today. He didn't even go to his office.'

'What's the matter?' I asked.

'He begins to feel very restless all of a sudden. His legs go weak and his hands start to tremble. He gets such strong attacks of this restlessness and discomfort that it seems his life is in danger.'

Mother, Simran and I exchanged looks. These were the symptoms of my own condition, which had troubled me for so many years.

'What do the doctors say?' Simran asked.

'The doctors all believe that there is nothing wrong with him. His heart, his blood pressure, his blood sugar are all fine. They say that all these years he has nurtured a delusion that he is ill.'

Again we exchanged glances. The doctors had said exactly the same things to me all these years.

'This morning Dr Bose came and said that now there was only one thing left to do. We have to consult a good neurologist.'

'And?' I asked.

'We've called Dr Sukhdev Singh, the top neurologist at Willingdon Hospital. He's coming at five today. Let's see what he says.'

At about a quarter to six in the evening, I glanced out of the drawing-room window and saw a doctor carrying a bag getting into a car.

'Simran,' I called out to my wife. 'I think the neurologist has seen Shaukat Hussain sahib. We should go to their house and ask after him.'

'I will also come with you,' Mother said. She was clearly keen to see what opinion the neurologist had given on the condition that our neighbour and I shared.

Shaukat Hussain sahib was lying in bed. When he saw us, he propped himself up on a pillow. On seeing us in her home, the begum seemed to forget all about her husband's illness.

'Please sit here. Be comfortable. Mother, you please sit here,' she fussed over us.

'What did the neurologist say?' asked Simran.

'Well, he started by checking the heart and blood pressure,' the begum related. 'Then he wanted to know my husband's entire history, right from childhood. "Who used to scold you during your childhood? Did anybody hit you? Did any servant frighten you when you were alone at home? Was your grandfather a very angry man? Was the atmosphere at home happy or terrifying? Was there any teacher whom you feared? Did you have any accident or tragedy in your childhood or youth?" When my husband replied in the negative to all these questions, the doctor was lost in thought. Then it was as if a sudden light came on in his mind and he asked, "Where were you during Partition?"'

The begum fell silent suddenly. As if some wild animal had jumped at her from the dark past. We waited as she gathered herself. When she spoke, there was a quiver in her voice.

'He told the doctor that he was in Moradabad then. A mob of rioters had burnt down his ancestral haveli. They killed his father and two uncles, and raped his sister-in-law and two unmarried sisters.'

Everyone knows that Simran is foolish. Her eyes immediately fill up with a veritable storm of tears at any sad story. And that's exactly what happened. The tears were flowing freely down her cheeks. I saw, then, that tears had welled up in Mother's eyes too.

'And then?' I asked, my voice choked with emotion.

'Then it appeared the doctor had got a grip on the problem. He wanted to know every detail of those evil days and terrible nights. His opinion was that the horror and fear of the Partition riots has settled deep into my husband's subconscious mind, and it is this that causes these bouts of restlessness and despair. He said that it's not a delusional belief but a serious psychological condition that needs to be treated properly. And that it can be cured.'

I looked at Simran, she looked at me, and Mother looked at both of us. Our looks said that in one fell swoop, my own condition had been diagnosed.

'I am convinced of the neurologist's advice,' the begum continued. 'It was only after Partition that my husband began to suffer these bouts. In the months of August–September, the time when these riots took place, he always suffers.'

Wiping the tears from her face with her dupatta, Simran said, 'You will be surprised to learn that my husband suffers from the same problem. All of a sudden he loses heart. "I'm dying," he says. "Call the doctor, do something." All these years, no doctor has been able to understand his problem.'

Holding back the rush of tears, Mother added, 'We also saw a lot of bloodshed during the Partition riots. We suffered big blows, terrible losses. It appears our two families have the same illness.'

'We have the same illness,' I said in my mother's support, 'because we belong to one community.'

Seeing the quizzical looks in the eyes of Simran and my mother, I continued, 'I am right. There are only two communities in this world: the cruel and the meek. Our two families belong to the community of the meek.'

I saw that Shaukat Hussain was nodding in agreement.

'Bhabhi jaan,' I said involuntarily, and then I hesitated. 'Can I take the liberty of calling you Bhabhi jaan?'

'Of course, Bhai sahib. Why not?'

'Bhabhi jaan, this is a happy moment. A wise neurologist has diagnosed the illness in both our families. Diagnosis is half the cure. The rest is just a matter of time. And then, once we're totally cured, Shaukat Hussain sahib and I will go for long walks from Satya Marg to Shanti Path. So, like I said, it's a happy moment. Give us something sweet.'

'Why not, Bhai sahib,' the begum replied. 'I'll get some fruit, and some dry fruit too.'

'Forget those,' I said. 'If you're going to give us something sweet, then do it properly.'

'But how?' the begum asked, a trifle helplessly.

'Maybe some halwa with raisins, or some kheer with coconut and almonds, or a nice dish of sevian.'

The begum looked at Simran and then at Mother. The open smiles on both their faces were supporting my request.

'We understand your problem, Bhabhi jaan,' I said. 'Making any of these dishes takes time. We're in no hurry. We're as comfortable as we would be in our own home. We'll content ourselves with tea and biscuits until the real sweet dish is ready.'

The begum jumped with joy and rushed happily towards the kitchen, calling out, 'I'll be back in an instant,' as she went.

That Third Thing

Mirza sahib was feeling very sad that day. Actually, 'sad' does not quite describe his condition: he was deeply depressed. Ever since he had read the previous day's newspaper, he had descended into the dark hell of hopelessness, and could not see the faintest ray of hope.

Though the newspaper continued to speak of the victories of Pakistan's army, Mirza sahib's knowing eye had read much between the lines that supported the claims of All India Radio. Perhaps it was true that the Indian army had captured thirty-six Pakistani posts in the Kargil sector and one in the Poochan sector; Pakistan had given up everything in the Chhamb sector; despite the large numbers of tanks and aircraft deployed to capture Akhnoor, the Pakistani forces had not managed a foothold on the eastern bank of the Tawi. On the other hand, the Indian forces moving towards Sialkot had reached the outskirts of Shakargarh, and, in that sector, India had captured 325 square miles of Pakistani territory. The Indians had also captured the bridge on the Ravi on the Dera Baba Nanak front. At Hussainiwalla, the Pakistanis had managed to capture only a couple of posts across the Sutlej when their progress had been stopped by the enemy. The most disappointing situation was in Sindh, where, according to All India Radio, Pakistan had washed its hands off nearly two thousand square miles of territory. On the eastern front, the Indian forces were moving towards Dhaka from all directions and, God forbid, East Pakistan was probably on its last legs.

The crisp parantha made by the begum herself was turning to ashes in Mirza sahib's mouth, and the fragrant, cardamom-laced tea tasted bitter. While eating his breakfast he was waiting for the newspaper vendor, but without the hope that he used to have in the early days of the war when the paper would be full of Pakistan's achievements and India's losses. Over the last three or four days, the paper had lost its zest and there were increasing doubts about Pakistani claims.

The thud on the veranda outside indicated that the newspaper man had delivered the paper. Mirza sahib's heart was in his mouth. He wondered what new calamity would greet him. He fervently wished for some news that would change the course of this war completely.

His heart was in his mouth as soon as he saw the banner headline on the front page. Breathing hard, he read through the columns quickly. Now this was some real news, unlike the nonsense they had been trotting out earlier. For the first time the newspaper had lived up to its responsibility. For once, America had given proof of its friendship for Pakistan. America was truly incomparable. It had checkmated India with just one move. It had wiped out all of India's plots by simply turning the Seventh Fleet towards the Bay of Bengal.

Thrilled at the news, he jumped up to share these happy tidings with the begum, but then stopped halfway to the kitchen. For the last two days they had neither exchanged a look nor a word. Two days ago, when Mirza sahib had been lost in the newspaper at the breakfast table, the begum had started berating him about some irrelevant matter. They had had such a heated exchange that they had not yet got over it. His entire life, it seemed, had passed in this antagonism, this fighting. Ceasefires had taken place but never had true peace been established. His married life, Mirza sahib thought, was like India–Pakistan relations. War would continue to smoulder even during ceasefire. The only cause of this lifelong battle was the begum's sharp tongue. When Mirza sahib had been charmed before marriage by her sandalwood complexion and her warm smile, he had not seen the long tongue hidden behind that smile. Life would be so peaceful, Mirza sahib often found himself wishing, if two things did not exist in the world—the begum's tongue and the Indian army. Then he could be truly happy in this charming lane of Kucha Laila Majnu in the lovely town of Lahore in the beautiful Pakistan made by the Qaid-e-Azam.

No, he decided, he would not share this good news with the begum. She deserved to be kept away from this happiness just for her bad temper.

His eldest son, Nadeem, had gone to ascertain the result of his examination at the office of the Public Service Commission. His young daughter, Naheed, was playing with pebbles, sitting in the courtyard, throwing up one and gathering the others in her hand. She had little idea of international politics, so there was no point sharing the news of the Seventh Fleet with her. But it was no longer possible for him to keep the entire burden of this important development to himself. It was extremely important for his physical and mental health that this news be shared immediately. Taking his sherwani off the hook and pulling on his shoes, he quickly left the house for the residence of his bosom friend, Vakil sahib, or rather Choudhry Fazal Karim, advocate, High Court.

Vakil sahib's residence was in Chowk Mati, after Kucha Laila Majnu. He was reading the English newspaper at the breakfast table, and greeted Mirza sahib.

'This is telepathy. I was thinking of going to your house.'

It was obvious from Vakil sahib's face that he had already read the entire news report that appeared under the banner headline, and had been similarly impatient to share the news with someone. The two friends looked at each other through their spectacles and shared their bursting joy.

'This is great, Vakil sahib,' said Mirza sahib. 'America has stood by us. They have made up for all their past mistakes.'

'The point to note, Mirza sahib, is that the aircraft carrier Enterprise in the Seventh Fleet has nuclear-armed aircraft,' Vakil sahib pointed out.

'I say,' said an energized Mirza sahib, 'that they should drop a nuclear bomb on Delhi. At least this All India Radio would shut up.'

'No,' said Vakil sahib, with a lawyer's cold, analytical intellect. 'That way the entire Muslim population of Delhi would also be killed.'

Mirza sahib's enthusiasm flagged a bit. It would be great to throw a nuclear bomb on India's capital but Vakil sahib had a point.

'Okay, forget Delhi,' Mirza sahib said, magnanimously sparing the city. 'But how about a nuclear bomb on the Indian army heading towards Dhaka?'

'No, Mirza sahib.' The advocate from the High Court presented a lawyerly objection. 'The nuclear bomb will destroy the civilian population too. And you are forgetting that the civilian population of East Pakistan is made up of Muslims.'

'Not Muslims, Vakil sahib,' Mirza sahib responded hotly, 'but Bengalis. Bangladeshis! I have no sympathy with those traitors.'

'Also remember, Mirza sahib, that there are a hundred thousand Pakistani soldiers in East Pakistan. A nuclear explosion can harm them too.'

Disappointed and speechless, Mirza sahib responded, 'Then, if nuclear bombs are not to be used, what is the use of nuclear-armed aircraft?'

'As far as I can make out,' Vakil sahib said, 'it isn't America's purpose to jump into the war but only to show its strength in the Bay of Bengal.'

'Only a show?' Mirza sahib asked. 'What earthly good is a show?'

'It is very useful,' Vakil sahib responded in a sagely tone. 'By sending its Seventh Fleet into the Bay of Bengal, America has warned India that it should refrain from war, otherwise America, with the strength of its forces and nuclear bombs, will side with Pakistan.'

Mirza sahib got the point, and his lost enthusiasm returned. At least America had reprimanded India to desist from its daily mischief or else... If the Indians cared for their lives, they would now give up the dream of capturing Dhaka, or would have to bring out their fleet to tackle the American nuclear fleet. They were trying to bully Pakistan, thinking it was alone. With Allah's grace, they would now see that Pakistan was not alone. A superpower like America was on its side.

When Mirza sahib returned home, his spirits were still soaring with the thought of the Seventh Fleet, and his steps scarcely touched the ground. He heard another bit of good news as soon as he crossed the threshold of his home, and his heart's joy knew no bounds. Nadeem had been selected for the Pakistan Foreign Service. He had stood sixth in the competitive examination held by the public service commission. Today he had made his father's dreams come true: the dream that Mirza sahib had expressed when he had first held him and blessed the newborn, 'With Allah's grace, you will be a deputy commissioner.' He himself had served as a sub-divisional clerk in the canal department all his life, but in his dreams he had always imagined Nadeem as a magistrate, deputy commissioner, judge or ambassador. And today, Nadeem had realized those dreams. Mirza sahib had suffered many deprivations and denied himself much to see Nadeem through college. For many years he hadn't got a new sherwani stitched for himself, nor bought a new pair of shoes. Ever since Nadeem had started going to college, Mirza sahib had worn his son's old sherwanis and shoes. He would stay awake half the night to keep Nadeem company as he studied, just in case the boy felt lonely or needed something.

Today he had received recompense for all those deprivations, all those sleepless nights. After a few years, perhaps, Nadeem would end up as Pakistan's ambassador to America. Then Mirza sahib would retire, and go and live with him.

There was hustle-bustle in the house. Neighbours were coming in to convey their congratulations. The begum had sent Juman to the market to buy sweets, and was uncontrollably happy as she distributed these to the neighbours. She took a laddoo and, with the tips of her sandalwood-coloured fingers, put it fully into Mirza sahib's mouth and smiled into his spectacles. His spectacles shone. He recalled those youthful days before his marriage when he would suffer all day and all night, wounded by that smile.

All day, intoxicated by happiness, Mirza sahib soared in the heavens. This intoxication did not leave him even as he lay down on his bed, already half asleep. Suddenly someone picked one corner of his quilt, and a fragrance seemed to enter his bed. Not only a fragrance but also warmth and the smoothness of sandalwood. Mirza sahib liked the begum's way of making up after a fight. She would use this method only once in a while, but when she did Mirza sahib would forgive all the harsh words of her sharp tongue. Today he was already delirious with joy. The begum had just added to it. Today had truly been an exceptional day, crowded with joys. This loving union with the begum and before that Nadeem's glorious success and before that—before that there had been something else, too. But try as he might, Mirza sahib could not recall that third thing.

Gondlanwala

Shabbir lay on the bed for a long time, one arm under his head, staring vacantly at the ceiling. His face was serious, and his heart despondent. This time, coming to Gondlanwala had brought him no happiness. He normally came from Lyallpur to his maternal grandparents' village during the holidays, when it was time for the Marhi fair, with its famous wrestling bouts. It was the wrestling bouts and the wrestlers' great feats of strength that attracted him most to the fair. Gondlanwala was a village of Sikh wrestlers, who were known throughout the area for their prowess. During the fair, they would wrestle each other and put on an exhibition of their strength, twirling huge dumb-bells and clubs, and lifting massive weights. At first he didn't understand the terms for the different varieties of weights and equipment, but now he even knew what a 'magra' was—a weight made of a strong wooden bar with a heavy bag of soil attached to each end. During the last fair, he had managed to lift a magra. He had been keen on physical activity since childhood, and had by now developed a strong, muscled body through regular exercise, even though he was barely eighteen.

Even if he had waited for the holidays and come at the time of the Marhi fair, he wouldn't have been much better off. Pakistan had already been created, and all the Sikh wrestlers had left the village and were sitting in a refugee camp in Hafizabad. Gondlanwala couldn't be called either a Sikh or a Muslim village; it was a village of Gondal Jats, and they could be Sikhs as well as Muslims. For centuries they had lived like brothers. But now the country's partition had given a new meaning to their identity. They were no longer Gondal Jats, only Sikhs or Muslims. No, it would not have helped even if he had come during Marhi.

He had come with his mother for his grandfather's last rites. They had not been able to arrive in time for the funeral. By the time the telegram had reached them in their holdings in the Sandalbar region, the old man had been buried.

Choudhry Karim Bakhsh's death shook Gondlanwala. Nobody could believe that the man was no more. Even at sixty, he had been as strong as a lion. The healthy eating and outdoor life of his youth had ensured that his face still shone like heated bronze. His blood would race and his spirit swoon in ecstasy as he willingly threw himself into work in the fields, despite his age and the availability of sufficient labourers. He had done no wrong in his life, had never hurt anyone and had followed the path of honesty and truth. Not only was his body fresh, a pure soul too dwelt in it; he symbolized decency to the people of the area. Nobody had ever opposed him, and even the wise would seek his advice. He had looked as if he could go on another twenty years or so. But he was gone in an instant...

Shabbir's grandmother had told him and his mother the story of his grandfather's untimely death when they had reached Gondlanwala the previous evening at dusk.

Looting and killing had begun in the other villages in the area as soon as Pakistan came into existence. Choudhry Karim Bakhsh knew that his son Manzoor and his group of layabout friends were involved in the violence. He told Manzoor off several times—even shouted at him—but Manzoor did not back off. Karim Bakhsh knew that Manzoor and his group of thugs wouldn't hesitate to ransack Gondlanwala. So while there was still time, he sent the Sikh families of the village to the refugee camp at Hafizabad under the protection of some men he could trust.

But then one day, he heard that Manzoor had abducted the unmarried daughter of Surjan Shah Lamba from the village of Qazi da Kot. The choudhry was blind with rage.

'Oh, you spawn of evil!' the choudhry's voice cracked. 'Why have you done this terrible thing?'

Manzoor raised his brown eyes and replied, 'Bapu, why do you curse yourself? If I am the spawn of evil, then who is the evil?'

'Shut up, you son of a dog!' Karim Bakhsh roared. 'Where is the girl?'

'Girl?'

'Yes. Surjan Shah's daughter, the one you've carried off.'

'I didn't carry her off,' Mansoor narrowed his eyes further. 'My mare carried her. I just put her on the horse.'

'You evil, wretched boy! Talking back? I wish you had drowned instead of forcing yourself on the girl.'

'I did not force her. There she was, clinging to the dead bodies of her parents and brothers, sobbing away. I picked her up and tried to comfort her, and she fainted in my arms. So I put her on my mare.'

'Where have you hidden her?'

'Why do you want to know? I brought the girl back for myself. What right do you have to start salivating at the thought of her?'

'Dog! Thug! Pimp! I will tear you to pieces!' Karim Bakhsh grabbed Manzoor by the collar and shook him hard. 'Tell me where the girl is. I'm going to take her to her uncle, Jagira Gondal, in the Hafizabad Camp.'

'Let go of me!' Manzoor screamed.

'Let go? I'll skin you alive!'

Manzoor Ali was built like an ox and was proud of his youth. But his excesses had taken their toll on his body, and he knew that he could not match his father's iron strength.

'I didn't bring her just so I could have some fun,' Manzoor stuttered in his own defence. 'I will marry her properly.'

'Bravo! You will marry her! You killed her parents and brothers, and now you'll marry her?' Karim Bakhsh tightened his hold on his son's collar. 'You'll only marry her if I don't kill you first.'

'Please, let go of my collar. I cannot breathe,' Manzoor yelled again.

With that, Manzoor Ali smashed his fist into his father's face. Blood began to flow from the choudhry's nose.

Karim Bakhsh pounced on Manzoor and started to beat him mercilessly. His rage had not yet subsided when Manzoor ran out of the house, screaming and yelling at the top of his voice.

The choudhry was breathing hard. Then all of a sudden, he felt a sharp pain in his chest, and fell dead on the floor.

Shabbir's grandmother also told them that now, the entire village knew that the accursed Manzoor had hidden the Lambas' girl at the choudhrys' well. Near the well, there was a kaccha thatched shed, where Jumma, one of the choudhry's labourers, lived. Next to it, Manzoor had constructed a pukka room where he used to indulge in drinking sessions with his friends. Many of the villagers had seen the abducted girl peeping through the bars of that room's window.

Suddenly, Shabbir stopped gazing vacantly at the ceiling, and stood up from his bed. He shoved his feet into his slippers and left the house. His quick strides took him to the well of the choudhrys. Through the barred window, he saw a thin, pale and fragile girl sitting on a wooden bed, her face streaked with tears. Jumma's wife, Saida Bibi, was trying to feed her. But the girl pushed away the bowl of rice and cup of tea with a listless hand. Saida Bibi gave up and walked out with the dishes. When she passed Shabbir, he saw that her eyes were full of tears.

Jumma saw Shabbir from where he had been tending to the lentil crop and came over to him, the hoe still in his hands.

In a condoling tone, he said, 'It has been a big shock—this news about the choudhry.'

'It's God's will,' Shabbir replied.

'The choudhry was a very fine man, but he did not understand Islam much.' Jumma shook his head dismissively, as if he himself were a great scholar of Islam.

Shabbir was speechless. He raised an eyebrow towards Jumma.

'Now see,' Jumma carried on by way of explanation, 'if he understood Islam then why did he fight with his son over this act of charity.'

'Act of charity?'

'Of course,' Jumma affirmed. 'The act of charity that Manzoor Ali and his fellow crusaders are performing.'

'Crusaders!' Shabbir's anger had been roused. 'You call those skunks, those evildoers, those murderers, those rapists—crusaders? They are not performing acts of charity; they are demeaning Islam.'

Jumma again shook his head sadly and said, 'It seems to me that you understand Islam only as much as your grandfather did.'

Maulvi Qutbuddin saw Shabbir from the dirt track that ran alongside the field, and stepped towards him to express his condolences. Jumma, meanwhile, saw Manzoor Ali approaching on his mare from the other direction and started heading towards the paddy fields in the distance.

'So, Shabbir,' Manzoor Ali asked, getting off his mare, 'how come you are here?'

'Nothing; I was restless. I thought I would go for a ride, but the stable is empty. Where is grandfather's Dula?'

Dula was the name of the choudhry's horse.

'I've sold Dula.'

'Sold him? But why?'

'Just sold him.'

'When?'

'Whenever.'

Shabbir recalled that Dula was a rebellious and self-respecting animal. He never allowed anyone but Choudhry Karim Bakhsh to ride him. He had never taken to Manzoor Ali. Once, when Manzoor had tried to mount him roughly, Dula had bitten him in the calf. Manzoor had burned with fever for a month and a half because of that bite, and had barely escaped the jaws of death. Shabbir knew that Manzoor had sold off Dula to avenge that insult. And he must have done so in the past few days. Nobody would have dared raise a covetous eye towards Dula while the choudhry was still alive.

'Then, Uncle, I will have to ride your mare today.'

'No, young man,' Manzoor warned. 'My Naazo is very touchy. And you are the precious only son of my only sister. If something were to happen to you, your mother wouldn't let me live.'

'You are not worried about me, Uncle, you are worried about your mare. But I promise not to tire her too much. As long as she doesn't behave too badly with me, I won't spur her too hard.'

'You? Tire her? She will tire you! And it's she who will behave badly with you. Look at how you brag, and that too without sprouting a moustache!'

'I am going to ride her today, come what may,' Shabbir was insistent.

'Back off, boy,' Manzoor cautioned. 'Seems you don't know anything about Naazo. She doesn't let anyone touch her except me. Why are you playing with death?'

Shabbir had heard tales of Naazo's friskiness. He knew that even the best riders of the area shuddered at her name. In fact, judging from her rebellious spirit, she may well have been a close relative of Dula. But Shabbir had dealt with frisky horses on their holdings in Sandalbar. His reckless sense of youth was ready for the challenge.

'Don't worry about my life, Uncle. Just take off the saddle. I prefer to ride without one.'

The young boy's challenge cut Manzoor Ali to the quick. Let him die if he wants, he thought. Let him go to hell. My duty was to warn him. The villagers already hold me responsible for my father's death. If they blame me for this, it's no big deal.

Manzoor Ali noticed that the night rain had softened the ground. Even if the boy fell, he wouldn't die.

He took off the mare's saddle. 'Damn you, then! Don't say afterwards that Uncle didn't warn you. Go ahead and ride this little devil, if you are so keen on breaking your bones. See the Chimnis' well over there? Ride to it, then jump the canal. After that, go around Saida's well, jump the canal again and come back here. Stay within my sight and Maulvi Qutbuddin's sight the whole time. If you come back in one piece, I'll reward you.'

'What'll you give me?'

'Whatever you ask.'

'Swear?' Shabbir asked, but he wondered if an oath by a man like Manzoor Ali was of any use.

'I swear on the Holy Quran, to Allah,' Manzoor swore with his hand on his chest.

But just then it struck him. What would he do if Shabbir asked for the mare as reward? Then he dismissed the thought. The boy would never have the courage to ask for so big a reward.

'You'll give me whatever I ask?'

'Yes. But what if you come back with your bones broken, all covered in the mud from the ditch?'

'Then I will clean your stable and dispose of Naazo's manure for a full year.'

'Don't go back on your word later.'

'Swear.' Shabbir took an oath.

'A beardless boy's oath has no value. We need a witness.'

'What witness?'

'Who can be a better witness than Maulvi Qutbuddin? Speak, Maulvi, do you accept?'

The maulvi nodded in agreement.

'I, too, accept,' said Shabbir and leapt on to the mare.

The mare moved her ears affectionately and started walking, taking small steps and putting on airs, as if she were happy to carry the light weight of Shabbir on her back. He thought, This mare has heard of my skill as a rider, and is afraid to gallop.

'No, no, Naazo,' Shabbir urged, 'this won't do. Try a bit harder! Let's see what you are made of.'

And so saying, he dug both his heels hard into the mare's sides. Immediately, he felt a storm stirring under him and knew that the mare was about to come into her own. The horse jumped into the air like a ball. Then she planted her forelegs on the ground and bucked, but Shabbir managed to cling to her body. Then she shot off like a bullet.

Like a flash of lightning, the mare bolted past the well of the Chimnis. Then she leapt across the canal in a single bound. Her anger rose with each passing minute, as she felt Shabbir still on her back. Circling Saida's well, the mare leapt back across the ditch. Then she decided to play a trick. She began to leap repeatedly from one side of the canal to the other. Shabbir dug his heels deep into the horse's sides with all his strength and clasped his arms tight around her neck. He began to tire quickly as she jumped and jumped, and he felt like he was about to die.

'Keep at it,' he told the mare. 'I will not die alone. I will take you with me.'

By this time, Shabbir was panting and every bone in his body hurt, each muscle crying out in pain. He was about to lose heart when the mare changed her behaviour again. She wasn't tired, but it was as if she had taken pity on the boy. She turned toward the choudhrys' well, where her owner was waiting for her, walking softly like a swallow flying in the sky.

'Well done, boy,' said Manzoor Ali, in a tone laden with defeat. 'You have kept intact the honour of Sandalbar.'

'My reward,' said Shabbir as soon as he had caught his breath.

'Ask. Whatever you want. But just don't ask for the mare,' said Manzoor, already going back on his word.

'No. What would I do with the mare?'

Mansoor Ali sighed in relief.

'Otherwise, you can ask for anything in both this world and the next.'

Shabbir thought of this world and the next. In both places, he saw only one thing: a thin, pale, sad face, stained and streaked with tears.

'Give me the Lamba girl.'

Manzoor Ali was dumbstruck. He couldn't believe his ears.

'What did you say?'

'You heard what I said perfectly well, Uncle.'

'Have you gone mad? I'm going to marry her. What would you do with her? She is four years older than you.'

'I will take her to her uncle, Jagir Singh, in the Hafizabad Camp.'

'You are as stupid as your grandfather.'

'Be careful, Uncle, you are going back on your oath. You swore.'

'Yes, I did swear. But how could I have known that you had such evil in you?'

'Evil or truth, Maulvi Qutbuddin can decide. You yourself made him the witness.'

'Maulvi,' said Manzoor, 'do you want to live in this village or not?'

'I do.'

'Then think before you speak.'

The maulvi was a slight man, but he had a spine of steel. He was afraid of no one but Allah. He had truly understood Islam, and had followed the path of truth and justice all his life. His integrity was well known in the area.

'The boy is right,' he said. 'You're going back on your word.'

'Just you wait, Maulvi, I'll show you.' Grabbing the maulvi by his collar, Manzoor Ali lifted him off the ground with a single motion.

'Kill me if you want,' the maulvi screamed. 'You are an evildoer. You have insulted Islam. You'll pay the price on the Day of Judgement.'

'I see, Maulvi,' Manzoor Ali said, putting the maulvi back on the ground. 'But you'll pay the price right now.' He punched the maulvi hard in the face, and the maulvi fell on to the strip of raised earth between the fields.

Shabbir couldn't hold back any longer. He sprang at Manzoor like an eagle. Powered by his steely muscles, his fists pounded Manzoor's face and body. The uncle couldn't hold his own against his nephew's strength and speed. Shabbir beat Manzoor until he fainted and fell into the field of lentils.

In a flash, Shabbir unbolted the door of the room and brought the girl out.

'Let's go, sister. Let me take you to your uncle. Hurry up before it's too late.'

He picked up the wavering, stumbling girl and put her on the mare, then leapt on the mare himself, and spurred the horse towards Hafizabad.

'Go, my children, may Allah protect you.' The blessings of Jumma the labourer's wife, Saida, accompanied them as they went.

The Crimson Tonga

Before they left Rawalpindi, my aunt and uncle came to meet me in Lal Kurti cantonment.

That was in September '47, after Pakistan had already come into existence. The killings that had taken place six months before, in March, were matched in ferocity only by the Noakhali riots. Hindu and Sikh villages such as Narhali, Duberan, Kallar, Thoa Khalsa and Dera Khalsa had been reduced to smouldering ruins by murderous mobs, whipped up by fanatic slogans.

My aunt's village, Phulra, was among the handful that had survived. The main reason these villages had been spared was that they lay in hilly terrain: the narrow, steep trails made it difficult for large mobs to gather for attacks. In any case, peasants were so poor in these hilly areas that even the merchants and moneylenders weren't rich enough to make the crossing of such difficult terrain worthwhile.

The British Raj was in its death throes but it hadn't yet given up the ghost. It still had enough life in it to rescue Hindus and Sikhs from the surviving villages in Rawalpindi division and bring them to a newly constructed large refugee camp near a village called Wah, on the road from 'Pindi to Peshawar, not far from the Hassan Abdal Railway Station. Later, this refugee camp became well known as Wah Camp.

My aunt and uncle had spent the six months between March and September '47 in Wah Camp. The travails of life in the camp had left their shadows on their faces. My aunt's eyes still had the same light, but the glow that used to emanate from her face was now marred by wrinkles and furrows. My uncle's white turban had lost its smartness and its pristine whiteness, and his beard had lost its earlier shine.

'We went to the house in New Colony first,' my aunt said. 'The Muslim neighbours told us that you had started living in your office in Lal Kurti cantonment.'

It was true. I had begun to live in the compound of my office at the army's services selection board. For four and a half years I had worked at the army headquarters in Delhi, all the while yearning for Rawalpindi—the town where I had been born, in whose lanes and bazaars I had passed my childhood, youth and early manhood. My homesick longing came to an end suddenly one day in February '47, when I got the news that I had been posted to the board's office in Rawalpindi. My joy knew no bounds, and I rushed back to Rawalpindi. The following month, the villages around Rawalpindi were consumed by violence. It was only due to the strict measures taken by the decent and enlightened Muslim deputy commissioner that the town itself had been spared. But two months before Pakistan was born, Hindu and Sikh families began to abandon the city. Locking up their shops and houses, carrying what they could with them, they left for Patiala. The once-flourishing lively lanes and colonies now wore a haunted look. Some of my Muslim friends appealed to me that I, too, should move into the barracks of my office in the cantonment until the whirlwind of violence had passed.

I related all this to my aunt.

'Get ready, come with us,' she said. 'Throw a few things into a suitcase and come with us to Patiala.'

'No,' I told her. 'It's difficult for me to leave just yet.'

'Difficult? It was difficult for your uncle too, who used to say that nothing will ever happen here. "If the Muslims kill all the Hindus and Sikhs, then whom will they rule over?" he used to ask. Even after everything had transpired here, he still wouldn't move. "Rulers change, populations don't move," he used to say. Six months in Wah Camp has brought him to his senses. Now he cannot wait to get to Patiala.'

My uncle kept nodding in silent agreement.

'You are right,' I said. 'But it's a question of my job. I cannot leave yet.'

'To hell with jobs! Your life is worth everything. If you save your life, there will be no shortage of jobs.'

I couldn't deny that she was right. But I wanted to keep my livelihood when I left Pakistan. I didn't want to lose my job and end up living on charity in some refugee camp.

'Another week or so,' I told my aunt. 'You go to Patiala; I'll be there before you know it.'

'Who knows what can happen in a week?' said my aunt despondently. 'We didn't come to make a social call: we came to take you with us to Patiala.'

I reiterated my predicament. The employees of the services selection board had been asked to indicate their preference for serving the government of either Pakistan or India before 15 August. This decision could be revoked if they changed their mind over the next six months. Most of the employees of the board belonged to the Pothohar region, and couldn't bear to leave their birthplace and their properties to move across the Ravi. So they all chose to serve the Government of Pakistan, emboldened by the knowledge that they could still change their decision over the next six months if they wanted.

The chairman of the board hadn't yet sent our acceptances to the army headquarters when suddenly the direction of the wind changed. Rawalpindi began to empty. Houses began to be boarded up. The lanes and neighbourhoods wore a deserted look. Rumours about the fires of Lahore and the killings in Sheikhupura became rife. Fear descended into our hearts and grew until it became a monster. So the employees made up their mind to go to the chairman and tell him of their intention to change their earlier decision.

The chairman, a Muslim colonel, stared at us in anger, as if we were somehow betraying the newly formed state of Pakistan. But he couldn't do anything, since he knew that the government had given us the right to change our decision. Fuming, he sent off our new applications quickly to Delhi. That was about fifteen days ago. Any day now we hoped to receive acceptance from Delhi, and be free to leave.

I explained all this to my aunt.

'I don't understand all these official matters,' she said. 'All I understand is that you should leave with us right now. It's not right that we old people should run and save our lives while a young man like you stays in this danger.'

'There is no danger in Rawalpindi town,' I consoled her. 'The deputy commissioner is a God-fearing Muslim. Even in March he didn't let the town come to harm. This time, I hear that he has warned all the gang leaders in the city that he would be merciless with them if any violence broke out.'

My aunt was not satisfied but she relented in the face of my resolve. She got up to say farewell. I touched her feet and then bent down to say goodbye to my uncle. He patted my back.

'May God take care of you,' my aunt blessed me and kissed my face.

Something happened within me when she kissed me. I didn't want them to leave, not right then. I wanted them to sit with me, to stay. Some strange emotion had taken hold of me. I couldn't understand it, but I couldn't wish it away either.

Looking at my watch, I said, 'The refugee-special train to Amritsar isn't till five-thirty. I know it's crowded and you need to be well in time to get seats and space for your luggage. But it's only a quarter to three. The tonga will take only ten minutes from here. Stay a while longer.'

When they sat down, a sudden fancy caught hold of me and I said to my aunt, 'Tell me a story about my childhood. You've related them many times before, but I still like them so much when I hear them from you.'

My aunt's face lit up in front of me. The frowns and wrinkles that had been etched on it by Wah Camp seemed to vanish. She was back in my childhood, and her youth. I felt as if I could see a faint crimson glow around her face. All of a sudden she looked like a newly-wed girl.

She smiled. 'You were only two and a half then. You would put a towel on a wooden stool and wave the little hand fan over it. We had a small brass vessel on which we used to put a rubber nipple, so that you could drink milk from it. Glass bottles were not much in use then. You would fill that vessel with water. Then you would circumambulate the stool while sprinkling water on the ground. "What are you doing, little man?" I would ask. "Bhakti, bhakti," you would reply.'

'And what did that mean?' I teased my aunt.

'You should know. I don't,' she replied.

'Okay, now tell me another one,' I insisted like a child.

'Which one?'

'About the crimson tonga.'

'You were even younger then, not yet two. There was a church behind our house in the New Colony. It had a large compound surrounded by a low boundary wall. There was a tonga stand beside the wall, where about fifteen or twenty tongas would be waiting for customers. I would hold you near the rear window of the upper floor of the house and ask you, "Which tonga do you want, little man?" And each time you would give the same answer, "The crimson tonga."'

When they finally got up to leave, I went with them to the main road. The tonga was waiting for them, their baggage already loaded on to it. The coachman had nodded off while waiting. I was happy to see that it wasn't just any coachman but Khairati Lal, who was distantly related to my uncle.

When I got back to the barracks, I saw the board's watchman Dilawar running towards me. Someone was asking for me on the office phone. I went across. It was Khairati Lal, calling from the railway station.

'Our tonga was attacked,' he said breathlessly. 'Just outside the station, near the tonga stand.'

Then his voice broke.

'Where are my uncle and aunt?' I asked repeatedly. But I got only a tearful silence in reply.

Hurriedly, I called for the office jeep. I took Lance Naik Ali Akbar with me as driver. It took us about five minutes to reach the station, and in that endless time I tried to prepare myself for the worst.

A crowd had gathered around the tonga. Without a word, they parted to let me pass. Instead of my aunt and uncle, I found two bloodied bodies. My uncle's on the road, and my aunt's on the back seat of the tonga. There was a deep gash at my aunt's temple. Khairati Lal's faded tonga had turned crimson with their blood.

I fell to my knees and touched my lips to my aunt's feet.

'You forgot, Aunt, the crimson tonga was meant to be for me.'

The Butcher

When I stepped into the drawing room, I sensed a strange tension in the air. It occurred to me then that the tension was radiating from the faces of the guests and had invaded the entire atmosphere. Their faces seemed to say, *We are tired of looking around. There is no girl who can match our very handsome son. We are ready for yet another disappointment today.*

The boy was truly handsome, one in a million.

'This is my elder brother.' Tripat introduced me to the guests. 'When we were in Tanzania, he was Neeti's local guardian in Delhi. And we don't take any decisions in our family without his agreement.'

The boy's father gave me a cold look. I took no notice because I was staring at the boy. Beauty had always been my weakness, whether in a man or a woman.

We, too, had searched far and wide for a match for Neeti, but had not found anyone suitable.

When she walked in from the bedroom door, it seemed as though the moon itself had come in through an open window. Dressed in jeans and a cream blouse, she was quite a picture. The life on her face! The cut of her features! Her eyes, as if someone had dissolved the golden sun in sapphire waters!

The listless faces of the guests lit up with sudden interest. The boy's face turned dark red. His eyes took on a dreamy look.

'This is our Neeti,' I said. 'Her name is Navneet, we just like to call her Neeti. An innocent girl, without any guile. Not at all like her nickname!'

Neeti looked at me with sweet reproach and said, 'Uncle, there you go again, starting already!'

Her voice, as bright as the sound of tinkling silver bells, further shook the guests. They had been staring fixedly at her. Now their eyes shone with joy.

'Oh, yes,' I continued, 'she is now doing her master's in literature from St Stephen's College. She topped her BA Honours with a first class. Keats and T.S. Eliot are her favourite poets, and in Punjabi she worships Mohan Singh.'

The guests, who till then had been sitting uncomfortably on the edges of their chairs and formally looking away from the dishes on the table, loaded with sweets, now settled back comfortably and began to fill their plates merrily. Their happiness was unbounded. They chirped with glee, and every time they stole a look at Neeti a new lilt would enter their voices.

A beautiful face and sharp features can overwhelm anybody, and you are no exception, I thought.

But all I said was, 'Please try these sweets. A new kind, called pakeezah.'

'And our boy,' the boy's mother was telling Tripat, 'says that he wants a very simple wedding. No ceremonies, no dowry. But the girl should be exceptionally beautiful.'

The boy looked down, trying to hide his face in his plate of sweets.

'Of course, my dear sister,' the boy's mother continued with a proprietary tone in her voice. 'What's the use of material things in the long run? But a daughter-in-law should be such that if she sits in the kitchen her light emanates all the way to the courtyard.'

With that, she threw an enveloping look towards Neeti.

I don't want to give the impression that only the guests were happy. We, too, were very agreeable to the match. Tripat's bright and unworried face bore witness to her happiness. And my silent brother-in-law, who could write long notes on the files in his ministry but couldn't string together two sentences of small talk, couldn't hide his happiness either. We had waited and looked for a long time, but at last it seemed that we had reached our destination.

The boy's mother was hugging Tripat; the boy and Neeti were surreptitiously examining each other and the boy's father was relating stories about his department to me. He had sloughed off his cold behaviour like an old skin, and now he was warm and voluble. Matters soon came to such a pass that instead of waiting for us to fill their plates, they began to fill ours.

Extending the plate of rasgullas towards me, the boy's father said, 'Here, please have these rasgullas. They're very good.

'Seeing you, I recall a Bengali joke,' he continued. 'There were two Bengali babus eating rasgullas...' He began to laugh at the thought of the rest of the joke, an uncontrolled, wild laughter. As he laughed tears began to stream from his eyes, his brown pupils became golden, his pale cheeks began to shine like seashells and an overlapped tooth in his lower jaw revealed itself.

A memory flashed across my mind... In October '47, I had accompanied an army convoy from Delhi to Amritsar. The government had established a new army organization charged with rescuing Hindus and Sikhs from the newly formed Pakistan. This organization had its headquarters in Amritsar. My parents and siblings were in Rawalpindi. I wanted to reach Amritsar and do my best to get them out. There were no trains or buses running to Amritsar because of the riots. After someone used a bit of influence, I was allowed to travel with the army convoy. There was another man besides the driver in the truck I was travelling in, a handsome young man who laughed at the drop of a hat. His laughter had brightness, it had life. I was transfixed. When he laughed, tears would stream from his eyes, his brown pupils would become golden, his pale cheeks would began to shine like seashells and the overlapped tooth in his lower jaw would reveal itself.

The convoy had suddenly stopped somewhere between Ludhiana and Jalandhar. There was a great commotion in the fields beside the road. Some men, staves in hand, were searching the field as if for some hunted animal. One of them held a sword. Then I saw a poor-looking Muslim step out of the field. He tried to run, but he was frozen with fear and couldn't move. The next moment the sword was poised above his head like death itself.

He fell at the feet of the man holding the sword and begged, 'For the sake of the Guru, O Sardar, have mercy on me. I have young children.'

It seemed as if he would die of fear itself. The man with the sword hesitated, and I thought his soul had rebelled against the evil deed.

'Go, run away,' he told the unfortunate man, pushing him away from his legs.

In the same moment I saw that the face of the young man with me in the truck had turned bright red, like super-heated iron. In an instant he jumped out of the truck, pulled the sword out of the other man's hand and cut the poor Muslim to pieces.

Returning to his seat in the truck, he said, 'Last March, these cruel people killed eight of my family members in Kahuta.'

The boy's mother was telling Tripat, 'Let's not fiddle about. We should fix the wedding straight away. Long engagements are no longer the custom. We are fortunate that we have met people who are just like our family, gentle people.'

The boy's father was nodding firmly in agreement, testifying to his family's gentleness.

But a fire had erupted inside me, and I screamed out, 'You! Gentle people? I've known you for years. You're butchers! Murderers! Get out of here! We won't give our lovely daughter to butchers!'

The Crusader

A soft knock sounded on the door. Khalil had just gotten up to open it when his father, Choudhry Umra, stopped him.

'Don't open it, for the sake of your ancestors.'

For a moment Khalil paused. Then he felt ashamed of his hesitation.

'Why should I not? No mob is going to attack us. Those who had to suffer have suffered.'

'Don't open it, fool.' The choudhry stared hard at him. 'I'm telling you, don't do it. Already they cannot stand me and my views. They have tasted blood. If any Gondal or Sansi comes in, we won't be able to do a thing.'

The soft knock sounded again. Khalil unbolted the door. The choudhry was embarrassed to see that it was only Reshma, his sister-in-law's daughter. To hide his embarrassment he went out into the courtyard.

Khalil did not recognize her at first. The face of the once happy-go-lucky young girl was careworn.

'Reshma, is all well?'

'Something awful has happened, brother,' she answered, trembling like a leaf. 'As soon as I heard of it I rushed to you, without even waiting to put on my shoes. Do something if you can.'

'But what has happened?' Khalil put his hand on her back to console her.

'That useless Bashir, the son of the ironsmith Dina. He... Preeto...Preeto...' Preeto's outraged modesty rankled like the tip of an arrow in Reshma's heart. She couldn't complete the sentence.

'Preeto, the moneylender's daughter?'

'Yes, my best friend from childhood. Bashir's gang of Gondals has killed Rama Shah and his wife Mathura Devi, and looted the haveli. The Gondals finished their looting and went back to Gondlanwala, but Bashir has locked up Preeto in the living room of the haveli. I implore you, brother, for the sake of Allah, do something. Daggers pierce my heart each time I think of her.'

She saw the blood rise to Khalil's face.

'You go home, Reshma,' he said, 'and don't worry. If Allah wills, Preeto will sleep at your house tonight.'

First, Khalil got Fazlu the wrestler to keep an eye on the Shah's house. Fazlu's skills as a wrestler were renowned throughout the area. He had subdued several young bulls like Bashir. He had lived the high life in his youth, but after marriage he had turned into a religious and honest man. Now he earned his livelihood by running a tonga.

Walking towards the house of his uncle, Khuda Bakhsh, Khalil wondered what sort of a Pakistan was this that had entered their village like some maddened bull, trampling humanity under its hooves and turning everything upside down?

Choudhry Khuda Bakhsh Varaich lay listless on a cot. Khalil had never seen him this way before. The skin now hung loose on his jaws, and the wrinkles on his face looked like furrows ploughed deep into sandy soil. He seemed to have aged fifteen years in the last ten days.

Khuda Bakhsh had already heard of Preeto's abduction. 'Listen to me, boy, there are no two ways about it: daughters are common to all. Those who commit atrocities on daughters invite God's retribution.'

Khalil saw that tears were shining in the old man's henna-coloured beard, and his voice seemed to be coming from the grave.

'God's retribution will come when it will, Uncle, but what's killing me now is that these mobs went through this village shouting "*Allahu Akbar*" and demeaning Islam, and we did nothing.'

'I tried what I could, son.' Khuda Bakhsh's head shook uncontrollably. 'But I am old now. My days are over. When I had first got the news I went to Gondlanwala village. I beseeched the Gondals to desist from violence and looting. I begged them in the name of God and the Prophet, and I begged them in the name of this white beard. I put my turban, the honour of my ancestors, in the dust at their feet. But they paid me no heed. There was a time when nobody would have dared go against the word of my grandfather or his father. That's how much goodwill they had earned in these villages. And today, my honour turned to dust in a second. I told the Gondals, "The Hindus and Sikhs of my village have not harmed you. Tomorrow, we will send them with a refugee column, and it will be my responsibility. But please, for the sake of the Prophet of Medina, do not kill them, do not loot them. They are closer to me than my own people. I have come to you with this request. Please honour the fact that I did that." But they replied, "We didn't invite you to come here. You're the one going around spouting nonsense for the sake of infidels. This is the sort of Muslim you are. You will suffer badly on the Day of Judgement." Insulted and dishonoured, I came back from Gondlanwala. I still can't forget the moment when one of their young men grabbed my beard.'

Khalil didn't say anything. He couldn't say anything.

'With the fear of the Englishman gone, every rogue thinks

he can do what he wants. I say that if this Pakistan is to survive and flourish, we'll have to put an end to what these depraved villains are doing. I mean, even from our own village this bastard Bashir has joined them. What a fine man his father Dina is, and what an utter scoundrel the son has turned out to be. If I could I would strip men like him and have them beaten up in front of the whole village.'

On hearing Bashir's name, anger flared up in Khalil's eyes.

'Uncle, just let me have your gun. I swear, Uncle, I'll teach him a lesson by smashing his face in before his foul hands get a chance to ravage Preeto.'

'Be careful, son,' Khuda Bakhsh warned. 'That Bashir is evil.'

With the gun in his hand, Khalil felt the courage of some crusader bubbling up inside him.

'Don't worry Uncle. I'll take his measure today. Evildoers are always on the up until the true holy warriors charge into battle. I swear by the Holy Quran that I'll take my life in my hands today.'

Rama Shah's sitting room was next to the dharamshala's well. There was a veranda in front of the sitting room, which could accommodate four or five cots. In the corner stood a broken-down wooden bed, which the looters had not thought worth carrying off. Crouching behind this bed, Khalil wondered wryly why they had left it there. They could have used it for fuel in the tandoor for four or five days instead.

Bashir unlocked the door of the living room and was about to pick up the lantern from the floor of the veranda when Fazlu the wrestler, who had been hiding near the well, ran and caught him in a tight hold, throwing him down on to the ground. Bashir tried to free himself from the wrestler's hold, but Fazlu had muscles of steel. Khalil came out from behind the old bed and put the double-barrelled gun to Bashir's temple. When Bashir had turned towards the haveli at deep dusk, he had already drunk half a bottle of spirits, but at the sight of the gun the alcohol in his veins turned to water.

'Speak, you bloody wretch,' Khalil said tersely. 'You insult to our faith!'

In the yellow light of the lantern, Khalil's face shone like copper. The silver pendant in his neck seemed to be made of gold.

The touch of the double-barrelled gun and Khalil's fiery gaze shook Bashir. He thought first of the gang he had looted and murdered with. They were all sitting in Gondlanwala and Qazi da Kot enjoying themselves, and he was the only one who had been caught. If his companions had been with him, this impudent choudhry whelp wouldn't even have dared to look at him.

'But what have I done wrong, Choudhry?' Of necessity he spoke humbly, and his voice wavered like his spirit.

'What have you done? What you've done wrong is that you are a blot on humanity. The likes of you are the shame of this new Pakistan. Where is Preeto?' Sparks seemed to fly from Khalil's angry words.

'Well done, Choudhry! Getting all worked up about that infidel girl, are you? We won't get in your way. You can enjoy her for the first few months. When you tire of her you can pass her on to us.'

Khalil shoved the barrel into Bashir's temple. Fazlu, too, hit him twice powerfully in the face. Two of Bashir's front teeth fell out.

'Speak, you bastard. Where have you hidden the girl?'

Bashir was raging inside, but he knew that if he made the slightest move or tried to escape, Khalil would shoot him straight in the head. And nothing would happen to the choudhrys for killing him: everyone knew they were powerful and influential men.

'I will tell you,' he said, in a defeated tone. 'But don't shoot me.'

Only the thin white slivers of Bashir's eyes were picked up by the light of the lantern; the rest of his face was contorted with fear.

'A bullet would be an easy death for you,' Khalil said sternly. 'The likes of you should be chopped up into pieces.'

Bashir sat quietly in submission. All his evil intentions seemed to have melted away. Spreading his hands helplessly, he silently gestured towards the door of the living room.

Khalil spat on the ground with hatred and removed the gun from Bashir's temple. Fazlu kept his knee dug deep into Bashir's chest.

Opening the door of the living room, Khalil raised the flame of the lantern. All the contents of the room had been looted. Preeto was doubled up in one corner of the bare floor, sobbing and drained of all colour.

'Get up, sister! Reshma is waiting for you.'

Coming out, he shoved the barrel of the gun into Bashir's side again.

'Listen, you foul villain. If you're going to live in the village, then live like a proper human being. If you don't, I'll be your worst nightmare.'

The touch of honest humanity opened the floodgates inside Preeto. When balm was applied to the wounds caused by depravity, she cried inconsolably. For a long time Reshma held her tight, and calmed her sobbing.

Khalil wanted to take Preeto away from the village immediately. Anything was liable to happen in blind, lawless days like these.

Preeto told Reshma that the previous week she had received a letter from her maternal uncle saying that he and his family had reached Kamoki Refugee Camp. Neither Khalil nor Reshma could think of anything better than to take Preeto there. The train to Kamoki was due to reach Gujranwala station at one in the morning. At midnight, Khalil and Preeto left the village on Fazlu the wrestler's tonga. Dawn had just broken when they reached Kamoki Camp and found her maternal uncle.

Preeto broke down as she hugged her uncle. Her howls pierced Khalil's heart. After her family had calmed her down somewhat, she got hold of herself for a moment and looked towards Khalil. She couldn't manage even a single word. Her dust-covered lips trembled for an instant as if to say, 'May you live long, my brother. I will pray for you as long as I live.'

Hope

A strange restlessness, some deep dejection had taken hold of me that day, and I could not fathom why. More than anything else, an immense loneliness seemed to be swallowing me up; though, considering where we lived, it was difficult to feel lonely.

Helpless as straws buffeted in the huge refugee wave that followed the dreadful aftermath of the country's partition, people had clung to whichever shore that came to hand. We had somehow reached Delhi. Some were carried as far as Kanyakumari, and others ended up even further, across the Indian Ocean, on the islands of Andaman and Nicobar, and began to live the life of prisoners of earlier days. Their fault lay in that they were inhabitants of the northwestern part of the country that had been the victim of an accursed political decision of departing rulers, and were left at the mercy of an angry fate. They had been on the wrong side of the line which had been drawn to divide the country. To come from the wrong to the right side, to cross that bloody line, they had had to pay a very heavy price; everybody's fault was the same, but each one paid a different price.

We were fortunate that we found a place in Delhi. In the capital of free India, under the eye of the central government, we didn't have to face too much trouble. We found a room in the Lady Hardinge hostel near the railway station. This hostel was normally reserved for the attendants of patients admitted to Lady Hardinge Hospital, and there were many rules of admission. But the wave of refugees broke all rules; in some cases, as many as three families occupied a room. Even as the hostel employees watched helplessly, it was turned into a refugee camp in the space of a day. Troubled hearts found solace in the company of fellow-sufferers and the days began to pass swiftly in the hustle-bustle of the refugee camp. Nobody found time to sit alone, relive the recent atrocities and shed tears of blood.

That day I was alone at home. My husband used to spend the entire day in office. After standing for weeks outside the employment agency office, he had managed to get a job. We had been barely married a year and I was pregnant. Under these circumstances, it would have been natural to feel low. But so involved was I in the throbbing life of that refugee camp that I didn't have time to be sad.

But that day, for some reason, I had no heart for anything. My wandering gaze fell on the half-open door of the neighbouring room, and I understood the cause of my dejection. An old man of about sixty lived in that room. He had come there the day after we had started living in the camp. No one seemed to know him, and he had never been seen talking to or even looking towards anybody. He would pass by quietly, eyes lowered, lost in faraway thoughts. Gradually, he had become the focus of everybody's curiosity. But till now no one had found out anything about him. Not a rumour, not a word. He remained as much a mystery today as he had been on his first day. In this sea of humanity, where everyone shared their tragedies with one another, he stood alone.

His remote personality didn't permit anyone to come near him, to bar his way, look into his eyes and ask, 'Where've you come from? How did you come? What all did you go through? What wounds, what sorrows are wrapped up in your troubled heart?'

No one had the courage to step up and ask, 'Why are you alone at this age? Like the hollow trunk of an old tree, you have drifted in this wave to the shore alone. Where are your children? Your relatives?'

Nor could anyone ask, 'Why don't you speak? Why don't you look up? What killer blow has made you bend down forever? Whose terrible hands have caused your head to tremble so?'

His personality may have been remote, but it was pleasant. I had liked him from the first day itself. I found something pure and decent in his face. A bright glow seemed to emanate even from his unwashed clothes, and my heart would always fill with respect at this sight. My father had passed away when I was a child, but for some reason I felt that had he been living now, he would have been like this person.

I hadn't seen the old man all morning and was finding it difficult to get through the day. His absence had created a strange emptiness. I knew that I liked him, but I hadn't realized until then how much. My worried gaze kept returning to the half-open door, and my heart sank at the thought that he may be ill.

Finally, I pushed open the door slightly. After some hesitation, I stepped inside. My fears were proved right. He was ill. He lay curled up on a badly crushed blanket on an old string cot in the corner, his turban pillowing his head. The sound of my entering the room made him open his eyes. His bloodshot eyes told me that he had a high fever. I felt his pulse. I was right again. Covering him with the blanket, I began to gently press his head.

A slight smile appeared on his lips. They trembled and fluttered and he spoke, 'Navneet, my daughter, you have come?'

I didn't say anything, could not say anything.

He spoke again, 'Navjot did not come?'

With an effort I replied, 'My name is not Navneet.'

The hint of a smile on his lips vanished. Those fevered eyes searched my face.

'Who are you?' he asked in a defeated tone.

I told him my name.

I felt a burning sigh against my wrist. Then his eyes, heavy-lidded with fever, closed again.

I left the room to try to get a doctor. My husband wasn't back yet. I asked the young Sindhi boy next door to fetch the doctor and made some tea. Clearly, he hadn't eaten or drunk anything since the morning.

That fever of a day and a night left him very weak. He couldn't get up from the cot for another week or so. I had the good fortune to serve him for those days. I saw him up close, got to know him. His life had been a closed book to me, but now when I turned one page, I kept on turning. He didn't stop me. I got a chance to peep into a great soul. The soul that had once been so powerful and creative that it had given birth to souls like Navneet and Navjot. Now, when I saw that spirit in poverty and despair, I lost my balance. My heart was shaken as if by an earthquake, the walls of my existence cracked open, and my beliefs and values lost their bearings.

Navneet and Navjot began to live in my imagination. Their bright foreheads, their sharp and intelligent features, their fearless and rancour-free spirits took over my consciousness. I could see thousands of impure hands of communal violence reaching out to besmirch the honour of that lone girl, even as she clung to her brother. That barbarous mob would do its worst, but would not be able to separate brother and sister from each other. Then some strong arm would impale a spear in the boy's back. The sharp spear would cross its target and go through both brother and sister. Those two pearls of life, strung on the same spear, would writhe in pain, while the same tyrannical hands reached out for the old father's head.

That bloody drama would play in my head all day in an unbroken sequence. At night, the two pearls would toss and turn on a spear, in that zone where I lay between wakefulness and sleep. All night, all day, I would tremble and clench my hands until my nails began to bite into my palms.

I knew that this state of mind was dangerous for me, especially since my child was due any day. But try as I might, I couldn't get those images out of my head. Most troubling was the confusion in my mind: my objectives, values and beliefs had all been clouded over. I was lost in some thick fog and search as I might, I couldn't see a single path that could lead me through it.

A father had given all his ideals, his values to his two children. His entire experience, all his toil, all the brightness of his life had been poured into them. He had squeezed into them the essence of the world's philosophies, civilizations, religions. Like lotus flowers, he had kept them above the muddy waters of superstition, fear, intolerance and narrow-mindedness. Then that dreamy-eyed father had begun to dream of a brave new world based on the foundations of his children. And then...

The next day when I went to his room, he was reading the newspaper. Perhaps it wouldn't be correct to call it a newspaper, though. It was a scrap of an old newspaper, which I had spread on the teapoy, setting his medicine bottles on it. Some report in that old paper had caught his attention. He was so engrossed in it that he didn't notice me entering the room. I saw that a smile had spread gradually across his face, a living smile that reached all the way to his eyes. Instead of being happy at the sight, I began to worry. I had seen this cheerfulness for the first time on that face, and my instinct told me that it couldn't be a happy development.

'You look very happy today,' I said, trying to divert his attention.

'You haven't read this news.' He impatiently shoved the newspaper towards me. 'Scientists have now developed a bomb which is ten times more destructive than the atomic bomb. Now this world will be destroyed very soon.' Then, with an insane eagerness, his eyes began to go through the report again.

'Why do you feel like that?' I couldn't stop myself from asking. 'Life is not going to be defeated by atomic bombs or hydrogen bombs. The development of these bombs is only a warning to life and you will see that, in response, it will give birth to new powers that will slay these bombs.'

The smile vanished from his face. He looked at me, then at the report. Then again at me, and then got lost again in the news.

After a while he spoke again, as if he hadn't heard what I had said, 'Scientists are hopeful that, in the next six months, they will produce so many hydrogen bombs that the world can then be destroyed in one go. Just think about it,' he was lost again in that happy thought, 'the entire world—in one go—only six months from now.'

I couldn't say anything more. I didn't want to take away his moment of happiness. Besides, I was overtaken by a flood of pain that very moment, pain sent by my child in its hurry to be born. My legs were trembling, cold sweat broke out on my brow; I felt that my child would arrive even as I stood there.

'Please, somehow,' I heard myself saying, 'get me quickly to the Lady Hardinge hospital. My husband is in office. Give him a call.'

I gave birth to twins, a girl and a boy. I barely survived their birth, and had to stay in the hospital for many days. But he didn't come to see me even once. I thought that he had forgotten me. Then one day, he appeared, holding a newspaper in his hand. He sat on the chair next to the bed. Staring vacantly around him, he made no effort to ask after me, nor did he express any desire to see the children. When at last he turned his attention to me, I complained, 'I've been waiting so many days. You didn't come to see me. You've been very busy?'

'Yes,' he replied. 'Very busy.'

'With what?'

His eyes brightened up and he said, 'I was reading about hydrogen bombs. With great happiness I have reached the conclusion that the world will now last only a few days.'

I fell silent. After a while I heard myself saying, 'Do you know what I have named my son and daughter?'

He looked up. There was no curiosity, no question mark in his gaze.

I said, 'I call this boy Navjot, and this girl Navneet.'

His face paled. For a moment his head stopped trembling, then began to tremble again, ever harder than before. Then his eyes misted over. He reached forward to take both children in his lap, and his eyes began to shed tears, like merciful clouds. He kept smiling happily at me through the veil of tears.

'I read in today's newspaper that the leaders and people of many countries have raised their voice against hydrogen bombs,' he said. 'It seems that, at long last, this weapon will be snatched away from the hands of tyrants. You were right. Life cannot be defeated by atomic and hydrogen bombs. Soon, life will give birth to powerful new forces, which will slay every hydrogen bomb in existence.'

The Minor Gandhis

Standing in one corner of the casualty ward in Irwin Hospital, Begma was praying fervently.

'O Great God, for the sake of Your Prophet, have mercy on me. Accept the prayer of this worthless slave. O Merciful One, O Bountiful One, give back the health of my son. I am a sinner. I do not deserve Your mercies, O King of both the worlds...'

All of a sudden she could not concentrate on the prayer. Someone was shouting and screaming in the ward. She saw that two hospital workers were putting a freshly wounded man from a stretcher on to the bed—the third bed in the opposite row—that had been vacated earlier the same afternoon. The wounded man's trousers were torn in several places and splattered with blood. Tossing his head on the pillow he screamed, 'Oh, someone kill me, please. Give me a poison injection. I cannot bear this pain any more.'

When Begma enquired, a hospital worker told her that the man had been riding his bicycle down Ring Road when a truck had hit him from behind. Both his legs had multiple fractures.

Begma knew that the wounded man would cry and wail and call out for death all night. But the next morning, when he would have been operated upon, his legs put in casts, and given painkilling injections, he would calm down. In the last three or four months, hundreds of wounded had come into this ward and gone away fully recovered. Hit by trucks, buses or scooters, with their legs, arms, ankles, knees and backs crushed, they would come here and go back good as new. Most of them would come in screaming, but there would be some who would grit their teeth and endure the terrible pain in silence, their faces pale. When they would return from the surgery on the stretcher, their eyes would be shut and their necks limp under the anaesthesia. Then it would seem as if they would never again open their eyes or lift their heads. But one by one they would recover and vacate their beds for the next man. Only Begma's son was destined to hang between life and death for months.

Many other patients besides her son had been brought to the hospital in an unconscious state. Some had their hair clotted in their own blood. But they would regain consciousness after their wounds had been bandaged and they had been given two or three units of blood. After that, their recovery would be a matter of time. The surprising thing was that there wasn't even the sign of a blow from the lathi on her son's head. Nor had he shed a single drop of blood. The doctors had been unable to diagnose his unconscious state. They had tried everything. Now they would only look up silently towards the ceiling in response to the question in her eyes as if to say, 'Now it's in God's hands. The matter is no longer in our control.' It said something for their humanity that, despite the fact that three and a half months had passed, they hadn't given up hope.

Begma lived with the constant fear that any time some doctor would turn around and say, 'Take this living corpse home. There is no point keeping him in the hospital any more. Vacate this bed now. We are in dire need of beds.'

It was true that, for the last three and a half months, Sadeq had been one of the living dead. Not once had he blinked his eyes over this long period, not once had he opened them. The only sign of life in his body was the slight movement of his chest with his soft breathing. For the last three and a half months she had lived in dread of the thought that, in some evil moment, this mildly heaving chest would also stop moving and her world would be plunged into darkness. Whenever the thought crossed her mind, her own heart would stop and she would stand up in fright. She would put her ear to his chest and listen for his heartbeat. At that time it would seem to her that the heartbeat had actually stopped and whatever she was hearing was an illusion. She would then put her fingers below his nostrils and try to feel his breath. The warm breath would comfort her. She would sit down by his bedside and start counting her beads again.

She had been counting beads, praying to Allah, beseeching Him. It is said that when medicines do not work then prayers do the job. But her earnest and sincere prayers had been unsuccessful. Allah had paid no heed. Why did He not listen? He could do anything. In a moment He could turn a desert into a garden. By His will He had parted the sea for Moses to walk through. Had human sins, human atrocities so soured His heart that He now refused to listen to the prayers of His creatures? Then she would think, nobody ever had all their prayers answered. Which prayer to answer and which to ignore, that too was in the hands of God. If God would answer man's every prayer, then man would make God do anything and would, in fact, become a sort of God himself.

Often a thought would cross her subconscious mind. Perhaps she should pray, 'O Merciful One, I cannot bear it any more. Either you bring my son back to his senses or let death liberate him from this torture. I cannot see him in this condition any more.'

But this prayer never travelled from her subconscious to her lips. In fact she would begin to curse herself. What sort of a mother was she, wishing death for her son? Her son was unconscious, true, but he was alive, he was breathing. And who knew when that blessed moment might come when he would open his eyes?

Her eyes remained on the heaving chest of her supine son and her mind turned to the past. Memories of three and a half months ago would play havoc with her mind every day. A dark storm had been unleashed on the country when the dream of freedom had been actualized after centuries. Caught in the grip of the monster of communal passion, the nation had been engulfed in bloodshed, and the mourning had silenced the celebrations of freedom. When the entire country was in flames, how could the capital escape?

October had just begun; only a month and a half had elapsed since the tricolour had been unfurled on the Red Fort on 15 August when Delhi, too, succumbed to the flames. Muslim shops were looted in its lanes and bazaars. Many colonies were torched. For three days and three nights the life and honour of Muslims was torn to shreds by butchers in the name of religion. The army took control of the city on the fourth day. They rescued the remaining Muslims from the affected areas and brought them to Tees Hazari Camp.

A military truck had come to take her family too, but Hakim sahib had hidden them the moment the riots had begun. Just where Kucha Ram Lakhàn opened into Sitaram Bazaar stood Hakim Chiranji Lal's three-storeyed house with its balconies. It faced into Sitaram Bazaar. Begma used to live in the first house in Kucha Ram Lakhan. In fact, the Kucha was named after the great-grandfather of the hakim. Just as the looting and killing started in the capital, the hakim made arrangements for Begma and her family to move into two rooms on the third floor of his house. No incident took place in Kucha Ram Lakhan during those three hellish days and nights. The hearts of the Muslim inhabitants trembled in the cold grip of fear, but nobody raised a hand towards their life or property, nor made any move to dishonour their women. Then when the army came, all the Muslim families were moved to Tees Hazari Camp. Except Begma's family. Hakim sahib did not agree to sending them to the camp.

'You are very keen to suffer in that camp?' he taunted them. 'You are not comfortable in my shabby dwelling? Stay even if you are uncomfortable. If someone sets fire to the house, we will burn first on the lower floors and only then will the flames reach you.'

'No, Hakim sahib.' Sadeq had stepped forward with folded hands. 'Permit us to leave, please. Why do you take on this danger for our sake?'

'Dangers are taken on for one's own, young man,' Hakim sahib replied, taking Sadeq's folded hands in his. 'Do you consider us outsiders? For me Sadeq is just like my son, Ram Swarup.'

It was Hakim sahib's greatness that he showed so much love and affection and did not let them leave his house. There was really no relationship that they had with him. True, they had been neighbours for many generations. If there was any other relationship, it was that Begma had been the midwife for Ram Swarup's wife Sushila for all her deliveries. Sushila had never agreed to go to any hospital; she had ultimate confidence in Begma's skilful hands. After all, hadn't Ram Swarup and his sister Kusum, who now lived in Bijnor, been born into Begma's hands? So were all four of Ram Swarup's sons born this way, and the entire family addressed Begma as Amma. In those difficult days, the third floor of Hakim sahib's house had seemed no less secure than any fort to Begma and her family.

A lamp of hope was lit in those dark days when Gandhi ji went on a fast unto death against the Delhi riots. The conditions in Delhi began to improve, to the extent that Muslim families began leaving the security of the Tees Hazari Camp to return to their homes in the lanes of Delhi. Some even began to work again; after all, one needs to work to feed oneself. Families cannot be fed by sitting idle in the security of the house. Thinking along these lines, Sadeq, too, brought his fruit handcart to its usual place outside Hakim sahib's shop. In the dusky twilight, three men with long bamboo staves appeared out of nowhere. The first blow caught him right in the middle of his head, and he fell down unconscious in the street. They hit him many times and, leaving him for dead, sauntered off into the next lane.

Hearing the commotion, Hakim sahib had come out of his shop. Quickly he had put Sadeq in a tonga and taken him to the casualty ward of Irwin Hospital. Leaving him in the care of the doctors, he had returned in the same tonga to give the bad news to Begma.

Begma had gone numb upon hearing the tidings, her daughter-in-law Waheeda had swooned and fallen to the floor and two-year-old Raeesa had started whimpering. Hakim sahib had mixed some rose essence in cold water and splashed it on Waheeda's face. When she had regained consciousness, Hakim sahib had comforted them all. He had carefully seen that there was no wound on Sadeq's head or body. Not a drop of his blood had been spilt. A blow on the head often resulted in the loss of consciousness. He was in the good hands of the skilful doctors of Irwin Hospital. God willing, he would recover and be back in a few days.

That night itself, Begma had put her mattress next to the corner bed in the casualty ward of Irwin Hospital. For two and a half months Waheeda, carrying two-year-old Raeesa in her arms, had brought her food and tea three times a day. As the days passed, Waheeda had grown pale and weak; it seemed she was losing hope. Often she would fall into Begma's arms and sob uncontrollably. She would cry silently because of the other patients in the ward, but those silent tears would tear Begma apart. But try as she might, she could not sob herself. She began to wonder of what dust Allah had made her that no matter what sorrow she encountered, she was unable to cry. Even when Sadeq's father had died at the height of his manhood after drinking poisoned hooch, she had not let out a wail. Last month, when her son-in-law Maqbool had been killed in the Meerut riots, again she had not shed a tear. She had asked Maqbool so many times to take a truck and bring the family to them in Delhi. They would have faced their fate together, whatever it brought. But he kept sending her messages that she should come to Meerut and stay with them till order was restored. He argued that they were not safe among the Hindus of Kucha Ram Lakhan, while in Begum Pul in Meerut they were fully secure in a population that was 90 per cent Muslim.

But fate had spared neither Maqbool in Begum Pul nor Sadeq in Kucha Ram Lakhan. And nobody had heard Begma wail when Maqbool died, nor did she howl for Sadeq. Yet when she would rest her back against her son's bed and face the wall, alone with her sorrows, the fever would rise from her heart to her head and her tears would run down her wrinkled cheeks. She would not try to stop them then, nor would they have stopped if she had tried.

Despite the entreaties of her parents, Waheeda had not moved in with them in Kucha Khanam. She continued to stay alone with Raeesa in her home in Kucha Ram Lakhan, returning from Hakim sahib's third storey once Begma moved to the hospital. She had nothing to fear now. Fate had already dealt its worst blow.

Then Begma recalled the morning when not Waheeda but Hakim sahib's wife Saraswati Devi had brought her breakfast. She had told Begma that the previous night Waheeda had taken the train to Pakistan with her parents. She had told Hakim sahib's family, but had given no sign of her intentions to Begma. Poor Waheeda, fragile and young, had cracked in two and a half months. The strong entreaties of her parents had worn down her resistance. Extreme sorrow, Begma thought, can easily twist human relationships.

If Waheeda had told her, Begma would never have stopped her from going to Pakistan. But she must have been afraid that her intention would falter in front of Begma.

Yes, Waheeda had gone away to Pakistan. But Begma was a mother. Her Pakistan was that corner of the casualty ward where her son lay.

She had held Saraswati Devi's feet and asked her to promise that she would never again bother to bring food and tea for her to the hospital.

'What's the use of my eating anything? For so many days, Sadeq has not swallowed a bite. They insert the glucose tube, then they take it off. I don't know what he is living on. Even the food Waheeda brought would not go down my throat. Yours, even less. I am already weighed down by your debt. For God's sake, don't make me a bigger sinner. I will get something from the vendors standing outside and carry on.'

Saraswati Devi respected her entreaties and did not bring food to the hospital again. But that same evening Roshan came instead. A tiffin box dangling from his belt, he came in step by step, aided by his crutches. Roshan Lal was Hakim sahib's third grandson, fairer and better-looking than all his brothers and the most unfortunate. He had been born a bonny baby of twelve pounds. But he had fallen victim to the evil eye and gotten polio as a child. His right leg hung like a half-dead piece of flesh from his body. With the help of his left leg and his crutches he would take each step quickly and with great courage. When he was a class-eight student, three ruffians had made his life hell by calling him The Cripple. The cheerful boy could not take this insult for more than a week and had finally stopped going to school. Instead, he had taken his place as heir to Hakim sahib's healing practice. Ram Swarup had not been interested and had joined an insurance company, and the other grandsons were too embarrassed to sit in the shop.

Begma was dumbfounded when she saw Roshan Lal bringing her dinner. When she could utter a word she caressed Roshan's back and said, 'Roshan, my son, why did you bother?'

Roshan replied, 'Amma jaan, first you call me your son and then you ask why I bothered? Do children have no duty towards their mother?'

'But why did you come so far, from Sitaram Bazaar all the way to Irwin Hospital?'

'I didn't walk. The rickshaw wala brought me right into the hospital.'

'Okay, but don't do this again after today,' she said firmly.

'I will do this every morning and evening,' Roshan replied, holding her feet. 'Until Sadeq bhai is in hospital. Amma, I beg you not to try and stop me. Because I will not be stopped. I am your useless son, Amma, who could not even go to school. Don't take this duty away from me.'

For this last month, Roshan had brought her breakfast in the morning and dinner in the evening.

Begma was suddenly pulled away from these thoughts. The nurse, Dorothy, came into the ward in a fluster. Fear had added its pallid colour to her dusky complexion. She whispered something in Dr Bhaskar's ear. Dr Bhaskar had just then put his stethoscope on the back of the patient in the bed adjoining Sadeq's. When he heard the nurse, the stethoscope fell from his hand. He stood for a while in utter confusion and then hurriedly left the ward.

'What has happened?' Begma asked the nurse. 'Why are you so flustered?'

Sobbing, Dorothy said, 'Someone has shot Gandhi ji.'

'No!' Begma screamed. 'This is not true. How can it be? This cannot be!'

The messiah of humanity, who had taken the entire country's evil upon himself—how could anyone shoot him? But then a crucifix appeared before Begma's eyes and she saw that Jesus Christ was nailed to that crucifix. Then it was Mansur hanging on that cross. And now it was Gandhi ji's frail body on the crucifix. This world had always nailed the angels of goodness and kindness on the cross.

It was someone's vile and evil hand that had shot the prophet of peace and non-violence. Was it a Muslim's hand? The thought sent a chill through her body. As it was, the Muslims were suffering badly in Hindustan. Now riots would flare up again. Thousands of innocents would be killed. Then Begma heard Bishambar, the ward's sweeper, come in and inform the patients, 'Gandhi ji has been shot by a Sikh refugee. He has been caught. They say he has left huge properties in Peshawar and has come here full of anger. After firing the gun, he was heard shouting at the top of his voice, "Gandhi used to say: Pakistan over my dead body. Pakistan has been formed. Then why is he alive? That is why I have made him a dead body."'

Begma felt a slight relief in her heart.

Nobody would say anything to the Sikhs. If it had been a Muslim there would have been hell to pay.

Rattan Lal, lying on the bed next to Sadeq's, seemed more troubled by his curiosity than from the pain of his broken bones. He called out to Bishambar. Bishambar eagerly came and repeated the entire story in the same words. Today, Bishambar considered himself a very important man in the country, because in all of Hindustan he was the only one who knew who had shot Gandhi ji.

Then someone said, 'This is wrong. I just heard the radio on the way. Gandhi ji has been shot by a Hindu whose name is Nathuram Godse.'

Begma saw that the man who spoke was Roshan, who had just entered the ward with her tiffin hanging from his belt.

Bishambar's face fell. He could not argue against the official news heard on the radio. In a moment he had changed from a very important person to just Bishambar the sweeper.

Begma's eyes left Roshan's face and fell on Sadeq's. She could not believe what she saw. Sadeq's eyelashes were fluttering. Then he opened his eyes. He looked around himself in all directions and then spoke in a soft voice, 'Has Gandhi ji given up his fast unto death?'

Before she could stop him, Bishambar said loudly, 'Gandhi ji has been killed today.'

Sadeq's eyes shut again. He took a few difficult breaths, and then his chest stopped heaving.

Begma stood motionless, numbed by two blows. When she could think again, she felt that her son had done the right thing. He did not want to live in a world where prophets of peace and non-violence were shot to death. She, too, would not live in such a world any more. That would be the first thing she would do once she had buried her son. She would take her life with her own hands. It was no crime to commit suicide if the choice was to live in such a world.

Then her eyes fell on Roshan, who was holding Sadeq's body and crying. Something flashed across her mind. In that flash, she saw that Roshan, too, was a minor Gandhi. There must be thousands of such minor Gandhis in India who would get together and give a new shape to the country, to the world, to life.

Begma decided then that she would not jump into death's darkness. Instead, she would live in the light of minor Gandhis like Roshan.

Sikhism

Though it was called Mughal Chak, the village belonged to Sikhs. There were very few Mughals, meaning Muslims, who lived there; those who did were all landless labourers who tilled the lands and harvested the crops of Sikh landlords. The landlords included some wealthy Sikhs who had also been given land in the new canal colony of Mannawala in Sheikhupura district, where the soil was so fertile that it very nearly beggared belief. These powerful families spent time in either Mughal Chak or Mannawala, as their fancy took them, leaving their lands and crops in the hands of their clerks while they were away.

When Pakistan was established, the Muslims of the village told the Sikhs, 'There is absolutely no need for you to leave the village. No one will dare touch you while we are around.'

It even happened that when the Pakistani flag was unfurled on top of government buildings and houses in towns and villages on 15 August, the Muslims of Mughal Chak asked Zaildar Chet Singh to do the honours. This gave some relief to the village's worried Sikhs. Their minds began to harbour a new possibility. How did it matter that Pakistan had been formed? So what if the Muslims had become rulers? After all, hadn't Hindus and Sikhs lived under the Muslims for many centuries? When power changes hands, there is revolution, there is violence. But that was over now. Bad things had happened, but now that there was a legitimate government it would surely be a just and fair one. After all, the new country could hardly be without laws... Not even an Islamic state would let Muslims go on killing Hindus and Sikhs, taking their women and stealing their properties...

The truth was that they deluded themselves with such arguments because they did not want to leave their beloved land and property. And besides, there was no guarantee that even if they left the village they would reach Hindustan alive. They had heard of the killings in Sheikhupura and the looting and burning in Lahore. Caravans of refugees were being attacked on both sides of the border and trainloads were being massacred. The wisest thing was to stay in their ancestral homes and look after their land and property, hoping all the while for better days and leaving the rest to God.

But the times did not improve; in fact, they worsened. Finally one day, the Muslims of Mughal Chak said, 'Now you are in danger here. Thousands of Muslim refugees, ravaged and looted, have come from the other half of Punjab and settled in the surrounding villages. They are seething for revenge. Take your cash and valuables and go to the Gujranwala Refugee Camp before they decide to start settling scores. From there, you can get across the border by train or in one of the large caravans. It shames us to say this, but matters are no longer in our control.'

Our caravan of about a hundred and fifty left Mughal Chak at midnight. It stayed off the metalled main road and tried to find its way down dark paths. Nobody had brought along a flashlight or a lantern: we wanted to escape searching eyes by walking in complete darkness. But when we got close to the village of Qazi da Kot, the light from dozens of lanterns hit us in the face. A large crowd stood behind these lanterns, blocking our path. Somehow they had found us out.

In the blink of an eye, the zaildar's son Gurnam, Subedar-Major (retd) Shivdev Singh and Sardar Bakhshish Singh of Mannawala aimed their double-barrelled guns.

'Don't fire,' a voice commanded from the other side. 'We're armed too.' We saw four guns on their shoulders. 'We will happily shoot, but we don't want any violence.'

Our response was an unbroken silence. We stood with bated breath.

'We will most definitely rob you, but we won't kill you. However, there's one condition.'

Nobody from our side asked what the condition was.

'The condition is that you give us your arms and ammunition.'

Gurnam, the subedar-major and Bakhshish Singh exchanged silent glances and agreed that wisdom lay in taking these people at their word and handing over the guns.

As soon as our guns and bullet belts were in their hands, seven guns started firing at us. More than half the members of the caravan fell right there. I saw my father and my younger brother Sukhjit fall before my eyes. The bullets kept chasing those of us who tried to run.

Day had broken by the time I finished slinking through the corn and millet fields to the Gujranwala Refugee Camp. By afternoon another thirty or thirty-five members of the caravan had also reached it. My mother, sister and youngest brother Kultar were among them. We stayed in the camp for what seemed like an eternity. My mother mourned and cried for my father and Sukhjit like a madwoman. She would quieten down when she saw us, but her eyes showed that when we were not around nothing could stop her tears.

About three weeks later we joined a large caravan and made it across the border. At Dera Baba Nanak we found military trucks waiting to take us to Amritsar. On the way we encountered such a foul smell that the women covered their noses with their dupattas and the men with their hands, and the children began to vomit. I looked out from the truck and saw hundreds of bodies on both sides of the road—men, women, children, old people. These unclaimed bodies were swollen with the water of the rains and had been rotting for God alone knew how many days. The military trucks ploughed through the bodies for an interminably long time. The entire two-furlong-long caravan of Muslim refugees had been massacred.

In that instant, my soul sank in shame at the thought that most of the killers who had committed this atrocity claimed to belong to my religion. I was struck by a sudden memory of the previous April.

The riots of March '47 in Rawalpindi division had just ended. All the Hindu and Sikh villages had been razed to the ground. Their passions whipped up by religious slogans, the mobs had spared nothing. They had sprinkled kerosene oil on schools and burnt them down, children and all. In some villages, small handfuls of Sikhs had pulled out their swords and fought to death against hundreds. Women had jumped into wells to save their honour. Some fathers killed their daughters with their own swords before they turned to face the mobs. We were shocked when word reached Mughal Chak about the atrocities perpetrated in the villages of Rawalpindi division in March '47. We said, 'This is just a taste of the tyranny that the Muslim League will unleash in the entire country if they don't get Pakistan.'

What had happened in the villages of Rawalpindi could be repeated any time in any other district of West Punjab—Jhelum,

Wazirabad, Sheikhupura or Gujranwala. Unwilling to die unarmed, we took the swords from our storage trunks: Zaildar Chet Singh's grandson Dhanwant, Subedar-Major Shivdev Singh's eldest son Gurpratap and I. We were all contemporaries and had passed our FAs together from Guru Nanak Khalsa College of Gujranwala. We managed to get the swords out of their scabbards with great difficulty. Not only were they blunt but badly rusted too: nobody had needed them during the peaceful British Raj. What use were these blunted and rusted swords to us now? We decided to have them honed and sharpened.

'Why not ask Din Muhammad to do it?' suggested Dhanwant.

'Have you gone crazy?' Gurpratap was quick to snuff out the suggestion.

Din Muhammad was Mughal Chak's ironsmith. But at such a sensitive time there was no question at all of asking a Muslim ironsmith to hone our swords.

'Then what should we do?' I asked.

'I know,' said Gurpratap. 'Let us go to Gharjhakh. There's a Sikh Sikligar who makes swords, knives and other weapons. Nobody can make a blade as sharp as he can.'

Gharjhakh was at least twelve miles from Mughal Chak by way of side-paths through the fields. We started after breakfast and were knocking on the weapon-maker's door about two hours later.

It took him an hour and a half, but Sukha Singh the weapon-maker honed those three swords as if we were off to conquer Jamrud Fort.

On the way back to Mughal Chak we came upon three Muslim labourers who were harvesting wheat near the village of Qazi da Kot. Two of them took one look at us and began to run. Running hard, they jumped over the irrigation channel and vanished towards Qazi da Kot. The remaining companion, a weak-looking middle-aged man who had not stopped cutting the wheat, called after them, 'Come back you idiots! Why are you running away? Oh, what's wrong? Have you seen some ghost? Khair! Fiza! Come back, I say! There's no danger here.'

We stopped and watched them run, listened to him calling out to them to return. When his companions could no longer hear his shouts, the man turned towards us.

'Young men,' he called out, 'long may you live. Give me a hand and lift this bundle of wheat on to my back.'

We looked at one another with surprise on our faces. Instead of running away, this man was calling us towards him.

When we got closer to him, Gurpratap said, 'Your companions ran away as soon as they saw us. But you...?'

'They're idiots.' He was visibly embarrassed by what they had done.

'They were scared of us,' said Dhanwant.

'They're idiots,' he repeated.

'Why didn't you run away?' I asked.

'I'm not an idiot like them.'

'You're not scared?' Gurpratap asked.

'Of what?'

'You know what's happening nowadays,' Gurpratap insinuated. 'You're a Muslim, we're Sikhs. You weren't scared?'

'Why should I be afraid of Sikhs?' he responded with a smile.

'What?'

'Baba Nanak's Sikhs are all good people,' he said, and we saw that his smile had lit up his entire face.

'But we have swords in our hands,' I said. 'Your companions got scared of our swords and ran away.'

'They're complete idiots. I, on the other hand, know that your Guru gave you your swords and they are never raised against an innocent man.'

We exchanged glances again. Tears had welled up in our eyes.

And now, sitting in a military truck ploughing its way towards Amritsar through piles of Muslim corpses, I saw that the Muslim peasant had a better understanding of Sikhism than those who only looked like Sikhs and had committed this act of carnage between Dera Baba Nanak and the holy city of Amritsar.

Ek Onkar Satnam—1935

When Baqir Hussain brought the bowlful of khichri to Zeenat, he saw that she was asleep. Often she would stay up all night in a fever and then fall asleep during the day. For a while he gazed at his wife's weak, pale and lifeless face. She seemed like a candle that was melting away fast, and soon a burnt-out black wick would be all that was left of her. His soul trembled at the thought. Then his eye fell on the rapidly cooling khichri and he tried to get a grip on himself. It was already late afternoon, and she hadn't eaten anything since the morning except for two spoonfuls of cereal and a few sips of milk.

He softly caressed her burning forehead and gently pushed back a lock of hair that had fallen across her face. Zeenat started from her uneasy sleep. Her hot breath touched his hand and she opened her eyes. She looked around sadly for a moment, and spoke, 'Was it then a dream?'

Another hot sigh surged up to his forehead as he bent over his wife.

'What?'

'What I just saw.'

'What did you see?'

'I saw,' she continued in a voice full of yearning, 'that I was playing hide-and-seek with my childhood friends in my father's mango orchard in Amethi. It was my turn to seek and I caught someone straight away. When I removed the blindfold from my eyes, I saw that I was clutching a parrot in my hand, and an entire company of parrots was cackling in the mango grove. There was no sign of my friends.'

When she paused to catch her breath, Baqir Hussain tried to feed her a spoonful of the khichri.

'Not yet,' she pushed away the spoon. 'Let me finish remembering the dream.'

'Not done yet?'

'No.'

'What happened, then?' Baqir Hussain played along with his sick wife.

'Then the parrot in my hand flapped his wings and spoke. You know what it said?'

'The parrot?'

'Yes.'

'What did it say?'

'It said, "Sweet girl, if you let me go I will take you to Purqazi."'

There we go again, thought Baqir Hussain, but he did not let his irritation show on his face.

'The parrot flew in front, and I behind it. Across the Roorkee canal and then along the Muzaffarnagar road. We landed on a lorry loaded with sugar cane and settled down on the piles of cane. Then we chatted and sucked on the sugar cane all the way to Purqazi.'

The momentary light that had come into Zeenat's eyes at the memory of her dream vanished.

'No,' she said. 'I don't want rice. I don't want to eat anything. I am not hungry. But I beg you with all my heart, just take me to Purqazi once.'

A helpless sigh escaped Baqir Hussain. Getting up from

the stool, he came and sat on Zeenat's bed. For a long time he humoured her as if she were his young daughter, not his wife. All the while that his trembling fingers caressed Zeenat's hair, he was lost in thoughts of the past. If only he could fulfil Zeenat's wish! But why couldn't she understand, despite being an adult, that Purqazi was now in another country? It might as well be across the seven seas now that Pakistan had been created.

Earlier it was his mother who would carry on about Purqazi.

'Oh, please take me to Purqazi,' she would beg him. 'Either Purqazi, or leave me in Barabanki.'

Purqazi was where her husband was buried; her parents' graves were in Barabanki.

She would spread her dupatta and beseech God.

'*Ya Allah!* Take me away. Accept my dust, Great Sustainer. Free me from this exile however you can.'

She continued to consider Pakistan a foreign land during the year and a half that she lived there after crossing over. Baqir Hussain had tried to convince her that Pakistan had been made through Allah's will, and that true believers should consider it their good fortune to live in this country. He was amazed that neither his mother nor his wife could understand that simple thought. He had driven himself mad dealing with his mother, and now had to do the same with his wife.

For three months his mother had suffered from bloody dysentery, unable to leave her cot. No medicine, no folk remedy could cure her.

'Oh Baqir, may God give you a long life! Take me to Purqazi once. I will drink the water of my well and be good as new.'

At other times she would say, 'If not Purqazi, then leave me with my brothers and nephews in Barabanki.' In her half-conscious state she would forget that all her brothers and nephews had also migrated to Pakistan from Barabanki and were now settled in Mandi Bahauddin.

Zeenat had served her sick mother-in-law tirelessly. She would call on Allah before administering each dose of medicine. But Allah granted no respite, and all her prayers went unanswered. It was as if after creating Pakistan, Allah had decided to put cotton wool in his ears and relax.

Even when his mother was at death's door, Baqir Hussain thought he could hear her wheezing 'Purqazi' in every dying breath. Her death rattle, too, sounded like 'Purqazi, Purqazi', and her silent lips seemed to call out to Purqazi even when she lay wrapped in her burial shroud.

For that year and a half, she had grieved for Purqazi and for her three-year-old grandson Asad, who didn't survive the ordeal of migration from Hindustan to Pakistan. The amulet that hung from his neck had not been able to save the boy. The refugee caravan had been only seven miles away from the Pakistan border when Asad vomited blood twice and went to sleep forever. The loss of her grandson had taken the life out of the grandmother. She would lean against the wall of the courtyard with her head bent low for hours on end, staring at the cracks in the floor, as if waiting for one of them to open up and swallow her.

Zeenat took to her bed soon after her mother-in-law's funeral. A low-grade fever took hold of her, and she kept talking about Purqazi. In her last moments her mother-in-law had held her hand long and hard, as if she had been trying to transfer something into Zeenat. And now Zeenat had taken up where her mother-in-law had left off. She had kept the grief of Asad's death buried in some corner of her heart as long as Baqir's mother had been alive; now it burst forth like a powerful torrent. Like her mother-in-law before her, she seemed to have been utterly consumed by the twin sorrows of Purqazi and Asad.

The long fever had darkened her smooth complexion. Her eyes, which once sparkled with light like two lively lamps, were flat and clouded. Baqir Hussain recalled how Zeenat used to be in the liveliest of moods day and night in Purqazi, singing some song or the other even as she finished her household chores. His favourite had the lines:

> Master of my heart, bring a doctor from Delhi
> Who can manage to find my faltering pulse...

How easy it would have been to call a doctor from Delhi when they had lived in Purqazi! But now lines had been drawn, borders had been demarcated; Delhi might as well have been on another planet now. How could he bring a doctor from Delhi for his dying Zeenat?

In Purqazi nobody had even suffered from a headache. There, the old neem tree spread its benevolent shade across the courtyard. The neem balls ripened and yellowed and fell one by one, and their bittersweet smell dissolved in the air. During the monsoon, Zeenat would sway back and forth in the swing set up from the tree's thick branches, singing old folk songs:

> Master of my heart, don't get ensnared
> By that other woman's tresses...

Heating up the cold rice again on the fire, Baqir Hussain wondered what they had gained by coming to Pakistan. Only Allah could understand what they had been through. He hadn't found any decent employment so far in Daultala. He had tried to sell fruit on a cart for a few months, but it had come to nothing. Now he took on odd jobs to make ends meet. He had learnt masonry from his neighbour Khalid, who was from Barabanki and was a distant nephew of Baqir's mother. Khalid would take him along whenever he found work.

How well he used to do in Purqazi, with his fruit shop on the main road from Muzaffarnagar to Roorkee! It was well known that Purqazi had the cleanest and cheapest fruit. The cars and buses travelling from Delhi and Meerut to Dehradun and Mussoorie would halt on some pretext or the other in Purqazi, and he could often earn enough to get by for a day or so from the passengers of one bus alone. Those relatives of his who had stayed on in Purqazi after Partition were fortunate indeed. No one had taken their properties or abducted their daughters. People had said that Muslims wouldn't be able to get by in Hindustan after Partition, that everything would be confiscated from them, that they would be turned into field hands. All those rumours had proved untrue, and people continued to live in peace and quiet in their ancestral homes. Those like himself who had fled in fear had found only difficulties and problems.

The second time, too, Zeenat refused to eat. The third time she agreed to eat four spoonfuls, and by then the whole of the afternoon had passed.

Baqir Hussain carefully folded the brand-new green silk chaddar, embroidered with little white flowers and, wrapping it in one of Zeenat's dupattas, hurriedly left for the dargah.

The doctor at the government hospital in Daultala had not been able to find a cure for Zeenat. He had tried all sorts of different medicines, but they had turned out to be as useless as the prayers to Allah. Allah was supposed to hear even sinners' prayers. Baqir was not a sinner and, as far as he could make out, he had never done Satan's bidding. He had put all his belief in Allah and the Holy Quran. So why did Allah not heed his prayers? Baqir Hussain concluded that he needed an intermediary. An intercessor, a pir, who would make sure that his prayer reached Allah. Who could do that better than Sayyid Mehmood Ghazi, towards whose dargah his impatient steps were now leading him? The dargah was about half a furlong off the path that led from Daultala to Nata village. Before the formation of Pakistan, a lamp was lit every night at the dargah and a new chaddar gifted to the shrine every year. In those days, most of the inhabitants of the surrounding settlements—Sukho, Daultala, Sayyid—had been Hindu and Sikh. Only passing travellers and the Muslims of Nata village and its surrounding hamlets had paid attention to the existence of the shrine. But after Partition, when all the infidels had been pushed out of Pakistan, Sayyid Mehmood Ghazi's dargah had quickly become a major pilgrimage centre.

Ghazi miyan, it was said, had become a martyr more than three centuries ago. But his tomb had never seen better days, not even in the days of the Mughal empire. Even an annual Urs celebration had been inaugurated the previous year. During the Urs, people prayed for their wishes to come true, and all who did so went back fulfilled. The powerful and rich of Daultala, Sukho, Bhaun, Sayyid and Chakwal would bring gifts to the dargah. Women from whom evil spirits had been exorcised would come with donations. In the heat the floor would turn into a hot metal plate and the sky would rain down fire, but still such crowds would gather that one could hardly stand. Pilgrims would donate bouquets of flowers and garlands to decorate the tents. There would be shehnais, drums and cymbals. Singers and qawwals would come from far and wide. Ghazals and thumris would be sung.

The tradition was that whosoever had his wish fulfilled would present a chaddar to the tomb. This was fine for those who could afford to wait for their wish to be granted. For Baqir Hussain, each minute, each hour was crucial. He could not wait for Zeenat to recover her health. He feared that any moment Zeenat would breathe her last and plunge his world into darkness. That was why he had decided to put a chaddar on the tomb in advance, at the time of his appeal.

He respectfully unfurled the green chaddar with the little white flowers over the grave. Then he prayed for a long while with all his heart, 'Ghazi miyan, the doors of life are closing upon me one by one. Life is about to push me into a long dark tunnel. Save me however you can.'

A qawwali was being sung next to the grave at the same time:

> I sacrifice my life for you
> O Mehmood Ghazi

He stayed to listen to it and swayed to its rhythm. Then he began to sing along and clap his hands to the beat.

The sky had been absolutely clear. All of a sudden, dark clouds gathered out of nowhere and drops of rain began to fall on the hot, sweating crowd. The same thing had happened at the last Urs. It could only be a miracle of Sayyad Mehmood Ghazi.

When he returned home, he was witness to another of Ghazi miyan's miracles. A long, sharp flash of lightning lit up the front of his house. That flash seemed to illuminate everything deep inside Baqir Hussain. It struck him that the words '*Ek Onkar Satnam*—1935' (God is One, His Name is True—1935) were carved in the Gurmukhi script on a marble plaque fixed above the entrance. The house had been built by Sikhs in 1935.

He had lived in this house in Daultala for a year and a half, entered and exited it innumerable times. He had glanced at the yellowed slab of marble with its inscribed black writing countless times too. But his stupidity had prevented him from paying any attention to what it said. At last, on Ghazi miyan's recommendation, Allah had been inconvenienced to send a flash of celestial lightning to make him pay heed to this piece of infidel writing. Baqir Hussain felt that the voice of Allah Himself was echoing from the thundering clouds, 'Unfortunate man, I have heard your prayers. Don't worry, all your troubles will now end. See what my finger, turned into a flash of lightning, now points at.'

Muslims, he mused, usually carved '*Rahim Manzil*' or '*Rasul Manzil*' or '*Karim Manzil*' or '*Ya Allah*' on their newly constructed houses to keep away evil spirits and misfortunes. Similarly, the Sikh who had made this house had had his God's name carved into it to keep misfortune and illness away. That was all right while that infidel and his family had lived in this house. But now that he, a true Muslim believer in the Prophet and the Holy Quran, was living here, the inscription had become a curse. For a year and a half, he had suffered misfortunes and tribulations due to that inscription. For a year and a half, he had been walking on hot coals. How could he have harboured any hope of happiness when he had been living in a house with the stamp of infidelity above its entrance?

Inside the house he saw that Zeenat was fast asleep—or, more likely, unconscious in high fever. He picked the stepladder up from the courtyard and set it against the entrance of the house. Then he went inside to fetch a lantern, an adze and a chisel. Hanging the lantern from the protruding end of one of the steps he put the sharp edge of his chisel against the marble slab. With four or five blows of his mason's adze he had stripped away the first shape in the infidel inscription—*Ek Onkar*—from the marble plaque.

'What is this you are doing?' Zeenat's voice startled him. Baqir Hussain saw that she was standing in the doorway, staring up at him.

'Why have you come out in the rain? Go inside quickly. I'll be there in a minute.'

'But what are you doing?' Her voice was like a weak scream.

'I am rubbing out these black letters which have made our life hell.'

'But that is the name of God.'

'Yes. But the God of the infidels.'

'Is He different?'

'Stop babbling and go inside. If you get wet with your fever, you will get pneumonia.'

'Let me get pneumonia.'

'You won't go inside, then?'

'First stop this evil act.'

Baqir Hussain saw in the light of the lantern that her eyes were emitting sparks of anger. He had never seen his wife this angry before.

He decided that he'd better finish the job quickly and struck the chisel with his adze one more time. But Zeenat's argument had broken his concentration. He hit his thumb instead of the chisel and began to writhe in pain. The chisel dropped from his hands and fell at Zeenat's feet.

'Give me the chisel.' By now she had picked it up. 'Hand it to me, quick.'

'Get down. Now.'

'I'll only come down when I've finished the job.'

'If you won't come down, I'll split my skull open with this chisel.'

'Go on, do it,' the words escaped his mouth. It was as if he'd been possessed by spirits.

Zeenat held the chisel with both hands and hit herself on the forehead, once, twice, three times.

Baqir Hussain jumped down from the ladder. He could see red streams of blood flowing down her pallid face in the weak light of the lantern. He picked her up, laid her down on the bed and ran straight to the government doctor's house.

It took ten stitches to close the wound on her forehead. The doctor changed the bandage every three days. On the fourteenth day, when he finally removed the bandage, the wound had healed completely. Baqir saw the doctor off at the end of the lane and handed him his bag. When he got back, he noticed that instead of lying on her bed Zeenat was sitting on the cane stool in the courtyard with the early morning sun filtering on to her face through the concrete mesh atop the parapet.

'Feel my arm for a second,' she said with a weak smile.

'Why?'

'I think my fever has gone.' Zeenat pulled back her sleeve and extended her arm.

Baqir Hussain felt it. Her arm, which had been burning like an oven for the past two months, really was cool.

Feeling completely drained from astonishment, he sat down opposite her on the other cane stool.

What he saw when he looked up at her shook him to the marrow of his bones. The scar on her forehead formed the shape '*Ek Onkar*'. The stamp of the infidels had been rubbed off the face of his house and implanted on his wife's instead.

A Woman's Integrity

Sampooran Singh broke into a cold sweat at the first sound of the drum, and stars began to dance in front of his eyes. With the loose end of his turban he wiped the beads of sweat from around his eyes, but the stars would not go away. For a moment a faint hope touched his heart. Perhaps he had mistaken the roll of thunder for the sound of a drum. He stepped out of the room and on to the terrace. There wasn't the slightest sign of a cloud as far as the eye could see.

His spirit seemed to descend into a dark well of despair. His body began to give way. He felt that he lay dying, that he had already died. Actually, he had died the day he had received that letter from his brother-in-law in Patiala. Amolak Singh had written that he had searched all the refugee camps of Patiala, but had been unable to find either his sister or any of her daughters. This awful truth had settled in Sampooran Singh's heart when he heard later that the refugee special train of 29 July had been completely massacred at the Wazirabad station, and not a single person had crossed the border alive.

He had woken up too late. After the riots and killings of March '47 in the villages of Rawalpindi division, the surviving Hindu and Sikh families had locked up their homes and shops, and gone away to Patiala. In fact, Amolak Singh had taken his family away to Patiala as early as the beginning of April, and had even bought a small shop there. But like a fool, Sampooran Singh had doggedly clung to his double-storeyed house and his shop for grinding wheat and carding cotton in Tarlahi village. Eventually, when even the Hindus and Sikhs of Rawalpindi town itself had begun to flee, he had given heed to the appeals of his wife, and one morning put her and his daughters on the refugee special train from Rawalpindi to Amritsar. But by then it was too late; the refugee specials were being mowed down on both sides of the border.

He had not been living after that, only drawing one breath after another. Now, he was not even able to breathe. His body seemed to be a mere mound of dust. But just then, he felt the rising sound of the drum throbbing in each pore of his body. He was still alive; and if that was so, he should do something to stay alive. He should escape this terrible death that threatened to come at him from all sides, beating a drum as it came.

He ran to one edge of the terrace, then to the other, and then to the third, and then the fourth. There were terraces on three sides, but there was no common wall which he could jump over to escape; he had built his home and his godown on a free-standing plot. On the fourth side there was a corn field, extending into the slopes of the low hills. He wanted to go and hide in the field, but he knew that the crop was spare and he would be seen instantly. Then he thought about his godown, stacked till the roof with sacks of corn, wheat and barley. He could hide behind those sacks until the danger had passed. But he knew that the mob of thieves and murderers would loot the godown first, and the sacks would not hide him for too long. He did not want to die; he still wanted to live. He was surprised that, despite losing everything, he had not lost his love of life. If he could have known for certain that after death he would meet his wife and children on the other side, then he would have run to the mob himself and said, 'Here, plunge your daggers in my chest and cut me into pieces with your axes.' But death was a dark tunnel and nobody had seen its other end.

Then he thought of Noora. Why should he not go and hide in his house? But Noora's house was half a mile away from Tarlahi in the little hamlet. And Sampooran Singh saw that the mob had already crossed the hamlet, and was moving towards Tarlahi. All his routes of escape had been cut off.

Wildly, he began to shout for Noora. But he was shouting as if in a nightmare; nobody else could hear him. Fear had stifled his cries. Where was Noora? Why could he not hear him? In that moment of judgement, he felt that if there was a messiah, then it was his employee, Noor Mohammad.

Since the afternoon, Noora had opened up the flour grinder and begun to clean up some of its parts with kerosene oil. He had been waiting for customers, those who would want to grind their wheat or card their cotton, but not a single one had turned up. There had been a time—and that, too, not long ago, only six months earlier—when there would be a procession of customers from the surrounding hamlets who would want to come to this mechanized mill in Tarlahi, arguing with each other and appealing to Noora for an earlier turn. But since the riots began, customers were few and far between, and Noora yearned for the old days. The Hindus and Sikhs of the surrounding hamlets had moved to Patiala and only the rare one, bound by the love of house and land, was left in Tarlahi village. That morning, too, Noora had waited in vain for a customer. Finally, convinced that none would be coming, he had opened the store and taken out his tools. Then he had opened up the grinding machine and begun to clean its parts. His hands were busy with this job, but his thoughts were on

Sayida. For only a day or two in a year Sayida would not turn up to work at the mill, but on those days the place seemed bereft of all life, and Noora would find it hard to get through the day. She wouldn't stay away from work because of a headache or something like that: she would tie a tight thin bandage around her head and work from dawn to dusk, cleaning and preparing the wheat for grinding. But since last night, she had been tossing in a raging fever. Even then she had wanted to come, but Noora had sternly forbidden her from doing so.

Forbidden her he had, but now he was finding it difficult to get through the long day without her. It was as if her soul was breathing in his body. Their love was seven years old and their marriage three years, but still she lived in his heartbeat. Since the morning he'd had an inkling that his body was burning with her fever, and once in a while he had even heard himself moaning.

He recalled the day he had seen Sayida for the first time, when she had come to the mill with her mother. Zainab had not been feeling too well that day, and she had brought Sayida along to help her with the work. Sayida's young and fresh complexion, her shining large black eyes, and her finely cut chin and lips had left Noora breathless. Wrapped in a black dupatta, she had seemed a beautiful and sad Mariam to him. Whenever she came to the mill, the place would become a piece of heaven for Noora. Zainab had begun to fall ill often, and for four years Noora had devoted himself to taking care of her without bothering about his own comfort. Then, just before she breathed her last, Zainab had put Sayida's hand in his. Noora felt that the seven heavens had fallen into his lap.

Suddenly, the beat of a drum shook him from his reverie. This was no ordinary drumbeat. There was some evil and dreadful menace in it that set Noora atremble. Was the rumour true that the Muslims of the surrounding hamlets would loot Tarlahi after the Friday prayers? He thought of Sayida. She was alone at home. Before hell broke loose in the area, he should be with her.

Leaving his tools and the open parts of the mill where they were, he ran towards the door leading to the courtyard. But just then, he heard Sampooran Singh calling for him, 'Save me Nooreya, help me Noor Mohammad, for the sake of your Prophet, save me.'

Noora saw that the fear of death had made Sampooran Singh unrecognizable. Noora looked around himself quickly. There really was no place to hide from the mob—not in the machine room, not in the godown and not even in the living quarters of the house. Only the little store, with its tools and piles of empty sacks, offered some hope of safety. Noora pushed Sampooran Singh into that store and covered him with the empty sacks.

'Don't leave me alone, for the sake of the Holy Quran.'

Sampooran Singh needn't have said all this. Noora had eaten his salt for fourteen years and was not about to desert him in this moment of tribulation. He locked the store from inside and, covering himself with the empty sacks, lay down next to Sampooran Singh, hardly daring to breathe.

A volley of hellish voices burst in from the courtyard. In his hurry, Noora had forgotton to lock the outer door. In any case, the door would not have kept the rioters out; they would have jumped the low wall. *Kill them, burn it down, loot it now, put a torch to it*—amid all these shouts, once in a while, could also be heard the slogan '*Allahu Akbar*'. For a long time, they could hear the mob looting the sacks of wheat, corn and millet and running out into the courtyard. Then someone saw the tools on the ground and, picking up the heavy hammer, began to break the machine. Someone else's eye then fell on the closed door of the store, and soon the blows of the hammer were falling on the door.

'Come out, you Sikh.' Someone pulled Sampooran Singh from under the sacks.

'Don't do anything to him.' Noora leapt up in defence. 'Take everything you want, but spare his life.'

'Move out, you protector of an infidel!'

'May God's wrath be on him! What sort of a Muslim is he?'

'Supporter of this Sikh!'

'Let's finish him first.'

A strong hand caught Noora by the neck and banged his head twice against the wall of the store. When blood sprouted from his forehead, the man flung him on the ground. This was enough punishment for a misguided Muslim.

A young man held the point of his spear to Sampooran Singh's temple.

'Speak up. Where is your box, with the cash and the jewels?'

The mobsters began to push the trembling Sampooran Singh towards the house.

Noora lay unconscious on the floor of the store for a long while. When he recovered some sense, he thought that he was dead, surrounded by the silence of a graveyard. Then he heard the faraway echo of some holy slogan. He realized that the rioters were now looting the new settlement of the village, on the other side of the nullah. That meant he was not dead. He thought of Sampooran Singh, and stumbled to his feet. A baleful silence lay over the courtyard and the godown. Half-conscious, he stumbled through all the rooms of the house. Each room had been ransacked. In search of Sampooran Singh, Noora began to climb the steps to the terrace.

Sampooran Singh lay spreadeagled on the floor. His frightened gaze had frozen forever in his wide-open eyes. His hair was loose, and there was a large pool of blood under him. In fact, his entire body appeared to be covered with blood. Kneeling down, Noora gently shut the dead man's eyes.

Then he brought two armfuls of empty sacks from the store. He collected random pieces of wood from the courtyard and the godown—broken furniture, armrests and so on, and put them on the body. He picked up the vessel of kerosene oil, in which he had been cleaning the parts of the flour grinder, and emptied it on to the empty sacks. Then he set a match to the entire pile.

In the light of the flames he saw the colourful spinning wheel with brass knobs, which was hanging on the opposite wall. This was the spinning wheel that had belonged to Sampooran Singh's wife, of which Sayida had spoken so often. Sayida loved weaving, and would often busy herself with it till midnight in the winter, long after the evening meal was done. For years, she had yearned for such a spinning wheel, but in the last three years he had not been able to save enough money to fulfil her desire. He was surprised that the rioters, who had picked up even ordinary utensils from the kitchen, had left this beautiful spinning wheel behind.

He hesitated only for a moment. Then, extending both arms, he pulled the spinning wheel off the peg on the wall.

Sayida recognized his knock on the outer door and heaved a sigh of relief. But when she saw the spinning wheel on his shoulder, she forgot to ask about his well-being.

'What is this you have picked up and brought?' she asked, fixing him with a piercing gaze.

'A spinning wheel,' Noora replied in a sad tone, taking it off his shoulder and standing it on the floor.

'I can see that.'

'A colourful spinning wheel. With brass knobs. It has come on its own to fulfil your desire.'

His tone now had a touch of enthusiasm.

Sayida raised the flame of the lamp.

'But this is the Sardarni's spinning wheel.'

'Now it belongs to nobody. The brutes killed the Sardar too. I have just lit his pyre with my own hands on the terrace.'

'Then go and throw this too in that burning pyre. It will reach its owners. What were you thinking when you touched what belongs to someone else?'

Before the hatred that smouldered in Sayida's eyes could incinerate him, Noora thought it wise to pick up the spinning wheel and leave the house.

'Return what is not yours, and only then show me your face.' Sayida's words followed him.

The flames of the pyre had risen high, and the second story of the house was now on fire. Noora threw the spinning wheel into the flames and turned back towards his house. A woman stood for integrity, he thought. If women controlled the destiny of this world instead of men, then Tarlahi would still be a flourishing village, like it had been for centuries.

My Precious One

The sounds of the fury that had engulfed the village since dawn slowly turned to silence. And when the last of the slogan-shouting, screaming mob left the village, it was already dark.

Ali Mohammad unlocked the door and stepped out of the small room, trembling like a twig in a storm. His wife had banged on the door a few times and told him to come out, but Ali Mohammad had been unable to gather the courage. His response was to beg Barkate to come inside and hide with him instead. Now when he stepped out, he felt as if he was holding his life in his hands.

He watched as Barkate kneaded flour in a clay vessel. Her face was a pallid yellow in the faint light of the lantern, and her eyes were wide with fear. He was quaking, but he noticed that Barkate did not even tremble. Perhaps she, too, had trembled with fear, but now she seemed to have dissolved it all in household chores.

Barkate threw a glance in his direction and then returned to kneading the flour. She knew that her husband was built like a bull but had the heart of a sparrow. In any case, she didn't want to embarrass him by saying this.

'You are kneading flour?' Ali Mohammad asked, as if she were doing something very unusual.

Barkate nodded faintly in agreement.

'Whatever for?'

'Why does one normally knead floor?'

When Ali Mohammad did not reply, she continued, 'You want to eat roti, then?'

'*Roti*?' It was as if he was hearing the word for the first time.

Barkate patted the kneaded flour into shape and covered the clay vessel with an old broken plate. Then, wiping her hands on her thick black muslin dupatta, she examined her husband from head to toe.

She knew that there was no man as docile and harmless as her husband in the entire village of Qazi da Kot. He prayed five times a day and would not even step on a dead ant. That is why the whirlwind of terror that had swept the village had left him shaking like a piece of straw.

Barkate picked up the lantern and turned up the flame. Then, putting a hand on Ali Mohammad's shoulder, she said, 'Let's go.'

'Where?'

'Let's see what's happened to the village. Who knows what horrors have taken place.'

'No, no, I'm not going.' Ali Mohammad looked away and shot a longing glance at his hiding place.

'Why? What's there to be afraid of now? The looters are long gone.'

'No, no. I cannot bear to see it.'

'See what?'

'What they've done.'

'Then you go hide in your little corner. I'm going out. Who knows what's become of poor Khem Kaur and Beero.'

When he heard Khem Kaur's name, Ali Mohammad's whole body began to shake. He turned his head away from the little room and looked straight into Barkate's eyes. 'Hurry up. Let's go.'

They stepped out into the dark, deserted lanes of the village. It seemed the village had become hell itself. Scarcely silenced slogans seemed to hang in the air around them. The rain had fallen steadily till dawn, and the lanes were slippery with mud. They picked their way carefully through them, then stopped short outside the entrance to the gurdwara. A body lay face down on the threshold, as if prostrating in worship. From the black khadi turban and strap of his ceremonial sword, they made out that it was the body of the granthi of the gurdwara, Bhai Thakur Singh. The sight put paid to Ali Mohammad's quivering. Rage throbbed in his temples and he felt as if someone had plunged a blunt knife into his heart and twisted the blade off.

'Pigs!' he screamed. 'They are dragging Islam into the mud.'

Bhai Thakur Singh, who always had the name of God on his lips... What had those evil people achieved by killing such a good man? Ali Mohammad stood rooted to the spot. The body's shoulders and torso lay on the threshold. The rest lay in the lane, covered with mud. Ali Mohammad took the body by both feet and dragged it until all of it lay at the entrance. Then he turned it face up. In the light of the lamp, they could see the pallor of death on the face of the young man from Poonch, the face that used to glow with the redness of Kashmiri apples. There was a deep wound on his temple and a sharp sickle had dragged out his intestines from his side.

A dog's howl rose from the ruins of Qazi Noor Bakhsh's haveli and sent a chill up Ali Mohammad's spine. It seemed to him that the spirit of Qazi Noor Bakhsh, the man who had founded the village of Qazi da Kot, was lamenting the destruction of his village through this dog's howl. They scurried away from the ruins and the howling dog, and turned towards the lane that led to the Lamba courtyard.

There were only a handful of Hindu and Sikh houses in Qazi

da Kot, mostly clustered together in an area called the Lamba courtyard. Both of them were desperate to reach Khem Kaur's place as soon as possible. So they rushed past the other houses without bothering to stop. Without even looking inside, they knew that those houses had been destroyed. The doors had been broken down and the crazed mobs had taken everything, even the door-frames. They did not need to knock on Khem Kaur's door, since it, too, had been pulled out with its frame. It was the same for the doors to the hall, the storeroom and the kitchen. The house's frame was empty and hollow, like the face of a man whose eyeballs had been gouged out.

A dog lay dead on the floor between the hall and the kitchen. Barkate recognized the pitch-black fur; it was one of the Lamba courtyard dogs. There was a deep axe-wound on its neck and all its blood had seeped into the dirty floor.

Inside the hall they saw two female bodies, and Barkate's heart nearly burst. But when she looked carefully into the circle of the lamp's light, she was startled to see that Khem Kaur was still breathing. She was out cold and there was a wound on her forehead, but it wasn't too deep. It looked like she had been hit with a stick. They turned their attention from Khem Kaur to her young daughter Beero. Maybe she was alive too? There was no sign of a wound on her body, but the blood that trickled from her mouth had left a dark patch on her pale dupatta. Barkate felt the girl's forehead. She was so cold in death that it felt like touching a slab of marble in winter. Barkate took off her black muslin dupatta and covered Beero's body with it. She herself was short of breath. Ali Mohammad ground his teeth as he wondered whether this was all the doing of his co-religionists. The thought filled him with shame. He reproached himself endlessly with the thought that he had hidden himself in his room when the rioters had come charging into the village.

They could do nothing for Beero now. But they didn't waste a minute where Khem Kaur was concerned. Ali Mohammad lifted her weak and spare body on his broad shoulders and took her to their home. Barkate roasted some turmeric powder in ghee and applied it to Khem Kaur's wound. Then she tore a strip from an old cloth and bandaged the wound.

Khem Kaur lay unconscious all night. Her dry lips would occasionally begin to flutter, and sometime after midnight her body started to burn with fever. All night Ali Mohammad and Barkate sat by her side, their eyes vacant and their hands raised in prayer.

A woman as sweet-tempered as Khem Kaur, they both thought again and again, so soft-spoken, who would never rub anyone the wrong way. She had used her small holding of land to get through her widowhood with dignity. Ali Mohammad was her tenant. He cultivated her land and took a third of the produce. She had supported them in every hour of need, and not them alone; she had supported several needy families.

Many times Barkate had tied up her old silver bangles in her dupatta and taken them to her, saying, 'My niece is to be married this Friday night. I will have to give at least twenty rupees. Here, take my bangles as security.'

'Don't say stupid things, Barkate,' Khem Kaur would reply. 'I am not the kind of landlady who would charge interest, nor do I have any worries about you. I have never kept anyone's bangles, and I am not going to start with yours. Take as much money as you need.'

Why had this happened to such a good-hearted woman? Why does God visit such horrors on good people? Barkate was beginning to lose faith.

The first rays of the sun slowly sawed away at the darkness of the long night like a knife with a blunted blade. All day, Khem Kaur lay unconscious in fever. Barkate tried more than once to feed her a spoonful of hot milk but it would simply flow out the corners of her mouth.

She opened her eyes as the sun was setting. For a long time her unfocused gaze hovered on Barkate's face. When she found her voice, she said, 'Oh Barkate, where am I? My head is on fire and my bed is spinning around.'

Till now, Barkate had kept her distress bottled up inside her. Several times she had almost succumbed, but each time she determinedly gritted her teeth and controlled herself.

But faced with Khem Kaur's question, she could no longer control herself.

'What evil days are upon us? The days of the British Raj were so good, not even a sparrow could flap its wings out of turn. How I wish that we did not have this new country, that we did not have this Pakistan.'

Ali Mohammad did not utter a word, but his choked throat was expressing silent agreement with Barkate.

Hearing Barkate's words, Khem Kaur recalled everything.

'Oh my daughter!' she croaked. 'The beasts have taken my virgin daughter. I begged and pleaded in the name of God and the Prophet that they should spare her. Curse them, may they never have peace.'

'No, the wretches killed the girl on the spot. My husband and I saw her body lying in the main hall.'

A faint trace of grim satisfaction appeared on Khem Kaur's face and then vanished.

'No, no,' she wailed. 'They didn't kill me, an old woman. Why would they kill a young girl?'

Then a tiny window opened in her hazy consciousness. 'Oh,

yes. I did hear her say that she had found the little packet. She must have eaten the poison. Oh Barkate, show me my dead daughter's face. It will give me peace.'

Suddenly, Ali Mohammad broke down. He held his head and sobbed loudly. Barkate put a hand on his shoulder in an effort to calm him, but she was sobbing herself.

When they recovered their bearing, they could hear Khem Kaur saying, 'Oh Barkate, make some arrangements to cremate my daughter.'

The dusk had deepened. Ali Mohammad walked in front, a lantern in one hand and a container of ghee in the other. Barkate was supporting Khem Kaur with both hands. With tiny steps they proceeded towards her house.

They emptied the storeroom of its firewood and set up a pyre in the courtyard. Barkate put Beero's body, wrapped in the black dupatta, on the pyre.

'Oh daughter,' Khem Kaur wailed. 'I cuddled you in my arms when you were little. Oh my dearest, my pretty young bride, where am I sending you now?' The flames rose from the pyre and set Barkate's heart and mind on fire.

'May such a Pakistan burn!' she screamed. 'To hell with such a Pakistan.'

The flames lit up the floor near the kitchen, and Khem Kaur's eyes fell on the dead dog.

'Oh Moti... Oh butchers, you finished off my Moti too. Barkate, take my dupatta and cover my Moti with it. He is my brave little lion. It's because of him that my daughter's honour stayed intact. When they started breaking down the outer door, Beero couldn't find the packet of poison they had distributed in the gurdwara at the beginning of this month. Bhai Thakur Singh himself gave packets of poison to each of the girls. Beero had carefully tied hers to the corner of her dupatta, but when the time came she couldn't find the right dupatta. Moti kept those butchers at bay for a long time. He barked and snarled and tried to rip their throats out. Then he let out a final howl and fell silent. At that moment they broke down our door.'

Barkate and Ali Mohammad stared with desolate eyes, first at Khem Kaur, and then at the burning pyre.

'My brother, Ali Mohammad,' Khem Kaur said, 'put this loyal son of mine on the pyre too. I'm indebted to him: he gave his life for a few bites of dry roti that I fed him, the silly fool. Oh my Moti, my precious one, how will I ever repay what I owe you? May you find a place in heaven! And if you are ever born again, may you be born a dog. May God never give you this cursed human form!'

Azaan

The first bus from Malerkotla to Barnala was leaving at seven in the morning. Two of its regular passengers were heading towards the bus station. One of them was Bashir Ahmad, a sixty-five-year-old with a white beard, his upper lip shaved in accordance with the sharia, which had the effect of exaggerating the thickness of his lips. Walking alongside him, a basketful of vegetables on his head, was Fattu Musali, who was in his forties. Fattu appeared a simpleton at first sight, but occasionally a mulish glint flashed in his small, slightly squinting eyes.

They had been up at first light and had bought the vegetables in the wholesale market at Malerkotla, which was reputed to have the freshest vegetables in all of Punjab. Now all that freshness was stuffed in the basket atop Fattu's head, and the regular customers of Bashir Ahmad the vegetable-seller awaited it eagerly in Barnala.

Though technically the two were master and servant, this relationship had given way to something more intimate over their twenty-year-old association. Bashir Ahmad's life had become an open book for Fattu as the years passed, and if anything was still hidden from him then it must truly have been some horrible secret. Fattu had learned to recognize the ups and downs of life reflected in Bashir Ahmad's eyes. So when he saw the dark shadows in those eyes this morning, Fattu knew straight away that there must have been some serious argument with the begum last night or in the morning.

The angry thoughts rising in Bashir Ahmad's heart towards Rashida proved the truth of Fattu's analysis. When would this woman stop her demands? Earlier, she used to go on and on about Ambala where, in her childhood, she would go from Batala to visit her aunt and play her little-girl games with her cousin Zainab. The aunt and her entire family had long since migrated to Pakistan and settled down in Mandi Bahauddin, but Rashida would still insist on seeing the house associated with her childhood memories.

Since last week, though, she had forgotten Ambala and had started on Chandigarh. During Partition, Rashida's parents had left Batala and settled down in Sialkot. They had wanted Bashir Ahmad to join them in Batala with his wife and children so that they could all catch the train together. But Bashir Ahmad had written back saying that they were safe in Malerkotla, and that the conditions outside the state were so bad that leaving was a certain invitation to death.

Later they received news from Sialkot that Rashida's younger sister Zubeida had been married into the Gawalmandi neighbourhood in Rawalpindi. And only last week, the youngest sister Feroza had written a long letter describing how she and her husband had vacationed for ten days with Zubeida and seen Islamabad. Feroza had praised Islamabad to the skies, saying that even though she had not seen Chandigarh, those who had said Islamabad was better.

This morning Rashida had scaled down her demand to see Chandigarh as much as she possibly could.

'Fine. If not Chandigarh, then at least show me Barnala,' she had said.

'Barnala?' Bashir Ahmad's irritation knew no bounds. 'What are you going to do in Barnala?'

'Nothing. Just see it.'

'Is Barnala the Taj Mahal or something that you want to go and see it so badly?'

'As if you have shown me the Taj Mahal, or ever will.'

Unable to answer and filled with irritation, Bashir Ahmad had set off. Rashida's taunting voice had followed him right to the door.

'Fattu, my friend, tell me one thing: why are women so stupid?'

Fattu looked at him but had no answer. Bashir Ahmad realized that he had asked the wrong man. Fattu was over forty but he was still a bachelor; his life experience provided no answers to such questions.

Not waiting for even a ritualistic response from Fattu, Bashir Ahmad carried on, 'I'll tell you. A woman is just a basket-case of emotions.'

Again Fattu was silent.

'And you know what comes out when you open a basket?'

'What?'

'Snakes.'

Fattu started. He had obviously never considered a basket-case of emotions to be such a dangerous thing.

'And these snakes,' carried on Bashir Ahmad in a philosophical tone, 'then go on to poison married life.'

Fattu's intense relief showed on his face; he was fortunate not to be married.

'She's been at me since morning to at least take her to Barnala, if nowhere else. You tell me, is there any sense in this? One could well ask, what is there in Barnala that I should take her there?'

'You are right, Miyan ji,' Fattu said in agreement.

'She tells me, "You go every day, it wouldn't be the end of the world if you were to take me along once?" Tell me the truth, Fattu. Does anything that this woman says make any sense to you?'

Once again Bashir Ahmad felt that he was seeking advice about the problems of married life from the last person who would know what marriage was.

They walked along silently for a while. Then Fattu broke the silence.

'You know, Miyan ji, it's now forty-one years since Pakistan was born, before I was born. But even now I tremble slightly every time I have to set foot outside Malerkotla.'

'It's not like that, Fattu. We can go anywhere in Punjab. There is no danger to us. Not in Chandigarh, not in Ambala. But I ask you, what is there in these places? Sure, we go to Barnala every day, but that's for our livelihood. Otherwise we wouldn't even give it a second thought.'

They never spoke while on the bus. Their conversations took place only on the way to the bus stand or on the way back from it. In the bus they would huddle at the back, reserved and withdrawn into themselves. The emotional wounds that Partition had inflicted may have grown old, but that wariness had not yet gone. This was why they did not talk in the bus. They would simply look around at God's creation or retreat into the depths of their hearts.

Bashir Ahmad had just sat down on the rear seat when his eye fell on two children on the seat in front of him. One was about nine or ten, the other seven or eight. Both had innocent fair faces and little red patkas on their heads. On seeing them, a picture that Bashir Ahmad had seen hanging in many shops in Punjab flashed in his mind. The picture of the two young sons of Guru Gobind Singh being entombed in a wall on the orders of the bigoted nawab of Sirhind, Wazir Khan. He recalled that when he was in the fifth standard in Batala's Middle School, he had gone to a poetry evening with his Sikh classmates. There, a long-haired Muslim poet had recited a lengthy poem in Urdu about the martyrdom of the Guru's two sons. He still remembered that the poet's name was Jogi Allah Yar Khan, and that the poem had been called 'Shahidan-e-Wafa'. He could even recall that many of those sitting around him had started sobbing. That was the first time he had heard about Malerkotla, about how its nawab had raised his voice against the atrocity. The murder of innocent children was unacceptable in Islam, the nawab of Malerkotla had said. When his words had gone unheeded, he had walked out of the court of the governor of Sirhind in protest. That was why, Bashir Ahmad had later learnt, Malerkotla had been blessed by the Guru. That was why, during Partition, Malerkotla had been an island of love and coexistence when the rest of Punjab had been drowned by wave after wave of hatred. Therefore, Bashir Ahmad had taken his family from Batala to Malerkotla when the first reports of riots began to come in.

After alighting at the Barnala bus stand, he unchained his vegetable cart from the wooden pillar of Harnam Singh's tea shack, as he had done for the last forty years. Before boarding the late afternoon bus for Malerkotla, he would chain his cart to the pillar. Over these forty years he had seen an adolescent Harnam Singh turn into a man with a grey beard, all the while serving tea to bus passengers. Harnam Singh had never objected to Bashir using his shack, even though he himself had come from Pakistan as a destitute refugee.

Fattu piled up the vegetables neatly on the cart and stacked away the empty basket on its roof.

At high noon they were pushing the cart through the main bazaar of Barnala when Bashir Ahmad suddenly started. Holding Fattu by the arm, he stopped the cart.

'Fattu, did you just hear something?'

'No, Miyan ji.'

'Did you hear a call?'

'No, Miyan ji. What call?'

'The call to prayer, the azaan.'

Now it was Fattu's turn to be startled.

'Miyan ji, come to your senses. Azaan? In Barnala? The azaan is imprisoned in Malerkotla.'

'No, Fattu, I swear by the Holy Quran. Listen carefully.'

Fattu listened carefully, and then they rushed together to Barnala's main mosque.

After saying his prayers, Bashir Ahmad asked, 'Mulla ji, where are you from?' For a while, they couldn't stop asking questions.

'And no one stopped you from calling out the azaan in Barnala?'

'No, replied the mulla. 'On hearing the call for the Fajr prayer, some Hindus and Sikhs came and said that they welcomed my coming here. They didn't like that God's house had been deserted for so long.'

It was time for the three o'clock bus, and they turned towards the bus stand. For the first time, four cauliflowers and a kilo and a half of brinjals had been left unsold. If they had not gone to the mosque, they would have sold all this too.

'*Sat Sri Akal*, Sardar Harnam Singh ji,' Bashir Ahmad called out with folded hands. This greeting startled both Harnam Singh and Fattu. Miyan ji usually greeted the Sikh with a salaam, as he had this morning.

'Keep these,' Bashir Ahmad said, piling up the unsold vegetables on the counter of the tea shack. 'You can use them for making pakoras.'

'How much should I give you?' Harnam Singh asked, opening his cash box.

'Don't embarrass me, Sardar sahib! I've been tying my cart to your shop for years.'

'That hardly counts, Miyan ji!' Harnam Singh did not say anything else. He did not want to embarrass Bashir Ahmad by repeating his offer to pay.

When Fattu put the empty vegetable basket on the roof of the bus and stepped into the bus, he was stunned. There was no sign of Bashir Ahmad at his usual place on the rear seat. That seat was occupied by two women. Fattu was completely thrown. He had seen Bashir Ahmad board the bus. Had he got off again? He stepped off and looked around. Then he popped his head into the bus again.

'Here, Fattu. Here I am.'

It was Miyan ji's voice. Fattu was even more confused now. How could it be Miyan ji's voice when Miyan ji was not there?

Then Fattu saw to his astonishment that Miyan ji was spread out comfortably on the seat just behind the driver. He made a little bit of room and signalled to Fattu to sit next to him.

The driver twirled his moustache and looked back.

'Is everything all night, Miyan ji? Why have you given up the rear seat today? It's as if you've had it reserved all these years.'

'Reserved? No,' Bashir Ahmad said with a wry smile. 'It's just that it sort of became a habit.'

When he returned home, Bashir Ahmad saw that Rashida was in the kitchen, peeling garlic for the dal that simmered on the fire. He pulled up a cane stool and sat down near her. He had never done this before: he usually went straight through to the hallway, took off his turban and shoes and fell bone-tired on to the bed. The cane had begun to show through the frayed top of the seat, and the cloth cover had been rubbed to a dirty sheen through long use. But to Bashir Ahmad, it was as if he were sitting on a velvet-covered throne.

Rashida lifted her surprised eyes towards him. Bashir Ahmad saw that the morning frown had not left his wife's face. He began to attempt to cover that frown with his smile.

'Leave your cooking and get ready.'

'Get ready for what? For death?'

'Why death? For living.'

Rashida lifted her eyes.

'Tomorrow we will go to Barnala.'

'You do that every day.'

'No, us. Both of us.'

'Why? Is Fattu dead that you want me to carry the vegetable basket?'

'Tomorrow we won't be going to sell vegetables.'

'Then?'

'We'll go for an outing.'

Rashida stared at him in astonished silence.

'Yes, I swear by the Holy Quran, tomorrow I will show you Barnala, our own Barnala. And it won't be long before we go to Chandigarh, too.'

From Khanni to Bhikhi

Bhai Mohkam Singh, the granthi of the gurdwara in Khanni village, started in surprise when he saw Maulvi Ibadat Hussain of Patoki village at the gurdwara entrance. Although they had never actually met, he recognized Ibadat Hussain and wondered what had brought him there that day. Of course, he had heard that unlike other maulvis he wasn't an intolerant person, indeed, that he was a man of good intentions who always kept his promises. Before stepping in, the maulvi bowed down and touched the doorstep three times with his forehead.

'Bhai ji, I want to talk to you about a very important matter,' the maulvi began. He had taken off his shoes and, thanking God loudly, had sat down on the cot that Bhai Mohkam Singh had respectfully laid out for him in the courtyard of the gurdwara. 'You know, I am sure, of the bloodletting that has taken place in a few villages, and I am surprised that you are still here. The maulvis of the mosques in all the neighbouring villages are whipping up the passions of the faithful at prayer-times. They are saying that there is no place for infidels in Pakistan, created at the command of Allah himself, that Pakistan will be impure as long as it contains even a trace of the infidel. I have seen leaping flames and shining spears dancing in the eyes of the worshippers as they leave the mosques. Khanni village is at the top of their list, I hear.'

The maulvi paused to catch his breath and Mohkam Singh interjected, 'But where will we go?'

'I have thought of that too. You should go to Bhikhi in the dead of night. That village has proven to be wise and far-sighted. Many of its inhabitants locked up their homes and shops and moved to Sheikhupura Camp even before Pakistan came into being. Everyone who is left has gathered together in Bhikhi's big gurdwara. People from a few neighbouring villages have also joined them. If you can manage to get there too, some day soon the military trucks will evacuate you to Sheikhupura Camp or straight to the border. I have heard that a major caravan is going to leave from Sheikhupura Camp soon.'

Seeing Bhai Mohkam Singh lost in thought, the maulvi continued, 'Times are bad, Bhai ji. The poison of intolerance has spread far and wide, and has turned men into wild beasts. No one can be trusted these days. And staying here makes no sense. Don't delay any more. If you're going to leave, do it now; tomorrow spells death.'

In the evening, when the congregation gathered in the gurdwara for the evening prayers, the granthi apprised them of the situation. 'Just pack a few clothes in a bundle. Put your jewellery or valuables in a metal vessel and cover them with boiled gram or porridge. I can think of no better way to hide them.'

'And our animals and goods?' someone asked.

'Your animals, trunks, implements—all will have to be left here with your houses.'

This was how, that very evening, twenty-odd families prepared to leave Khanni. One of their ancestors had founded the village three generations before, and they were all related to each other in one way or the other. Apart from them there were a few families of

Muslim tenants with whom they left their animals.

'Take care, Zainab,' Moola Dei insisted, 'that my buffaloes don't lose weight. They are very choosy about what kind of fodder they eat. They have been spoilt.'

'Come, Bibi.' Zainab sought to set her mind at rest. 'This is hardly a problem; we'll take care of them as if they were our own. Let them eat the best fodder to their heart's content. With Allah's grace you'll come back quickly and take care of your own homes and animals with your own hands.'

'And also the brown one doesn't eat from any stranger's hand,' Moola Dei carried on. 'Mix some salt with gram and fodder for her; also let her lick some flour from your hand. She will get used to you in a few days.'

The animals, too, seemed to weep, as if aware of the oncoming long separation from their owners.

'So, Barkate,' Tej Kaur was saying, 'this is goodbye then. We have to leave and you have to stay. Who knows, this may be the last time we meet.'

'No, Aunt,' Barkate beseeched, 'why are you all going? This isn't right. For generations we have worked for you. In whose care are you leaving us? How I wish this accursed Pakistan had never been formed and you did not have to leave your homes.'

The yearning in Barkate's voice seemed to be calling the British Raj back.

'Hai!' lamented old Resham Bibi, sobbing uncontrollably, 'After you, we will not be able to get through a single meal. Your departure is tearing apart my insides. May Allah give you good luck and preserve you from all harm.'

The young girls found it the most difficult to part. Together they had picked and ginned cotton. Together they had spun and spooled the thread. Together they had played on the swings. Together they had crocheted cloth, and fashioned stools and all manners of baskets out of cane stalks. Now they clung to each other and cried uncontrollably.

'Come along.' The elders held them by the shoulders to separate them. 'It's getting late. If we survive and if it is in our fate, we will meet again.'

The girls wiped their eyes with their dupattas, eyes that were red from crying. The tears were still flowing on both sides when at midnight the caravan departed in pitch darkness. On both sides of the footpath through the fields were inky-black acres and acres of crops. They would not be harvesting these crops now. In the coming autumn others would plant the wheat, the gram and the vegetables. New owners would bring the animals out to feed on the fodder grown after the harvest. They were leaving it all behind; their destiny no longer lay on this fertile land.

Leading them was Granthi Mohkam Singh, his son Gurtej Singh and four or five other young men who had swords in their hands. After them walked the young girls of Khanni, little packets of poison tied to the ends of their dupattas, given to them by Bhai Mohkam Singh. If matters came to it, they would not hesitate to swallow the poison.

The frightening pitch-black night surrounded the path. The stars shone in the sky, but their light had little effect. Who could say if dawn would ever come?

Scared of the dark, the little children started screaming and their mothers muffled the screams with their shawls. From the black silhouettes of the trees came the call of sandpipers and the howl of jackals.

Then they walked past the village of Miyan Chak, home of the bloodthirsty Sansi and Rangarh tribes who could kill a man as easily as cutting a bushel of fodder from someone else's field. Beyond that village lay the deserted baoli of Patoki village, with its thick acacia grove, the hideout of the area's known dacoits. The jamun and mulberry trees stood like giants. It was as if men lay in ambush everywhere—against the tall trunks, behind the bushes and in the tall grass.

Near Bhikhi, the surroundings that had seemed so frightening in the darkness softened in the early morning light, and as the sun rose they entered the fallow pasture outside the village. Stepping into the narrow lane of the village, Bhai Mohkam Singh said, 'All right brothers, we have reached Bhikhi safe and sound. Now the rest is in God's hands.'

Entering the gurdwara they felt the tension draining away. Some inhabitants of Bhikhi and some people from a couple of other ravaged villages in the area were already inside. After the initial awkwardness wore off, the new arrivals mixed with them as if they had been living in the same village for generations. As best as they could they began to pass their days together, impatiently waiting for the military trucks. A fortnight passed without any trucks. But there were no untoward incidents either. Then one day, they came. On a cloudy grey afternoon, a large mob surrounded the gurdwara. Cries of '*Allahu Akbar*' rent the sky.

From inside the gurdwara came the answering slogan, '*Bole so nihal...Sat Sri Akal.*' But these voices were trembling with fear.

'Don't be frightened,' someone from the mob shouted. 'We won't harm you. All we want is your cash and jewellery. Tie it all in bundles and throw them out of the windows, and we will leave. Oh, one more thing: those of you who have swords, hang them out from the windows too.'

Those inside heard this and knew what it meant. But they didn't make even a sound in response.

'Think it over,' shouted the same man. 'You won't get a better deal than this. Hand over your cash and jewellery, and your lives and your women's honour will be safe. You'll regret it afterwards if you don't.'

After much whispered discussion, the women fished out their jewellery from their storage vessels, tied it up in bundles and threw them out from the windows.

After a while the same man shouted again, 'That was a wise move. Now make another wise move and give us your swords. We swear on the Holy Quran that not a hair on your heads will be harmed.'

'Never!' It was the old reader of the Bhikhi gurdwara, Bhai Chet Singh, his hand tightening its grip on his sword. 'How can we trust a thief's oath? These people don't know the first thing about Islam.'

'Never!' Bhai Mohkam Singh seconded. 'It was on the basis of such a faithless oath that the Khalsa left Anandgarh—and see what happened to them!'

'Never!' It was young Gurtej, Mohkam Singh's son. 'I will never surrender my sword.'

But all the other men threw their swords out from the windows.

Almost immediately they began to smell kerosene oil. Then the flames began to leap on all sides. Bhai Chet Singh, Bhai Mohkam Singh and Gurtej Singh pulled out their swords and rushed to take up positions at the entrance. When the mob broke through the door, the three leapt upon them. Eight or ten bodies lay on the ground before they themselves were speared to death. The girls untied their little poison packets and emptied them into their mouths, falling into a deep, eternal sleep on the floor of the main hall. The unarmed men were cut down like fodder. The women begged and pleaded but found no mercy. Some young men tried to jump from the parapet and run. Among them was Master Surat Singh of Bhikhi's middle school, who had been running a high fever for the last eight days. It was a wonder that he found enough strength to run, but he managed to leave even the young men behind.

Those among the mob who had mares gave chase to the escapees. Two mares caught up with Master Surat Singh. He was lying face down on the ground, his upper body barely propped up by both elbows. One of the riders, Shaukat, saw his fevered eyes, his pale complexion and his white beard, and took pity on him.

'Let him go, Aslam. He's a sick old man.'

Master Surat Singh heard him and found the strength to speak. He folded his hands and begged them, 'Yes, I am old and sick. Do not kill me, for the sake of your Prophet.'

Aslam drew back his spear and plunged it into the chest of the begging schoolmaster.

'So that's another job done, then,' said Shaukat, his tone betraying his unhappiness with Aslam.

'No, Shaukat,' Aslam defended, trying to explain himself. 'By the Holy Quran, I wasn't going to kill this old man. But who is an infidel to take the pure name of our Prophet with his unholy tongue?'

❧

Sympathy

Nihal Dei was sitting on the steps of Guru Ramdas Sarai with her face towards Harmandir Sahib, praying to Guru Ramdas. Somehow she had made it here, struggling along in the caravans, barely getting by in the refugee camps. Fortunately, she had managed to get a roof above her head in Ramdas Sarai. She spent half the day helping in the langar, and prayed the rest of the time for her daughter and son-in-law.

'You shouldn't leave everything to God,' said Krishan Lal, as he passed by. 'You have to make some effort yourself too.'

Krishan Lal, his wife Krishna and their two children were staying in the same room in which Nihal Dei had got a bed. Like her, they too were suffering and consumed with grief. After being forced out from Daska they had barely managed to get across the border in a long caravan. Their baby had fallen sick all of a sudden: he threw up twice, and they left his body in a bundle under a roadside tree for the dogs and the vultures. Nihal Dei and Krishna were bowed down by grief and racked with longing. Sharing their sorrows had created a strong bond between them. Krishan Lal and his wife had both begun to address Nihal Dei as Tai, or elder aunt.

Krishan Lal rarely spoke. But whenever he did, his atheistic views were obvious. After seeing the bloodletting that had accompanied Partition, he had little faith left in God. Which is why he had said to the praying Nihal Dei, 'You shouldn't leave everything to God. You have to make some effort yourself too.'

'If I could have done something myself, I would have done it long ago. Now I can only rely on God.'

'That's what I am saying. You can't just rely on God. Listen to me and get over to Rambagh. The government has a military office there. This office sends trucks to rescue people who have been left behind in Pakistan. Go and meet one of the officers there.'

'Really? Then be a good son and take me to Rambagh.'

'Tai, today I don't have time. Someone has told me about a burnt-down Muslim house in Katra Jaimal Singh. I'm going to take it over.'

'Then how will I go alone?'

'There's nothing wrong with going on your own. Just ask around and you'll get there. You can ask for directions all the way to England!'

Nihal Dei didn't waste any time and, asking around, reached Rambagh. She saw a huge crowd of refugees there, divided into several groups. The office was in an old building fenced off with barbed wire. An armed guard blocked the narrow gap through the fence. When she tried to hurry past the guard, he extended an arm to stop her.

'May you have a long life. Let this poor woman go in. I need to meet an officer.'

'No one can go inside, Mai. These are the colonel's orders.'

'But my daughter and son-in-law have been left behind in Pakistan. I have to appeal for help.'

'Mai, I've already told you. No one is permitted to go inside.'

Nihal Dei opened a knot at the corner of her torn and soiled dupatta and took out some money.

'Here, two and a half rupees. That's all I have.'

'Even if you give me two and a half thousand,' the soldier said harshly, 'I wouldn't let you inside. Now move on! Look at how many people there are over there, shouting away. Go and join them!'

The groups of refugees were indeed shouting. One group would shout, 'Save Okara!' When they got tired, another newly gathered group would shout, 'Save Montgomery!' Then, 'Save Mandi Bahauddin!'; 'Save Ghakhar!'; 'Save Arifwala!', as each group took its turn. The shouts would travel through the barbed wire and bounce back off the thick wall of the old building.

Nihal Dei went from group to group, begging, 'Brothers, someone shout for Cheecho ki Maliyan. My daughter and son-in-law are stuck there.'

But no one paid any heed to the old woman.

Finally someone said, 'Be patient, Mai. We'll shout out your village's name in a second.' But then he went and joined the group which was shouting, 'Save Wazirabad!'

Here, everybody is wrapped up in his own problem, Nihal Dei reflected. But then she immediately regretted her thought. She was blaming them unjustly. They were all as unfortunate as she, suffering from the same grief and separation.

'Save Cheecho ki Maliyan!' she tried to shout. But her cry was so weak that she barely heard it herself.

A man passing through Hall Bazaar in town stopped before a refugee roasting corncobs on the roadside. He bought a corncob for two annas and munched it as he passed through the Sheranwala Gate and over the rail bridge towards Rambagh. He had heard that the refugees from Pakistan had turned Rambagh into a lively place. I've got nothing to do, he thought. Why don't I go see the action? He listened to the refugees' different dialects and ways of speaking for a while, but quickly got bored and turned to go. Right then Nihal Dei accosted him. He had just passed her when she grabbed him by the arm.

'May you have a long life, son. Just listen to me for a second.'

'Go on, Mai.'

'Are you from Kamoki?' There was hope in her tone.

'No,' he replied coldly.

'I got this feeling that I have seen you in Kamoki.'

'I have never been to Kamoki,' he said with an added note of irritation.

'Then son, which village are you from?'

'From nowhere, Mai. Let me pass.'

'No, I mean which part of Pakistan are you from?'

'I've not come from Pakistan,' he said with disgust. 'It's these people here making all the noise who have come from Pakistan. I'm from Amritsar.'

'Okay son, if you are born of this city of the Guru, then do one thing for me.'

'What?'

'Here, take these two and a half rupees first,' the old woman said as she pulled out all her savings from the knot in the dupatta. 'Then I'll tell you what to do too.'

'Two and a half rupees!' The man turned up his nose. 'Who's going to do anything for two and half rupees these days! That won't even buy a single meal.'

Nihal Dei's hands were damp with cold sweat. That was all the money she had. Then all of a sudden, a faint hope lit up her face.

'Hold on, son. I've got something else to give you.' She took the silver earrings from her ears.

'Forget it, Mai. What would I do with these worthless four-anna earrings?'

'They're not worthless, son. These are pure silver.'

'Tell me the truth, Mai.'

'I'll swear by the Guru if you want.'

As he held out his hand to take the earrings, his corncob fell to the ground.

'Don't try to fool me, Mai. They look like they're made of nickel. Plus I've already lost my corncob.'

'Oh son, I don't lie with this head of grey hair. You can show them to a jeweller if you wish.'

The man put the earrings and the two and a half rupees in the inner pocket of his kurta. Then he picked up the corncob, dusted it off and started munching on it again. 'So what do you want done?'

'See how people are shouting out the names of their villages? May you live long and enjoy your youth, please shout once for Cheecho ki Maliyan.'

'What's that?'

'What did you say?'

'What's this Cheech Macholi?'

'Not Cheech Macholi, Cheecho ki Maliyan.'

'But what is it?'

'It's a village in Pakistan. My daughter is married there. We sent her to her in-laws last December. They have a haveli in the grain market there.'

'So what am I supposed to do?'

'What did you say?'

'What am I supposed to do about this haveli in the grain market?'

'Just call out "Save Cheecho ki Maliyan!" once.'

'Is that all?'

'Make sure you call out loudly like all these people. The officers sitting inside have to be able to hear it.'

'Hang on. Let me finish my corn first.'

Nihal Dei watched him finishing the corncob with hopeful eyes.

At last he flung the cob aside, cupped both hands to his mouth and shouted, 'Save Cheecho ki Chaliyan!'

'Not Chaliyan, my dear son, but Maliyan.'

'Maliyan?'

'Yes.'

'Correct?'

'Yes.'

'Save Cheekho ki Maliyan!' he shouted the second time.

'Not Cheekho, son. Cheecho. Cheecho ki Maliyan.'

'This is a really difficult name; I won't be able to say it. Take your two and a half rupees back.'

A cold sweat again broke out on Nihal Dei's palms.

'No, my good son,' she begged. 'Try again. You will get it right now with your mother's blessings.'

The third time the man shouted at the top of his voice, 'Save Cheecho ki Maliyan!'

'Is that correct, Mai?'

'May you have a long life and enjoy your youth,' Nihal Dei blessed him. 'You have calmed my heart.'

When she turned to leave Rambagh, a sudden doubt crossed her mind. What if the truck drivers didn't know the way to Cheecho ki Maliyan? But she comforted herself that they could always ask passers-by. You can get directions all the way to England, after all. Then another doubt: what if the officers inside the building didn't hear the shout of Cheecho ki Maliyan? No, surely they must have heard. That good man had really shouted with all his might. Cheecho ki Maliyan had surely been entered in the register in the office. That's what those officers are there for. They had probably even sent off the trucks already.

With an easy mind and quick steps, Nihal Dei set off towards Guru Ramdas Sarai.

The Parade

It was still dark and the stars were visible in the sky when Abnash started walking towards Gurdwara Bangla Sahib. This had become her routine ever since she had come from 'Pindi with her children to stay with her sister-in-law in Delhi. It happened to be her only refuge from the worries that constantly buffeted her. There, in the house of the child Guru, the alleviator of suffering, she would stand among the pilgrims' shoes and pray and beg for the safety of her husband and two elder sons in 'Pindi, and her newly-wed daughter and son-in-law in Abbottabad.

She would usually run into someone or the other on his way from Paharganj to the gurdwara. But today the roads were bare and deserted. In fact, all of Delhi had virtually become desolate over the past two days, ever since the anti-Muslim riots had started. Her sister-in-law had warned her against venturing out on the streets alone just as she had the day before. But she couldn't break her routine. And what did she have to fear in free India anyhow? Danger was the lot of those who had been left on the other side of the Line of Control, in Jinnah's Pakistan.

Her sister-in-law's husband had not bothered to warn her, even for the sake of formality. In fact, for the last three months, he had been cold towards her and her children. His behaviour had become increasingly rough and bitter as the days passed and the hope of her husband and sons surviving dimmed. He was obviously worried at the thought that he might be saddled with looking after her and the children forever. Since last evening, in fact, he had sat in high dudgeon. A number of houses in Paharganj and the adjoining colony of Multani Dhanda had been abandoned following the riots and arson, and he had managed to take over one which had been looted but not burnt down. He wanted Abnash and her children to move there.

'No, Bhaiya ji,' Abnash had said with firm humility, 'I couldn't even conceive of taking over some poor soul's looted house. Let my husband come. Then we will rent something, even if it's a broken-down hut.'

Even her sister-in-law was no longer as warm and sweet as she used to be. Once in a while she would even comment sarcastically on the fact that Abnash had abandoned her brother and her two dear nephews in the moment of danger. Her sister-in-law did not know how hard Abnash had tried; that she had been appealing to her husband since June, when the decision to form Pakistan had been taken and the date of 15 August fixed. From that time onwards people had begun to leave Rawalpindi for Patiala, locking up their homes and shops. In a matter of days, the flourishing, prosperous lanes had taken on a deserted look. Abnash had wanted the entire family to leave 'Pindi, but she had not been able to convince her husband. He was worried about his job and the jobs of his two elder sons. It was as if he wanted to take their employment with them to Patiala or Delhi. He did not want to live on government charity in refugee camps.

'To hell with these jobs,' she had said. 'Our own lives, our dignity are beyond all price: if we manage to survive, we can find new jobs.'

Her husband explained that the entire staff of the bank was

on duty, even though they had sent off their families. As the bank manager, he could not leave without orders from his headquarters. Some days he would say, 'You take the younger children and go to Harbans in Delhi. We'll be fine here. After all, if the Muslims kill all the Hindus and Sikhs, whom will they rule over? Governments change but people don't move.'

She had seen no sense in his arguments. Deluding himself was an old habit of his. She had pleaded and begged, but he had stubbornly held on to his idealistic beliefs. In the end she had given up, and come with her four young children to her sister-in-law's in Delhi at the end of June.

She had lived a blighted life for the past three months, struggling through storms of sobs by day and relentless waves of tears by night. Somehow she had pulled through on the strength of a thin thread of hope. Then the news grew worse. The fires of Lahore, the massacre in Sheikhupura, the wholesale killings on refugee trains at Wazirabad, Lala Musa and Gujrat. Then the letters from 'Pindi and Abbottabad stopped, and there was no word from anywhere else. She no longer knew if her husband, two sons, daughter and son-in-law were alive or had been chalked up to Pakistan's account. Each day that dawned was already soiled, and even the piercing sunlight of August and September appeared to be shrouded in a fog. At night her worries surrounded her like flaming pyres.

Occasionally one of her sister-in-law's neighbours would say, 'May God give comfort to all, but surely now only the lucky can get across from that side. Those who were going to come have come, and those who were meant to stay have stayed.'

Abnash would then dissolve in regrets. 'Oh, why did I leave my husband and protector, and my sons, to park myself in this foreign land with these little ones. I put too much value on my own life. God only knows what would have happened to us in

Pakistan. But at least we would have been together, whether we lived or died.'

Abnash was lost in these thoughts all the way back from Gurdwara Bangla Sahib. But when she crossed the chowk at Baird Road and Market Road, she jumped with a start. In front of the gate of Lady Hardinge Hospital was a sight that shocked her to the core of her being: it was the dead body of a Pathan. His eyes were wide open and a dark pool of blood had congealed under his head. She had not seen the body on her way to the gurdwara because it had been dark then. This grotesque sight was the first thing to greet her with the coming of dawn. When she turned from Panchkuian Road into Paharganj, she saw three more Muslim bodies lying spreadeagled in the middle of the road. This was the first time she had seen bodies of people who had been murdered. When she entered the house, she was trembling like a leaf.

The sun had barely risen when news about the riots began to spread. From the balcony across the road, the wife of the lame lawyer was telling Abnash's sister-in-law that Muslims' shops were being looted in Paharganj, that the rioters had finished off the Muslim colony in Multani Dhanda and were now looting and burning the few Muslim houses of Chuna Mandi. Anyone who tried to escape the flames was immediately dispatched straight to Pakistan with the thrust of a knife.

Abnash's heart sank as she listened.

Then they heard a drum beating in the lane below.

'Now what?' she sobbed. 'Why this drum beating?'

'There is going to be a parade,' said the wife of the overseer who lived below them. She had climbed up the staircase to be able to peep into the lane.

'A parade?' Abnash asked. 'Whose parade?'

'Two Muslis,' the overseer's wife said with glee.

The word 'Musli' rankled with Abnash. This word was a

message of enmity, a sign of hate. It wouldn't kill people to use the word 'Musalmani' for a Muslim woman. Similarly she did not like it when Muslims used the word 'Sikhra' for Sikhs and 'Kirar' for Hindus. These words were all wrapped up in the poison of communalism, a poison which had now sunk deep into people's souls.

'A parade of two Muslim women?' she asked in disbelief.

'Yes,' said the overseer's wife, making no attempt to hide her glee. 'After stripping the worthless wretches.'

Abnash swooned and fell to the floor in a heap.

Her sister-in-law splashed water on her face, pressed and rubbed her hands and feet, and barely managed to hold her mouth open so that she wouldn't bite her tongue.

When Abnash regained consciousness she said, 'Oh, throw those girls a dupatta or a sheet, and tell them not to beat that drum. It feels like it's beating inside me.'

For some reason, Abnash had assumed that only Muslims were capable of such terrible acts. To learn that Hindus and Sikhs were no laggards in committing atrocities tore her to shreds.

Nobody paid any heed to her. All these people were in favour of fanning a raging fire, it seemed to her. They didn't want to spoil the fun by putting out the flames. Those who had received their freedom while sitting in comfort in Delhi, and had celebrated the fifteenth of August by flying the tricolour on their own houses, saw the Delhi riots as a spectacle, and desperately wanted the spectacle to go on for their enjoyment. Only those who had themselves escaped the flames could understand what fire was and what it could do.

The shameless laughter of the overseer's wife ignited a different kind of fire inside Abnash.

'Such cruelty,' she screamed, 'and you all just sit here without a care in the world?'

'And what would you have us do?' the overseer's wife asked. 'This is what they deserve. This will teach them to make Pakistan.'

Another woman from the next house sneered, 'Let them call Jinnah now. Let him come and free them.'

The anguish in Abnash's heart flamed in her eyes. She quickly rose to her feet. She pulled the sheet and blanket off the bed in a single movement and rushed down the stairs. Her sister-in-law rushed after her, shouting at her to stop, but turned back at the end of their little street where the bazaar began.

Abnash ran to and fro, chasing the sound of the drumbeat. She did not even realize it when her dupatta slipped from her head and fell in the lane. She was panting and breathless as she crossed the bazaar of Tilak Street and Chuna Mandi. She finally caught up with the parade in Punjabi Lane. She stood for a second and looked at the howling mob, no better than cavemen with their weapons of bones. When those unfortunate girls tried to hide their nakedness with their hands, the crowd would poke long staves into their sides. Abnash ran into the crowd and snatched away the stave from a man's hand.

All of a sudden the drumbeat stopped.

The crowd's faces froze in astonishment when they beheld Abnash. She was no less stunned to realize that she was a lone woman against this crowd of howling wild men.

When the man whose stave she had snatched found his voice he said, 'Sister, what are you doing here?'

'Don't you dare call me sister,' she snapped. 'I am better off without brothers like you.'

'Bibi, you better go home,' a middle-aged thoughtful spectator said. 'This is no place for women.'

'And those are not women?' Abnash asked.

'They're different,' the thoughtful man argued. 'They're Muslis. We have to take revenge.'

'Revenge for what?'

'For the naked parades of our sisters and daughters in Pakistan.'

'And did these two girls go to Pakistan to tell people to parade your sisters and daughters?'

The man fell silent. It seemed that Abnash's words had hit home.

Another young man with a well-groomed beard spoke up, 'Bibi ji, you're a Sikh. I can see the karha on your wrist. What sympathy could you have for Muslims?'

'Oh, well done!' Abnash's voice was tinged with the sadness of a sigh. 'You really are giving the Hindu and Sikh religions a great name! And totally demeaning humanity.'

'Humanity?' the man shouted in anger. 'What humanity? Which humanity? What humanity did they show when they dishonoured our sisters? They are the ones who started these naked parades and nobody stopped them. We are only returning the favour.'

Some among the crowd, whose souls were not yet completely dead, had begun to shift their gaze. But most of them were staring at her with murderous eyes. Where had this wretched woman come from to spoil their fun?

'Fine,' said Abnash, 'return the favour then, take your revenge. But the only people who should be here to take revenge are the ones whose own sisters or daughters have been dishonoured in Pakistan. As for the rest, I plead to you with folded hands to return to your homes.'

Her tortured soul knew that those whose own sisters or daughters had been dishonoured would never commit the same evil toward the women of someone else's family.

The drum-beater was the first to leave the mob, then those in whose souls humanity still breathed faintly. And then the thinning crowd totally vanished.

Abnash looked at the two unfortunate girls with compassion. Numb with fear and trembling uncontrollably, they returned her gaze meekly.

She extended the sheet and the blanket toward them, but they did not take them. Fear, it seemed, had deprived them of all sense and thought. Abnash stepped forward and wrapped one in the blanket and the other in the sheet and, with one arm around each, led them with small steps to her sister-in-law's house. The first thing she did was to take out two pairs of clothes from her trunk and dress the girls. Then she and her sixteen-year-old son Gurdeep took the girls to the refugee camp at Tees Hazari and reunited them with their relatives.

When she returned home, a letter had arrived for her in the afternoon post. It was from her daughter Jasbir, in which she had written that with the grace of the Kalgiwala Guru, she and her husband had got out of Abbottabad and reached Amritsar safely.

This Problem of Kashmir

The week flew by as if time had grown wings. Naseem and Shabnam had reached Rawalpindi last Sunday, and the week since seemed to have passed in a day. Yes, it had been a week now, but the homesickness was just as strong; the hugs were still tight, the kisses still warm. The smiles were still as bright and the eyes twinkled with the same happiness as on the first day. The international border between two countries had been swept away by the flood of memories and yearnings.

The Toyota car stood idle, and the driver yawned away his time. Choudhry Abdul Razzaq had left for a week's political tour by the morning flight last Sunday. As a senior member of the Jamaat-e-Islami organization, it was mandatory for him to be present at certain functions. He could not change his programme just because his youngest sister-in-law had come from Malerkotla. Tahira had intended to accompany him this time to see their daughters Ishrat and Izzat, who were both married into rich Lahore business families. But she had changed her plans when she received Naseem's letter.

In his absence, Tahira made full use of the Toyota car and the driver. From dawn to dusk, she drove around with Naseem and Shabnam. They went to Murree hill station. They criss-crossed

Islamabad, and in passing Tahira showed them her two bungalows there, with the marble fountains on their lawns. They were rented out to two embassies, while the family continued to live in the old house in New Colony, which had been allotted to them by the government when they had come from Amritsar.

About 80 per cent of the inhabitants of Rawalpindi town had been Hindus and Sikhs before Pakistan came into being, so there had been no shortage of houses for the Muslim refugees who reached Rawalpindi. The house allotted to Choudhry sahib was not a particularly good one, because at that time he had not joined politics or made connections in the government. Only after Pakistan was created had Choudhry sahib realized the immense power of politics. The birth of this new Muslim country was no less than a miracle—a miracle performed by the Qaid-e-Azam Muhammad Ali Jinnah's political skill, which had lopped off India's head and dropped it into Islam's lap.

When he had lived in Amritsar as a wholesale silk dealer, Choudhry sahib had always regarded money as the greatest god. Now he had discovered the real secret—that there was an even bigger god than money, and it was politics. You could earn more in ten or fifteen years in politics than in seven generations in the wholesale silk trade. True, Choudhry sahib still had a shop in the Cloth Market in Rawalpindi's Purana Qila quarter. But this shop was only a front: his real income came from his political work. Some people were aware of this reality; on occasion, detractors and political rivals had tried to sully his name in the newspapers. But in the eyes of ordinary people, he was a simple, decent and religious man who had devoted his entire life to the service of Pakistan. These ordinary people were also unaware of the existence of those two luxurious bungalows in Islamabad. Choudhry sahib had given strict instructions to his wife, son and daughters not to mention these bungalows under any circumstances; he knew the importance of image in politics. For the past forty years he had continued to live in an old house without modern conveniences just to keep up the illusion of his simplicity and uprightness.

Knowing well the influence of Pakistan's army in its politics, Choudhry sahib had arranged for his only son Shahab, the youngest of his children, to become an army officer. He had become a captain, and his regiment was in Shakargarh, near Sialkot. Perhaps somewhere deep in his subconscious, Choudhry sahib harboured a secret wish that after Shahab was promoted to major general or lieutenant general, it might be his destiny to become the president of Pakistan. After all, the generals who had become presidents of Pakistan had been in no way better than his Shahab.

Tahira knew that Choudhry sahib would return from Lahore the next afternoon. As the hour approached her spirits flagged. She knew that Choudhry sahib would never agree to get Shahab married to Shabnam. The biggest problem with the proposal was that it had come from Malerkotla, and Malerkotla was in India. After forty years of marriage, she knew Choudhry sahib inside out. She could read his thoughts before he uttered them, as if his head were made not of flesh and bone but of clear glass. She knew that his life revolved around his hatred for India. He used to often say that India had not yet accepted the reality of Pakistan, that India's leaders still dreamt of swallowing up Pakistan to make a Greater India. In Choudhry sahib's opinion, Pakistan was still incomplete. He felt that Pakistan would only reach the stage of completion when it would be victorious in war and create not a Greater India but a Greater Pakistan. 'Study history,' he would say. 'History does not lie. Ever since Muhammad bin Qasim conquered Sind, we have always laid waste to Hindustan. Our great crusader, the idol-breaker Mahmud of Ghazni, raided the temples of Hindustan seventeen times and smashed their idols. No one could stand up to him. We ruled from Delhi for eight centuries, and if the foreigners hadn't tricked us out of our empire, the flag of Islam would still be flying over the whole of Hindustan. History has always repeated itself. It will repeat itself again. We can never forget that the Lal Qila is ours, the Qutub Minar is ours, the Taj Mahal is ours. Fatehpur Sikri and Ajmer Sharif belong to us, and we will not rest until we have them back.'

Occasionally some bright listener would dare to raise an objection, 'Oh Choudhry sahib, times have changed. What illusions are you under? Don't forget that the India of today is unified and seven times larger than Pakistan. India's army, navy and air force are three times the size of Pakistan's forces.'

Choudhry sahib would snap back, 'Size is not what matters on the battlefield. On the battlefield, bravery and the spirit of sacrifice count. Each warrior of Pakistan's army is better than ten Hindu soldiers because he is ready to die when he fights. Oh Miyan, battles are won by those who eat mutton and lamb. How will easterners who eat arhar dal, or South Indians who eat dosas and idlis fight?'

Three months earlier, when Naseem had proposed the match in a letter to Tahira and enclosed a photograph of Shabnam, Shahab was on leave in Rawalpindi. When she showed the photograph to her son, his heart missed a beat. When he was able to catch his breath, he said, 'Ammi, if this girl becomes your daughter-in-law, I will feel like I have been promoted to general.'

He kept the photograph in his wallet and took it away with him to Sialkot. But as he left he also said, 'Ammi, Shabnam is a fairy who has stepped down from the heavens, but I will not accept this match without Abba jaan's permission.'

Tahira knew his Abba jaan well. Moreover, the problem of Kashmir had hotted up again, and Choudhry sahib was particularly angry with India. So she could not gather the courage to talk about it to her husband.

She wrote to Naseem, 'Both Shahab and I liked the photo very much. I'll write more in my next letter after I discuss things with Choudhry sahib.'

There was no discussion with Choudhry sahib and no next letter. Then, the evening before Choudhry sahib was to take the morning flight to Lahore, they received a letter from Naseem saying that she was coming to Rawalpindi.

Tahira was left with no choice but to tell Choudhry sahib the real purpose of Naseem's visit. His face fell in surprise at what he had heard.

'Some people are in the habit of harbouring impossible dreams and hopes. Your sister is one of them. Wire them straight away that they should not bother catching the train. What's the use of travelling so far just to suffer disappointment? Better that she stay comfortably in Malerkotla.'

Tahira didn't send a telegram. It was obvious from Naseem's letter that she would already have boarded the train.

Tahira was enchanted with Shabnam. She was truly like the dew her name denoted: a dewdrop on a rose. When she passed close to Tahira wearing a turquoise phiren, it seemed to Tahira that a scent-laden breeze from Kashmir had wafted by. There was as much difference between Shabnam's photo and her in person as between seeing Kashmir on television and actually visiting it. Just looking upon her made one want to praise the Creator for his handiwork. It wasn't just that God had taken his time making her: He had, in fact, taken the day off just to create her. And after He finished making her, He was lost in wonder at how it was that another moon had come up in the sky. People said that the best daughter-in-law was one whose beauty would light up the whole house even if she sat in her own room. When she saw Shabnam, Tahira believed that such a thing was not an impossibility.

When Choudhry sahib returned from Lahore, he saw Naseem at the lunch table. He responded to her greeting without enthusiasm. He frowned at her violet sari with its flowery print. Tahira understood the frown: he hated saris. 'What kind of indecent dress is this?' he would say. 'It reeks of Hindu slavery.' Frowning and averting his gaze, Choudhry sahib began to stare at the two brass storks on the mantelpiece, as if they were hatching a conspiracy against Pakistan.

However, when Shabnam entered the room and came to the table, Choudhry sahib was dumbfounded. It was as if a window of light had opened into the room. He had thought that Allah had given all the beauty to the Arab countries, to Iran and to Pakistan, and that the Muslims who were left in India were no match. But one glimpse of this girl from Malerkotla unsettled him. The reality of the situation was indelibly stamped on his heart in that instant, and he knew that he would never find such a beauty in all of Pakistan no matter how long he searched. He forgot Naseem's violet sari. He forgot the brass storks, too, and the frown vanished from his brow. Tahira saw this change and her hopes began to rise again.

Choudhry sahib spent the entire afternoon on the top floor of the house, where he usually met members of the Jamaat-e-Islami and exchanged views on political issues. Tahira rarely went up there because it was more or less Choudhry sahib's political office. Late in the evening, when the last of the visitors had gone down the stairs, she went upstairs and touched on the topic of the proposal again. She saw Choudhry sahib smile and wondered if the sun had set in the east that day. She could not recall when she had last seen her husband smile. The further he had gone into the morass of politics, the more the smile had vanished from his face. He used to be a jolly man before he had entered politics, even more so before Pakistan was created. He even used to flirt and joke with Naseem, his young sister-in-law, when she was unmarried and they lived in Amritsar. But now for years his face had been set in grave seriousness.

'It seems you have no objection to this match.'

Choudhry sahib's smile widened. 'If you two sisters are bent on it then what objection could I have?'

It was clear that Choudhry Abdul Razzaq, the pillar of Jamaat-e-Islami, had not been able to withstand the impact of this young girl from Malerkotla and her narcissus-like eyes, her glowing cheeks and the cleft on her pointed chin.

Next morning Tahira sent Shekhu to Raja Bazaar to buy almonds, dates, coconuts and other dry fruits so that they could formally agree to Shabnam's engagement. He had hardly been gone ten minutes when the walls and the windows of the house began to shake.

'Earthquake!' Choudhry sahib screamed. 'Everybody sit on the floor!'

Scared stiff, not daring to breathe, they sat and waited, but the tremors did not stop. At the same time they began to hear explosions, as if heavy bombing was taking place. They could understand tremors in an earthquake, but not these explosions. When the tremors and explosions stopped, they rushed to the roof to see what damage the earthquake had done to the town. Other families had also come to their roofs and were staring in astonishment at a pillar of smoke, which stood like the Qutub Minar on the horizon. Nobody could understand what had actually happened. At that moment, climbing three steps at a time, an out-of-breath Shekhu came on to the roof. There were no dry fruits in his hands, and his face was pale with fear.

'Choudhry sahib! Choudhry sahib!' He seemed incapable of saying anything more.

'What is it, Shekhu? What is this all about?'

'We have been looted, Choudhry sahib,' Shekhu wailed. 'We have been finished.'

'But what has actually happened? What are these explosions and what is this smoke?'

'Oh, if only it were an earthquake,' Shekhu sobbed. 'This is not an earthquake, Choudhry sahib. This is the Day of Judgement itself.'

'Will you tell us something or not?'

'There is nothing left to say,' Shekhu banged his chest in despair. 'Pakistan was sleeping, and the enemy hit us.'

'Enemy? What enemy?'

Shekhu was so surprised at the stupidity of Choudhry sahib's question that he stopped wailing.

'India. Which other enemy does Pakistan have?'

'What has India done?'

'Don't ask.'

'Shekhu.' Choudhry sahib glared at him. 'If you don't speak up now, I will shoot you.'

'India has attacked Kahuta. Indian aeroplanes have destroyed our nuclear reactor. Shoot me, Choudhry sahib. My life has no meaning now.'

'Are you telling the truth?'

'It's not just me. Go out and listen. All of Rawalpindi is saying this, all of Islamabad is saying this, all of Pakistan is saying this.'

Choudhry Abdul Razzaq slipped on his shoes and left the house. When he returned after about half an hour, his eyes were raining fire and his face was pale. He caught Tahira firmly by the arm and pulled her upstairs.

'Tell your Indian sister and niece to get out of here immediately. Unfaithful, deceitful people! And they want to build a relationship with us? They have challenged a sleeping lion. They have put their hand into a snake pit. Tell them to take care of their own nuclear centres now: we will not rest until we have avenged Kahuta. By God's grace, Pakistan does not lack for long-range aeroplanes.'

Later, they heard on the Radio Pakistan afternoon bulletin that the rumours that Kahuta had been bombed were false. The truth was that a fire had broken out at the ammunition dump in Rawalpindi cantonment due to negligence, and a lot of ordnance had exploded. There was no foreign hand involved in the incident.

Tahira saw that the news had embarrassed Choudhry sahib deeply, and he left the house on the excuse of a party meeting.

After dinner he quickly went upstairs. Tahira followed him.

'What is your decision now?'

'It's fine. It was a misconception. It's all cleared up now. Perform your ceremony tomorrow morning.'

But the next morning before breakfast, Choudhry sahib called Tahira upstairs.

'This marriage cannot take place. It will not happen,' he yelled.

'What's the matter?' Tahira asked, grappling with her surprise. 'It seems you are not feeling too well. Did you not sleep properly?'

'There's nothing wrong with me, but...'

'But what?'

'This marriage cannot take place.'

'But you seemed thrilled with the idea last evening. I cannot understand you.' There was helplessness in Tahira's voice.

'Have you seen today's newspaper?'

'You must have read the entire world's newspapers by now, I suppose. But I want to know: what does a newspaper have to do with the engagement?'

'That is why I am telling you to read it. Read and see what they have done in Geneva. These Indians just can't stop playing their cheap, low tricks. Now they have convinced Pakistan's supporters, China and Iran, that they should prevail upon Pakistan not to push a resolution against India in the Human Rights Commission. So Pakistan has withdrawn the resolution under Chinese and Iranian pressure. See how the Indians' Chanakya policy works? Now Indian forces will violate human rights in Kashmir without any fear.'

'I want to talk to you about Shahab's engagement.' Tahira was close to tears by now. 'And you keep going on about your politics.'

'This is not politics. This is about knowing how to differentiate friends from foes. You don't marry your enemies. And this enmity won't vanish until the problem of Kashmir is resolved.'

When Tahira related all this to her sister, Naseem made up her mind that she would not marry Shabnam into this family even if they begged for the alliance. How could Shabnam ever be happy in a family where decisions changed from minute to minute? Though her visa allowed a longer stay, Naseem resolved to catch the evening train back.

All day Choudhry Abdul Razzaq did not leave the top floor of the house. His lunch and tea were sent upstairs.

Before her bags were loaded into the taxi, Naseem went upstairs to see Choudhry sahib. She said her goodbyes and turned to go. But then she stopped at the door and went back.

'Oh, I nearly forgot to say something. Tahira told me that you were talking about the Kashmir problem. I am not a politician like you, and I don't understand politics much either. But I can tell you one thing: by the time this Kashmir issue gets sorted out, Shabnam will have long been a grandmother many times over.'

Rumour

Chayya Devi felt, all of a sudden, that the rising sun of early November had been blotted out. Dark clouds seemed to have gathered in the clear blue sky as she listened to what Bimelendu had to say, the same dark clouds that had gathered in Dhaka thirty-seven years ago when Bimelendu's father had been on his way to get his asthma medicine from the government dispensary. The sun had been similarly eclipsed when her son-in-law Samir, the young handsome artist, had been stabbed by thugs, who had then shoved his weeping bride into a truck and taken her to some place, after which she had never been heard of again. Chayya Devi felt that twilight had descended upon Chittaranjan Park much before the appointed hour and consigned it to a deathly fear.

If the evening was so forbidding, how bloody would the next dawn be? Little pools of blood on the road, bodies lying on thresholds, smoke rising from half-burnt houses, vultures circling in the sky and the stench of roasting human flesh everywhere—Chayya Devi fainted at the thought.

Bimelendu splashed water on her face, pressed her hands and feet and, with a major effort, managed to unclench her teeth. It took her some time to gather her senses fully. Collapsing like this would not lead anywhere; she should do something. But what could she do? Then her eyes brightened.

'Come with me,' she said, putting a hand on Bimelendu's shoulder.

'Where to?'

'Wherever I go.'

Hooking her feet into slippers, Chayya Devi left the house, leaving it unlocked. This was no time to go out, Bimelendu thought, when the people of the colony had locked themselves in their houses. Only an occasional dog could be seen sniffing the baleful silence that had settled in all directions. Parting the silence with impatient steps, Chayya Devi advanced on the road that led from Chittaranjan Park to Greater Kailash. But when she turned towards the Greater Kailash gurdwara, Bimelendu's fears rose. With a few quick steps he caught his mother by the shoulder. By then she had reached the gate of the gurdwara.

'Let me be,' she said, holding the iron gate with both hands.

'Have you lost your mind, Mother?'

'Yes, I have lost my mind.'

'Turn back now. If somebody sees us we will not return home alive.'

'I do not want to return home alive. And you, too, will have to come in with me.'

'These people will kill us.'

'Let them kill us.'

'Mother, for the sake of Devi Durga, return home.'

'Never.'

'I will carry you away by force.'

'Don't you dare.' With some effort she freed herself from his grasp. Bimelendu felt as if the strength of the eight-armed Goddess had entered the weak old body of his mother.

In one burst she went into the main hall of the gurdwara. Bimelendu hesitated for a bit near the iron gate, torn and uncertain.

Then he also entered the gurdwara with fearful, small steps.

The secretary of the gurdwara stood up at the end of the kirtan. He seemed to be lost in thought. Greeting the congregation he said, 'This lady has come with her son from Chittaranjan Park. She wants to share a few words with the congregation. She refuses to tell me what she has to say. She insists that whatever she has to say will be said to the entire congregation. Come, respected lady.' The secretary motioned Chayya Devi to rise from where she sat near the stage.

The congregation leaned forward in curiosity. This was an unusual event. What was this lady from Chittaranjan Park, whose entire bearing was that of a Bengali woman, to the extent that a bunch of keys hung from one end of her black-bordered sari, doing in the middle of a Sikh congregation and what did she have to say?

The secretary adjusted the microphone for Chayya Devi's height. Bimelendu, too, came and stood behind his mother. He had tied over his head a blue handkerchief with a golden border, which a helper had handed him upon entering the gurdwara.

This was the first time in her life that Chayya Devi had got up to address a gathering. The voice she heard did not seem to be hers. It seemed to belong to someone else, not because it was coming through the sound system but because it was a trembling, hollow, dead voice. The blank expressions of the audience showed that they had neither heard nor understood the few sentences she had uttered. She stopped for a moment and turned back to look at Bimelendu. He stepped forward and held her by both shoulders from behind. His own hands were trembling but they gave great reassurance to the old woman. The trembling in her legs stilled a bit. With a huge effort she focused her mind and began again. This time the voice seemed to be her own.

'This is my first time in any gurdwara,' she said. 'I have often viewed them from the outside. In Dhaka and here, too, in Delhi. And I have always cherished your gurdwaras. It is nice to be inside one today. I have also closely read the poems written on Guru Gobind Singh by Rabindranath Tagore. Whenever I have looked upon a picture of the Harmandir in Amritsar, I have felt a sense of peace. This is the only reason I have been able to gather the courage to stand before you and make a request.'

She stopped again. What she had said so far had been easy. The next part appeared more difficult. She turned to look at her son again. Bimelendu did not know what his mother was going to say. But once again he gave her his full reassurance by looking into her eyes and gently squeezing her shoulders. With this she felt a wave of determination run through her, and she began to speak in an even and serious tone.

'You are well aware that Chittaranjan Park is the neighbouring colony. The people who live there came ravaged from East Bengal during the partition of the country. They are grief-stricken people who carry deep wounds in their souls. Wounds that never heal. Wounds that continue to fester. Go and take a look at Chittaranjan Park. The entire colony is shrouded in fear. The petrified people have begun to collect stones and bricks, bottles of water and soda on their roofs. They have heard rumours that tonight you are going to attack Chittaranjan Park and destroy it, and that's why you are all assembled in the gurdwara since the afternoon.'

The sound of a collective deep breath came from the congregation and people looked at each other in surprise. Then again they stared at the face of the old woman.

She felt her lips go dry and her resolve weaken. Again her legs weakened. Stepping forward beside his mother, Bimelendu took her hand in his. With her other hand, the old woman held on to the end of her sari so that it would not slip from her head. Passing her tongue over her lips and getting a hold of herself, she continued,

'We do not know much about you but we do know that you are a brave people. Your community has always protected the weak, the poor and the oppressed. What you have decided to do tonight has been motivated by the desire for revenge. Your desire for revenge is natural. My spirit has suffered since I came to know of the atrocities which have befallen you in Delhi from last night onwards. Last night, for you, has been another Partition, another birth of Pakistan. Maddened mobs have burnt your houses, your daughters have been dishonoured. You have been half-beaten to death with iron bars and then burnt alive with kerosene oil. Tyres dipped in petrol have been hung around your necks and set ablaze. These mobs have seen you dance the terrible dance of death. Your only fault was that the two persons who were caught for Indira Gandhi's assassination were Sikhs. Your desire for revenge is indeed natural. That's why I've come to you here today and brought my only son Bimelendu along with me. My request is that you satisfy your desire for revenge by killing the two of us. Cut us to pieces with your swords. Grind us to dust. We won't utter a sound. I have nothing more to offer you except my life and the life of my son. My husband and my son-in-law were killed in the Partition riots. My young newly-wed daughter fell in the hands of the mob that had set fire to our house. My two elder sons died of cholera in the refugee caravans. Bimelendu was then an infant in my arms. If they had been alive today I would have offered them all for you to exact your revenge. But for God's sake, do not attack Chittaranjan Park tonight. The people who live there are already burdened with pain and sorrow. They've never thought ill of you. They've never thought ill of anyone. Don't make a Pakistan again for them tonight. Who knows better than you what it means to have a Pakistan made twice in one's lifetime?'

Suddenly Chayya Devi fell silent. She bent her neck down, as if she was offering it to the sword of revenge. The congregation was stunned, but its silence seemed to speak. Bimelendu was no less surprised than the congregation. He hadn't known until then that his mother had brought him to the gurdwara as a sacrificial lamb. Momentarily, he paled. But he didn't let go of his mother's hand. A magnetic energy seemed to seep into his being from his mother's spirit through her hand. Colour returned to his cheeks and his gaze became fearless.

The secretary rose and made the mother and son sit near the stage. He was so shaken that he could not find words to speak for a while. Finally he cleared his throat and greeted the congregation. Its members responded with a weak response; they, too, were overcome with emotion.

'That is a very weak reply to my Fateh,' the secretary's own voice was still aquiver with emotion. 'Respond in such a way that your Fateh echoes loud and clear, so that it reaches Chittaranjan Park and our brothers there realize that the Khalsa exists only for the glory of God. That this faith has been created by the command of the Timeless One. His forces never wreak terror on anyone. The Khalsa lives in the house of mercy, and history is witness that when the time for justice arrives, the Khalsa exacts revenge—but only from evil demons, not from the weak and oppressed.'

The response from the congregation this time was loud and resounding. The loud tones also helped the members get a grip on their emotions.

'To whatever this lady from Chittaranjan Park has said...' The secretary bent down to ask Chayya Devi her name. 'Yes, like I was saying, to whatever Chayya Devi has said, I will respond very briefly. The Sikh population has been gathering in the gurdwara since this afternoon only for its own safety, not to attack anyone. Another terrible night like the last one awaits us. We have gathered together in the gurdwara only so that we are not found defenceless or killed one by one; rather, we have come together so we can die protecting our families. Just like our brothers in Chittaranjan Park came as refugees from East Bengal, many of us came as refugees from West Punjab. Today, as far as we are concerned, Pakistan has been formed once again in free India. Our prayer is that those living in Chittaranjan Park should be happy for all time. They should never again have to face the tribulation and trial we are facing now. Any ill wind that is going to blow towards them should turn in our direction—'

The secretary stopped in mid-speech. Chayya Devi had risen and taken the mic from him with her trembling hands. Not only her hands but her entire being was atremble. This time she had to push herself up with both hands on her knees, as if there was no strength left in her at all, as if her body had accepted defeat. She sensed her vision becoming indistinct. She took off her spectacles. Yet it wasn't because of the spectacles but the tears that she couldn't see clearly. She brushed them aside and tried to say something but only a sob escaped her. Biting her lip, she held back her tears and, clearing her throat, began to speak.

'Brothers and sisters, I am ashamed that I doubted your intentions. I should've thought twice before believing in a rumour. But fear and grief had blinded me and I came straight to berate you. I have wrongly blamed you and ascribed bad intentions to you. I had gone mad. I have not blamed you but Guru Gobind Singh, I have accused the Golden Temple in Amritsar. I am your culprit. Punish me. I must be punished for this.'

The secretary stood up and gently put his hand on her shoulder. Then he pulled the mic towards himself and said, 'I will now request the president to present a garland from the Guru Granth Sahib to Bibi Chayya Devi.'

The president of the gurdwara committee was a man who was full of life. This life force was evident in his glowing complexion and shining visage. He was a very sensitive person, easily shaken by life's emotional moments. He got up, took the garland from the secretary's hands and presented it to Chayya Devi. Receiving it, she first kissed the garland, then touched it to her eyes and forehead. Such fragrance had never floated into her life before.

'Now I will request the president,' the secretary continued, 'to present a "siropa"—saffron turban and sword—to Chayya Devi's son, Shri Bimelendu.'

Bimelendu was already wearing a blue silk handkerchief on his head. As soon as he put the saffron turban around his neck his face took on a crimson hue. When he received the three-and-a-half-foot sword from the president, lightning seemed to sizzle through his body, as if the sword's steel had touched his soul even through the velvet cover.

The Border

The first light came unannounced. The sun's orb had not yet risen. The last star could still be seen twinkling in the hazy sky. The inky darkness had fled the east and was being sopped up by the horizon on the west. Then a pink edge appeared on the eastern horizon and coloured the sleeping fields of paddy and hemp. The sky began to fill with flocks of birds on their way to welcoming the rising sun. Then the entire orb of the sun seemed to spring up all at once.

Standing at the edge of the field, Prabhdayal bowed to the rising sun and felt its first rays kissing his face. His entire being seemed to expand as he inhaled the fresh breeze touched by the sun rays. It was an old habit of his to spend this magical and peaceful moment of dawn in the fields; it had the same effect on his soul as a shloka from the Gita or a verse from the Sukhmani.

A tall border of hemp surrounded the shorter paddy crop. With the first touch of the sun the stalks had snapped awake and were now softly singing as they swayed in the fresh breeze. Prabhdayal's soul was enraptured by this song. Even if the past was smeared with blood, there was still so much in life that was beautiful, so much to live for, so much to cherish.

His heart lifted as he watched the ripe paddy sway. This was the first crop of the new dwarf variety of rice in Ranbir Singh Pura tehsil, and it was so substantive that it would make up for all past deficiencies. Only three lakh quintals of rice had been produced in all of Jammu last year, but this year Ranbir Singh Pura tehsil alone hoped to produce four lakh quintals. In fact, the paddy that swayed in front of Prabhdayal's eyes promised to top even that estimate. Tomorrow morning he would begin to reap his crop and there would be heaps of paddy everywhere.

A sudden sound echoed in his ears. More than his ears, it was his heart and soul that heard it: the sound of the engine pulling the Sialkot–Narowal train. He heard this sound every day, and it always reminded him of the folk song, *'Look, look, the Narowal train/Has lit a fire in the old man's beard.'*

The thick smoke that spread out against the blue backdrop of the horizon did seem to him like an old man's burnt beard. For the last twenty-four years, ever since the day he had come and settled down in Suchetgarh village (in Ranbir Singh Pura tehsil), this train had run daily from Sialkot to Narowal, sketching out the same line of smoke above the horizon. And every day, as he watched this line, many lines of blood would streak across his consciousness. Sialkot and Narowal were so close to where he stood. But they were still so, so far away. To get to either would mean crossing an international border—the one between India and Pakistan—that was only half a mile away from his village, Suchetgarh.

Prabhdayal had fond childhood memories of Narowal and Sialkot. His maternal uncle had a cloth shop in Narowal, and his aunt with her laughing face used to make sweet pulao for him out of the seven-coloured sevian. His mother's family had lived in Sialkot, where his grandfather had owned a wholesale grocery store. Whenever Prabhdayal went to the shop, his grandfather would fill his lap with walnuts and small sugar patashas. He remembered how every morning he used to go with his mother's widowed sister to Babey di Ber gurdwara, and eat warm 'karah parshad'. But all these memories seemed to be from a past life. He had no uncle now, and his mother's family was gone. The Partition riots had taken them all. Now, even though he watched the train from Sialkot to Narowal go by every day, he felt no desire to go to either town. But it was also true that he liked to look in that direction, across the border, towards Sialkot, Narowal, Lahore, the Ravi River and the city of Jhelum, near which lay the little town of Sohawa and his own village, Phulra.

As he looked across the border, his gaze was suddenly pulled up short by the unexpected bustle and commotion in the Pakistani villages of Khasiri and Khanachak. He watched these villages every day. There was usually very little activity, perhaps a bull in harness at someone's well, a solitary labourer watering his field or the occasional bullock cart going by. But today there was frenetic activity early in the morning. Bullock carts were being loaded with beds, cots, stools, sacks and bedding. Beside them stood droves of cattle, sheep and goats. The villagers were running around with little bundles and small trunks on their heads, as if they were leaving to go settle somewhere else.

Prabhdayal stood at the edge of the field and numbly surveyed the scene. He had no idea what it all meant. He had seen caravans of bullock carts like these during Partition, when Pakistan was created. But that was twenty-four years ago. What could such caravans mean now?

There was a roll of thunder. Prabhdayal looked up. Was it going to rain? But there wasn't a spot of cloud in the sky. The clear blue sky of late October looked like a sunny lake. So then what was this thunder? What was going on today? Nothing seemed to make any sense to him. But when he shifted his gaze again across the border, he understood everything in an instant. Pakistani tanks were heading straight towards the border from the left side of Khanachak. Prabhdayal stood rooted to the spot, eyeing the tanks heading towards him. The earth shook so hard that he was sure even the crops in the fields could feel the tanks' rumbling. It seemed to him that the stalks of paddy were no longer swaying to the breeze, but had started to tremble with a vague, indefinable fear instead. Fear had stilled the breeze, too.

The tanks stopped at the border. Behind them was a convoy of armoured military trucks. Prabhdayal could clearly see the steel helmets and automatic rifles of the soldiers sitting in the trucks. All this could mean only one thing: war! War between Pakistan and India. The Bangladesh affair, which had dragged on for the last six months, was going to end in something after all.

Before he could gather himself, he began to swoon and his legs began to tremble uncontrollably; then the trembling took over his entire body, as if he were coming down with double pneumonia. The slight nip of late October now infiltrated his body like a winter frost. He wrapped his rough shawl around him and started towards the village, stumbling like a sleepwalker down the raised path that ran between his fields.

Reaching home, he fell back on to the cot in the courtyard and called out in a low, fearful voice,

'Ram Rakhi, Ram Rakhi.'

There was no response to his faint call. He strained to push a louder sound from his dry throat.

'Ram Rakhi, Ram Rakhi.'

There was still no response.

He made an effort to collect himself. The sound coming from the kitchen was not the churning of milk. This was the hour when Ram Rakhi went to the temple. Then what was this sound? He picked up the blanket from the foot of the cot and, wrapping it around himself, went in to investigate.

Prabhdayal's son Tilak Raj was sharpening the harvesting sickles on the kitchen grindstone. He was so absorbed in his work that he did not notice his father come in. Finally, he paused to test the edge of the sickle on his left thumb and started when he saw his father's face.

'What's the matter, Lala ji?'

'Nothing, son,' Prabhdayal averted his gaze. 'Where is your mother?'

Tilak Raj knew that something was the matter from the way his father had looked away.

'She has gone to the temple. Why are you looking so lost? You don't seem well. Get into a warm bed. I'll make you some tea.'

Pushing aside the sickles, he put the water to boil. Just then, from the window, he saw his mother walking back from the temple.

Ram Rakhi was surprised upon seeing the glass of tea in her son's hand. Then she saw her trembling husband, wrapped up in a blanket, his eyes wide with fear and his face chalk-white.

'Oh my God,' she exclaimed. 'What on earth has happened?'

Prabhdayal did not respond. He couldn't say anything. His voice seemed to die in his throat. When he had taken a few sips of tea he could speak, but the voice did not seem his own.

'War,' he said in a frightened tone. 'War is about to break out.'

'A war? Between whom?' asked Tilak Raj, as he moved to sit at the foot of the cot.

'War between India and Pakistan,' answered Prabhdayal, astounded at his son's ignorance. 'Who else?'

'Did an astrologer tell you this?' Ram Rakhi asked.

'No,' Prabhdayal's cracked voice had a rough edge. 'I have seen it with my own eyes. Pakistani troops are gathering at the border.'

'Now what?' Tilak Raj asked. 'We have to harvest the crop tomorrow.'

'To hell with the harvest,' Prabhdayal snapped at his son. 'Just pack up and run. Let us take the morning bus to Jammu. From there we will go to Asa Ram in Ludhiana.'

'What are you saying, Lala ji?' Tilak Raj shouted back. 'Leave our ripe crop and run away? This cannot be.'

'And the house, with everything in it?' Ram Rakhi said, wringing her hands. 'We left Pakistan with nothing but the clothes on our body.'

Prabhdayal turned to his wife.

'You're worried about things? You sacrificed your two elder sons to Pakistan. Now you don't want your third son to live?'

Ram Rakhi's legs began to tremble and she turned pale. The unfortunate events of twenty-four years ago rose starkly in her consciousness.

'You are right,' she said. 'To hell with our fields and our things. Our lives are everything. Let us go to Asa Ram in Ludhiana.'

They were both looking at their son. He looked at his mother and then at his father, and then turning back to his mother he said, 'The whole village is here. The entire village is carrying on its life.'

'If others want to shed their blood for their crops, let them. We have shed enough already.'

'But Lala ji,' Tilak Raj tried to soothe his father, 'I tell you, nothing will happen here. You are scared for nothing.'

'The same words,' Prabhdayal answered, 'exactly the same words I used to say before Pakistan was created. People had already left in fright for Patiala and Delhi. More than half of Phulra was empty. The elders said that we should leave before the fifteenth of August. But like a born idiot I kept saying, "Nothing will happen here. People are running scared for nothing." You can never fully know, never fully understand what happened there. You were only three years old then. But your mother and I will not forget what happened in ten lifetimes.'

Tilak Raj looked towards his mother, but there, too, he did

not find any support.

'Your father is right, son,' Ram Rakhi told him. 'He didn't listen to me then. I used to beg him day and night, "Lala ji, let's just go. The entire village has left." But he was obstinate and we suffered badly. Let it not be that you, too, don't listen and we suffer again.'

'I had taken an oath then,' Prabhdayal said, 'that I would never be foolhardy, that I wouldn't risk my life in the face of danger. I have shed tears of blood once because of my stupidity. I won't be that stupid again.'

Silence prevailed for a while. None of them spoke. Tilak Raj's heart did not want to accept the wisdom of his parents, but he felt forced to hold his tongue. Lost in thought, he stared at the cracks in the floor.

'I'd say,' Prabhdayal continued, 'that we take the cash and jewellery and leave for Jammu by today's bus. We will see what happens later.'

'Today's bus has already left,' Tilak Raj said. 'We'll have to put things off till tomorrow.'

Prabhdayal, too, put it off till the next day. There was no other choice. They spent all day gathering their clothes, bedding and utensils, and Tilak Raj kept going up to the terrace and sighing at the sight of his ripe crop.

The next morning they woke up while the stars were still out. The bus for Jammu left Suchetgarh at the crack of dawn, and there was still some last-minute packing to do.

Tilak Raj tore a piece of newspaper and laid it out at the base of the small metal trunk before putting in his daily prayer book, as well as the Gita and the Sukhmani. As he did that, his eye happened to fall on a story printed in the newspaper. The prime minister had appealed to all countries in the world for aid for the refugees from Bangladesh. His hands froze where they were. There was his country asking for food for the refugees, and he was about to leave hundreds of quintals of his own ripening crop of the new magic variety of rice, a crop he had sown standing ankle-deep in water until his back felt as if it would never straighten up again. That crop was dearer to him than life. It wasn't right. He would not let it happen. He swore on his back-breaking labour that he would harvest the entire crop himself. Each grain of this new rice would reach the wholesale market at Ranbir Singh Pura—even if he would have to pay with his life in the process.

He put his daily prayer book, the Gita and the Sukhmani back on the shelf and, picking up his sickle from the kitchen, darted towards the fields.

Vashist, Guru of the Clan

When the police started recovering stolen goods from the shacks, Mukandi Lal lost his nerve. At least, he reflected, there was no need to fear going to jail; you just had to cough up what you'd already swallowed. But that wasn't easy either: it could tear a man's insides to shreds. In fact, imprisonment with hard labour would be easier to handle. Where was the justice in trying to recover stolen goods after a month and a half? It was just cruelty. You could rightly ask, he thought, why allow it to be stolen in the first place if it was just going to be recovered in the end? In hindsight, those who had sold off the colour televisions and VCRs for five hundred rupees as they returned to Haryana had been wiser. Why had he not thought of that? He had clung on to the colour TV, and now the police would pull that colour TV out of his tight grasp and drag his wounded and bloodied heart along with it.

He had struggled so long in Delhi, Mukandi Lal thought. The government had tried its best to remove his poverty with countless plans and schemes. But poverty was so deadly that the more you tried to remove it the more it dug in, like some persistent wild bramble. Then finally, a day came, he thought, when the prime minister had to sacrifice her life for the unity and integrity of the country. Then the poor of Delhi and Kanpur got permission to make a valiant effort to remove their poverty with their own hands. And the result of this effort was that today colour TVs, VCRs, geysers, fridges and washing machines were being recovered from the hovels of those who had hitherto never managed to set their eyes on even a transistor radio.

Those slum dwellers had lived it up for a month or so. The government had removed their poverty, after all. Justice may have been delayed in God's world, but it had not been denied. There was joy in the slums: God had generously showered mercies beyond all expectation on them. The women of the slums, who a day earlier had been sweeping and cleaning the big villas, now basked in the sun all day and combed their hair as they looked at themselves in mirrors. But this move to recover the goods had spoilt things a bit.

No one knew where the recovered goods went. One thing was certain: the goods did not go back to the owners or their heirs because they had already left this world. They were in a place where they had no need for a TV, fridge, geyser or washing machine. One blow from an iron bar on their heads and they had fallen down, half-dead. Then, to end their suffering, the anti-poverty crusaders had taken pity, sprinkled petrol on them and burnt them alive.

Mukandi Lal had got word that day that the police would raid the Kalyanpuri slum early the next morning. He lost all appetite after that. He smoked bidi after bidi and ferried passengers in his three-wheeler as if in a daze. His mind was elsewhere. He narrowly escaped getting into an accident twice. But though he thought about it all day, he could see no way out. He was, however, determined on one account: he would give up his life if necessary, but he would not hand his TV over to the police.

After the hit from the bidis, it was not difficult to think of sacrificing his life for the sake of what was rightfully his. But it didn't seem such a good idea after he had returned the three-wheeler to its owner, paid the day's rent and started towards the dhaba, tired and hungry. Even powerful men pissed their pants when confronted by the police; how could Mukandi Lal face up to them? He recovered his wits a bit after eating his dinner, and the answer came to him in an instant as he slurped his steaming hot tea. He found it surprising that he had not hit on this simple solution the entire day.

He ran all the way to his hut. He tied up the TV in a torn blanket and put it on the seat of his three-wheeler. Then he drove his three-wheeler towards Model Town, where a friend of his, Jang Bahadur, worked as a security guard in the house of a rich merchant. Mukandi Lal had himself worked as a chauffeur in that house for a year and a half. But he had been turned out last year after it became known that he had forged receipts in cahoots with the local petrol pump.

Jang Bahadur stayed away from cheats. When Mukandi Lal had been thrown out the previous year, Jang Bahadur had not been able to get rid of the bitter taste in his mouth for days. He had had a special place in his heart for Mukandi Lal. Last year when the owners of the house had gone to Nainital, a gang of Sansi robbers had left Jang Bahadur half-dead, and it had been Mukandi Lal who had put him in a taxi and taken him to the hospital. He had needed two bottles of blood. If he had reached the hospital any later, Jang Bahadur would surely have had to cross the river of forgetfulness and present himself at the court of Yamaraja.

When Jang Bahadur heard that Mukandi Lal had participated in the killing and looting of innocent Sikhs in Delhi, his affection for him was seriously shaken. He criticized Mukandi Lal and cursed him, but he could not break the bond of friendship through which two bottles of red blood coursed.

Jang Bahadur firmly refused to keep the TV in his quarters.

Just imagine: stolen goods in the quarters of Seth Ram Prasad's security guard! It was out of the question. But as Mukandi Lal begged and beseeched, Jang Bahadar's resolve wilted. He was still shaking his head in the negative, but his 'no' seemed to have a lot of 'yes' in it.

'All right,' Jang Bahadur said at last. 'Seth and his family have gone to America for two months. You will have to remove this TV from here before their return.'

Mukandi Lal was ready to meet any condition. Two months was a long time. By then the police would have had enough of slum colonies, and finished its mission.

Mukandi Lal had been the owner of a colour TV for a month and a half, but he had not switched it on even once, because his hut in Kalyanpuri lacked electricity. When Jang Bahadur relented, it was a double gain for Mukandi Lal. Not only was the colour TV safe in the servant quarters of the villa but he, the owner of the TV, could now come and watch it whenever he liked.

The *Ramayana* was being shown on TV those days. Mukandi Lal had heard much praise for this show. It was watched in homes all over the country with infinite reverence. Every Sunday morning, between nine and ten when the show was on air, the streets and bazaars of Delhi would be deserted, as if all the citizens of Delhi had gone off on a pilgrimage to Ayodhya. Even three-wheelers would get passengers only after ten, when the show ended and activity resumed in Delhi. And when passengers talked amongst themselves about the show, the three-wheeler drivers could only sigh, since they possessed neither a television set nor the leisure to see the serial. He too used to suffer, his yearning doubly pronounced since he possessed a TV and still could not see the *Ramayana*. But now, God had answered his prayers. Now he would watch the *Ramayana* every Sunday with his friend Jang Bahadur, and no power on earth, no captain of police, would be able to stop him.

There were still six full days to next Sunday. Those six days seemed to Mukandi Lal to pass like an eternity. Each of the days came in turn—but Sunday, it seemed, would never come. It appeared to Mukandi Lal that the Ravana of Time had abducted his Sunday.

When at long last Sunday did arrive after a long Saturday evening and an even longer night, Mukandi Lal rose early, bathed, put a tilak on his forehead and dressed in a white kurta and dhoti. He usually reserved these clothes only to go to the temple on full-moon or no-moon nights. Once he was ready, he turned his three-wheeler towards Model Town. Many people tried to wave him down on the way, but he did not take any passengers. His soul was focused on his desire to see the *Ramayana*, and he did not want to disturb his calm concentration under any circumstances. He did stop on the way, but only to buy a garland of marigold flowers and some incense.

Untying the knotted torn bedcover, he released the television set. Then he wiped and cleaned and caressed it as if it were his beloved. Then he adorned it with the garland of marigolds. When he lit the incense and performed an aarti of the TV, Jang Bahadur's quarters were filled with the fragrance of musk and sandalwood.

When the TV was finally switched on after all these rituals, King Dashrath was sharing with his court his decision to abdicate in favour of Rama. In the next scene, a determined Rama was saying that he had no right to the throne during the lifetime of his honoured father, and he would not accept being anointed as king. Then Vashist, the clan's guru, came and told Rama that he should not be governed by emotion, but must do his duty.

When he saw Kulguru Vashist's long beard and bushy eyebrows, Mukandi Lal felt a flaming heat rise from his own half-shaven straggly beard. His jaw was gripped by fierce pain. The pain pulled him way back along the string of time to the Partition, when his parents had been killed in the Sheikhupura massacres. He had been ten years old then. The men of the army convoy had dragged him and his uncle out from under the pile of dead bodies. With much difficulty, they had managed to reach Delhi. His uncle was a born lazybones, incapable of hard work. They often ended up eating their lunch at the langar in Gurdwara Sisganj. Then, encouraged by his uncle, Mukandi would hide a pair of the congregation's shoes, slippers or sandals in his pyjamas, and walk out with a meek expression on his face. They would sell the footwear to a cobbler in Urdu bazaar, and that would take care of the evening meal. One day, one of the gurdwara volunteers caught him red-handed in the act of stealing shoes, and gave him such a resounding slap across his face that the world spun around in front of Mukandi Lal's eyes. His jaw hurt for a full month, and for the rest of his life Mukandi Lal dared not set foot near a gurdwara.

Now the long beard and bushy eyebrows of Kulguru Vashist reminded Mukandi Lal of that gurdwara worker, and he felt the fire of those hot fingers rising in his cheek again.

Jang Bahadur looked at Mukandi Lal's frightened eyes and asked, 'What's the matter? Are you unwell?'

'Nothing. It's nothing,' replied Mukandi Lal, rubbing his jaw.

Persuaded by Kulguru Vashist, Sri Ramachandra agreed to be anointed with the royal tilak. The ceremony was to take place the next morning. In accordance with tradition, Sri Rama and Sita were washing the Kulguru's feet before the ceremony.

Suddenly Mukandi Lal gripped his chest tightly with both arms, as if he had been struck a mighty blow. It seemed to Jang Bahadur that Mukandi Lal had lost consciousness and his body was giving up on him. He had begun to froth at the mouth, and his eyes were rolling wildly. At any moment, it seemed, he would go into a seizure. Mukandi Lal hit his own forehead hard with both his hands as Jang Bahadur watched, and shrieked in a hoarse voice, 'This is not Kulguru Vashist. It's the man whose villa I looted. The same white beard, the same silvery top-knot, the same glowing forehead—which I smashed with a thick iron rod. A torrent of blood, spewing forth...but that glow did not fade. See, Jang Bahadur, a trident is shining from his forehead. Oh, that trident has pierced my eyes! I cannot see anything any more. I have been blinded! I have gone blind!'

Parmeshwari

Parmeshwari watched Nasib Kaur coming down the steps, a glass of tea in her hand. Her step was lighter than usual, and there was a glow on her face. Parmeshwari knew the reason. First thing in the morning, Nasib Kaur's son Rajbir had brought an excellent Persian carpet from the Muslim choudhry's bungalow and had rushed back for more. Parmeshwari had seen him go up the stairs with the rolled-up carpet on his shoulder. And she had also heard Nasib Kaur shout after him as he had rushed down the steps, three at a time, 'Go, my son, go with all your mother's blessings, go as many times as you can.'

Then Nasib Kaur had turned to the young servant. 'You wretch, why don't you also go take advantage of this bounty? Look, even your pyjama is torn. If nothing else, go and get someone's pants.'

'No, Bibi,' the servant had answered, 'I can't do it.'

'Useless fellow, of no earthly use at all.'

That morning, the dark cloud that had been threatening Patiala for so long had finally burst. There was wild shouting in the lanes and the mobs rushed wildly to and fro. In Pakistan, the Muslims had killed and plundered the Hindus and Sikhs and now, here in Patiala, the Hindus and Sikhs were returning the favour. That was the reason for the new joy in Nasib Kaur's dim existence.

'You should come with me,' she remarked sharply to Parmeshwari now. 'Let's also go stand in the lane and see what's happening.'

'I don't feel like it,' Parmeshwari replied despondently, withdrawing to the corner of the room.

'Why don't you feel like it?'

'I can't bear to see the killing and the looting.'

'Why are you feeling so sad for those bloody Muslims now? Have they done any less to us in Pakistan?'

Parmeshwari felt like asking Nasib Kaur exactly what she knew about Pakistan. After all, Nasib Kaur was one of the lucky ones who had been given freedom while sitting in their own houses.

'Just take a look at yourself,' Nasib Kaur continued, noisily slurping her tea, 'they killed your husband. They took away your newly married daughter. You left behind two houses bursting at the seams with your stuff in Rawalpindi, and now you live in a rented room in my house here. How can you possibly feel anything for them?'

Parmeshwari tried in vain to swallow the bitter taste that choked her mouth. This was the same Nasib Kaur who went to the gurdwara every day and invoked God's name every time she sneezed. And now she was defending the actions of the murderous looting mob.

Rajbir rushed up the stairs again, lugging a radio in both hands. Nasib Kaur saw the mute reproach in Parmeshwari's eyes and tried to ignore it. But when it began to seem that the angry gaze would burn a hole in her, she spoke up, 'The whole world is looting. Will the world come to an end if my son grabs a little soundbox? And what was I just telling you?' Nasib Kaur gathered the creamy film that had congealed on her tea with her finger and flicked it to the floor. 'Why are you standing there trembling like a leaf about to vanish into the ground? Look at your son. He's been avenging himself to his heart's content.'

A sob escaped from Parmeshwari's half-open mouth, and there was a long pause before she could utter the words, 'My son? Who? Bhagwant?'

'Who else?'

'No. Bhagwant has gone to look for a job.'

'A job? Where? He was running with the mob, holding a sword in his hand. I saw him myself when I was looking over the wall on the terrace.'

'You must have been mistaken. My Bhagwant is not like that, he's not the type to hurt anyone.'

'I have not yet got cataract in these eyes. I can recognize Bhagwant. And I know what a sword looks like. A bloody one.'

The words pierced Parmeshwari's heart. She went into the room and opened the cupboard. The sword was missing. Quickly she pulled on her shoes, put a dupatta over her head and left the house.

'What's the matter with you? Where are you off to?' she could hear Nasib Kaur shouting after her.

She searched through the lanes and bazaars of Patiala as long as it was light but couldn't find Bhagwant anywhere. These lanes, these twists and turns were strange to her and she had no idea where they led to. In Patiala she only knew the lane from Nasib Kaur's house to Gurdwara Dukh Niwaran Sahib, down which she went barefoot every morning at dawn, on her way to pray for her abducted daughter. She seemed to be going round in circles now, passing the same lanes again and again, the same ugly scenes lacerating her soul repeatedly, until she returned to the house, tired, defeated and polluted by what she had seen.

She saw Bhagwant standing at the entrance of the house,

wiping the blood from his sword with a piece of sackcloth. He flexed the fingers of his right hand, numb from holding the sword for so long, and kneaded his tired wrist with his left hand. Then he entered the house and went up the stairs.

Parmeshwari felt as if the last drop of blood had been squeezed out of her body. She clung to the door for support. She waited for the dizziness to subside. Then, holding the wall, she began to climb the steps to the upper floor with trembling feet. As she came up to the room, she could hear Bhagwant relating his exploits to Rajbir. She halted in the shadow of the half-open door.

'If only you had seen them, if only you had heard them. How they begged for life, how they fell at my feet, how they beseeched me, begging in the name of "Waheguru". How strange "Waheguru" sounds from their lips. All of them, old and young,' he gasped breathlessly, 'we did them all in. The children were screaming. And then we gathered all the women together in one courtyard.'

Parmeshwari's breath was coming in short, angry bursts. She covered her mouth with her dupatta so they wouldn't hear her.

'One young girl,' Bhagwant continued, 'was as beautiful as a princess. She could have been made of gold. She wouldn't take off her clothes. Not even if we chopped her to pieces, she said. I nicked her neck with the tip of my sword and a long, thin line of blood appeared, but she still wouldn't do it. Then two of the boys held her and I tore off every last shred of her clothing. What a body!'

Parmeshwari felt as if a saw was slicing through her chest. But she held herself back, silent, behind the door.

'Then at high noon, we took out a procession of all those naked Muslim women. A procession of naked breasts. All types of naked breasts. Small and hard, big and soft. Virgin breasts, young breasts, middle-aged breasts. Oh, the sheer pleasure of that sight!'

Parmeshwari's anger gave her strength. The door banged

against the wall as she burst into the room.

'Damn you and the day you were born,' she screamed, her thin body taut and trembling. 'You are fond of looking at naked breasts, aren't you? Here, see them to your heart's content, you wretch.' She tore open all the buttons of her shirt and hung out her breasts. 'Why are you looking down now? Why didn't you look down then? Weren't they someone's mothers and sisters? Raise your eyes now and see the breasts that have fed you. If I had known then that I was feeding a demon, I would have strangled you.'

Bhagwant and Rajbir were frozen to the ground. Then Rajbir slid away quietly and went down the stairs.

Bhagwant at last said with a touch of anger, 'What have I done wrong? Why are you cursing me? Wasn't it the Muslims who took our Harbans from her in-laws' village? I don't even want to think about the terrible things those butchers must have done to my sister.'

Parmeshwari's eyes were like red-hot coals.

'If you were so brave then you should have gone and saved your sister from them. You should have taken revenge from those killers. But you were a coward: you ran away to Patiala to save your life. Where was your sword then?'

'You're on the Muslims' side, Mother. You don't even remember that last month the Muslims stabbed Father to death.'

'I haven't forgotten. You're the one with the weak memory: it was some Muslim thugs who stabbed your father in Rawalpindi. Patiala's Muslims didn't go to Rawalpindi to kill him.'

'But Mother...'

'Don't you ever call me mother again.' Parmeshwari was frothing at the mouth. 'I'm dead for you and you're dead for me. Didn't you see the steel bangle of your faith on your arm when you raised the sword of the tenth Guru on innocents, you butcher? I, your mother, curse you. May you die and may you...'

Parmeshwari swooned and fell down, unconscious.

Nasib Kaur, who had been listening, leaning against the wall, came into the room. First of all she tucked Parmeshwari's breasts inside her shirt and buttoned it up. Then she took some water from the bucket and began to splash it on Parmeshwari's face.

She and I

I remember that midwinter afternoon. Bent over the pile of registered letters on the counter, I was scribbling out the receipts furiously with the little piece of pencil clutched tight between my numb fingers. The rush of work had exhausted me. I wanted to throw the pile of envelopes on the floor and shout at the people in the queue beyond the little counter window, 'Pick up this junk or I will set fire to it. Yes, what do you think I am?'

Just then the postmaster called me and I went to see him, seething with resentment. At that moment I was ready to pick a fight with him. For a full month I had been been doing the job of two persons. Every day he would dangle the promise of an assistant. Today. Tomorrow. But none appeared, and my patience had worn thin.

'Lot of work?' he asked, wiping his glasses until they glistened.

'Yes, sir,' I replied, irritated.

He smiled. His smile had always taken away my bitterness. I felt the irritation leaving me. In fact, I almost smiled back.

'Seat this lady next to you,' he said, hooking his spectacles around his ears. 'She will learn the work slowly, and you, too, will get some help.'

I turned to the girl sitting on his right, whom I had not looked at yet; my mouth fell open with surprise. I had never dared to hope that my assistant would be a girl. Suddenly she raised her large dark eyes towards me and my heart took a leap. The entire staff of the post office was looking at her. She was the first girl on the staff.

I pushed my cushioned chair towards her. She took it without thanking me. I pulled up a rough wooden chair for myself and sat down. I saw that she was staring at the pile of registered letters, as if anxious to get her hands on them. Silently, I admired her hard-working nature. Then I handed her the basic rules for stamping registered letters and, clutching the bit of pencil again, began to fill in the receipts.

Shortly, there was no one left at the counter. I had finished the pile of letters. For me, this was hardly any work, just a pastime. Even if the entire town were to bring registered letters, I would write out the receipts in no time.

Twisting the little pencil in my hand I began to steal looks at her. She was lost in studying the rules. I was sorry that though I had worked so hard in her sight, she had paid no attention. The men in the queue had been staring at her under the pretence of having their letters registered, but she had been so absorbed in the rules that she had not looked up at anyone.

Everything has a limit, I thought. Such hard work is not good, and in any case it does not suit pretty young girls.

My stolen looks began to gather courage. Earlier they had been afraid that if they met those dark eyes, they would quickly have to withdraw. Now I felt that I was staring at some stone statue. Those sharp features were smooth, as if carved out of old ivory. And her complexion was transparent, something you could see through. A green vein twisted like a creeper on her fair neck.

I tried to make out the expression on that face. Disappointment? No. Happiness? No. It seemed that her face was beyond all emotion. I had the strange feeling then that the face was not alive; it was already dead. And a chill went up my spine at that thought. Uncomfortable, I twisted around in my chair. The sound of the creaking chair made her raise her eyes for a moment and look at me. It was a look without any emotion. Only a vast desolation. But those eyes were the only sign of life in that dead face.

I wanted to say something, but my tongue did not move. At that moment the clock in the postmaster's room struck four and I found some words.

'It's four o'clock,' I said, in a soft, wavering voice. 'Now you can go home.'

She was going to start reading the rules again. Silently, she shut the book, pushed it towards me and got up to go. Oh, that look of hers! Behind those ashes of grief I had also seen sparks of hatred. They had scalded my insides.

She went off but I was left with a bitter taste in my mouth. The chair was hurting me from all sides and the poster on the wall announcing National Savings Certificates seemed to be staring at me. She had left behind a strange suffocation, an air of mystery and an entire entangled web on the counter. Some assistant they had given me. It seemed that her cold, sad silences would deprive me of all will to work. I sat lost in the thought of the penetrating gaze of those desolate eyes, and did not even notice that a nail from the arm of the chair had pierced my wrist and drawn blood.

The next day she was there before me, once again reading the rules regarding the registration charges. She had taken the wooden chair, and had left the cane chair with the cushion for me.

'You please take this chair. You will be uncomfortable on that one.'

She gave me a quick glance and started reading again. Neither did she say a word nor did she make a move to leave the chair. Her indifference seemed to imply that I was a mere shadow and my words were but smoke.

'At least take this cushion,' a tone of appeal had crept into my voice. 'That seat is very rough.'

This time she did not even raise her eyes. I could have just been some barking dog. I may as well have been talking to the wall. She kept sitting on the chair in her obstinate silence.

Suddenly anger began to curdle inside me. A peon with a deformed face was standing at the counter, holding a pile of letters in his hand. For a moment I wanted to mimic his deformity and make him run away. Then I thought, perhaps the girl is deaf and dumb. Perhaps that was the cause, too, behind that lifeless face and those desolate eyes. My anger drained away.

I scribbled on a piece of paper and pushed it towards her, 'You must definitely take this cushioned chair. Your sitting on that wooden chair makes me very uncomfortable.'

On reading the note her eyes, those eyes with the long eyelashes, narrowed. Her face paled and I saw her lower lip tremble like some broken petal. With trembling fingers she wrote something on the other side of the paper and pushed it back towards me.

'I do not need your sympathy. Please keep it to yourself. I need work. I have read these rules thrice already.'

I felt as if I had run into a wall. The poster whirled around me. When I gathered my senses I put the pile of letters, the receipt book and the pencil in front of her.

Again I wrote on the piece of paper, 'Why don't you speak? I want to hear your voice.'

Her sharp eyebrows seemed to come closer and she frowned.

'Would you be good enough to keep to your work?' she wrote on the piece of paper.

'Why are you so cold?' I wrote back. 'From your lips I would have expected sweetness.'

As soon as she read that, her eyes filled with fear. Her cheeks became like freshly fluffed cotton wool and she might have barely stopped herself from screaming. The pencil slipped from her fingers and the face of the peon at the counter, who had been staring in wonder, appeared even more deformed.

At last she picked up the pencil and wrote with her trembling, bloodless fingers, 'For God's sake, why are you after me? What did I do to you? Like this broken-down chair on which I am sitting, I too want to just stay in one corner. I do not need sympathy or friendship. You can give me all your work but please leave me alone. For the sake of my old mother, please let me keep this job.'

Question marks appeared all around me and began to poke me in my eyes. I shut my eyes in pain. When I opened them again I could see only the flash of hatred in her quicksilver eyes, and my entire being burned in that flash. The fear I had seen in those eyes had made me doubt my own intentions. Fearfully I glanced at the girl, and then, ducking the blows of some unseen whip, stumbled away from my chair.

There was a small enclosed garden outside the post office. I stayed there a long while, trying to recover my balance. Blue linseed flowers were blooming in the shade of the hedge, and sunlight flowed in thin streams on the soft grass. I stood there, one arm around the trunk of the tamarind tree, drawing comfort from its solidity. A squirrel sat at my feet, munching on the unripe tamarind fruit and staring at my face. All seemed to be well again. I decided that I would ask the postmaster to change my duties. I would not be able to get along with that girl.

In fact, he called out himself as I passed, 'How is the lady assistant?'

I was stung to the quick.

'Lady assistant? She is no lady assistant. She is a mystery-filled wax doll, who will melt some day in the strong sunshine and reveal her true, frightening face.'

'What do you mean?' A slight frown had appeared on his face.

'I am surprised,' I said, 'that you gave the job to a deaf and dumb girl.'

'What rot are you talking?' Surprise had deepened the frown until it covered his entire face.

'I cannot do registered letters. Give me telegrams, give me insurance. I can even sit at the dispatch desk. But I cannot handle registered letters any more.'

He stared long at me in astonishment. Then he seemed to understand something. Putting down his pen, he asked me to sit down on the chair opposite him. Then he began to polish his glasses with unusual care. He did not realize that the tears filling his eyes had made his glasses misty. Blinking the tears away, he put both his elbows on the desk and said in a soft tone, 'It is not good to get irritated with this lady. She has had to suffer a lot in her short life, a lot that was terrible and hateful. She has been through hell.' He stopped and put his trembling, wrinkled hand on mine. 'No one else on the staff should get wind of this. I can tell you because I have faith in your wisdom.'

Holding his hand in mine, I conveyed my silent gratitude to his eyes.

'She used to stay with her mother in Abbottabad. She didn't have a father. They lived on the rent from their property. She was studying at college when the riots for Pakistan started. The monsters didn't let her return home. Crying and helpless, the mother came this side alone.

'She moved into a small room in our neighbourhood. This girl was freed after two years. What memories she must have brought with her you can guess, you who write stories and bring out the secrets hidden in the human heart.'

My tears fell on his hand. He looked up and said, 'I have great faith in your sympathetic heart. That is why I put her with you. You shouldn't be angry with her. Yes, she is strange because she has seen a very ugly side of life. She may never be able to be normal again with people. Her mother told my wife that even now she wakes up in fright at night and stares at the dark shadows, that the sight of every man makes her legs tremble, that sparks begin to fly from her eyes and she coils into herself.'

When I returned to my seat, she was bent over the pile of letters, lost to her surroundings and deeply engrossed in her work. The crowd on the other side of the counter was feasting on her sad beauty with its hungry eyes. Quietly, I sat on my chair. I put the receipt book in front of me, but could not clear the mist from my eyes; the small piece of pencil trembled and jerked in my hand. It was good that the registration counter was tucked away in a corner, else I would surely have attracted the curiosity of the entire staff.

Clouds of sadness had descended upon my heart. If they had shed their burden in one go, I would have felt lighter. But they only threatened to rain; the sadness rose to my head like some strong wine and I felt my entire being drip like a drenched piece of cloth. If only I could cry... I yearned to find some quiet corner and hold my head in my hands and cry.

There was no one at the counter. She had gone through the work quickly, or else I had lost track of time. I wanted to look towards her, but I didn't have the heart. But then my eyes gave way to temptation and, when she turned towards me, the gathered clouds opened up and great torrents of tears seemed to engulf my spirit. I threw my head down on my folded arms on the counter and began to cry.

Without raising my head I knew she was looking at me. But I could not hold my tears until my soul had been thoroughly drenched and then, when I looked up, I realized with a start that she was staring at me with eyes which were free of hatred and fear. For the first time I saw signs of life playing on that crystalline face, as if some rays of sunshine had lit up the heart of a frozen lake.

The next morning, again, she was there before me. When I arrived, she looked up at me and I saw her lips tremble. It seemed that, finally, she was about to speak. Then she took out a fresh piece of paper from the drawer and revived our correspondence.

'Yesterday, you cried. I wondered: can a man also cry? I was thinking of it all night. I thought I would ask you in the morning.'

'A man, too, is made of the same dust,' I wrote back in reply. 'Men and women inherit the same emotions and feelings.'

A sarcastic smile crossed her lips. She narrowed her eyes and I saw the sparks again.

'Men are symbols of control. Crying is for weak women. It's very easy to shed tears after all.'

'Men are also brothers,' I wrote. 'Born of the same parents, warm and with hearts like oceans, looking for the best matches for their dear sisters. Men are also fathers, who love their daughters even more than mothers do and cannot control their sobs when they give the daughters away in marriage. Men are also husbands, yearning, suffering in love.' Then I scratched out the last sentence and, pushing the paper towards her, tried to catch her changing expression from the corner of my eye.

A queer discomfort had taken hold of her, as if the link of some chain had slipped from her hands or some strange breeze had passed her by. Then the discomfort passed and her face set. A while later, I noted a softness in her eyes. She turned to the piece of paper to write.

'My father died when I was still a child. I had one brother who, too, died before I had grown up. My mother still gets by remembering him.'

After an astonished gap I was writing again, 'The merciless and ugly destiny that entrapped your innocent life like a serpent has shaken you deeply, but time and distance can heal the deepest and most poisonous wounds. You'll be well again.'

She seemed to shake with fear. She fixed me with a gaze that was startled and scared and watchful. A quick shadow passed within me. But the paper was in her hand, and, this time, I could not scratch out the sentence.

'The postmaster told me...' I took the paper from her hand and wrote. 'But do not worry. Look into my eyes. You will find belief.'

Then she looked into my eyes. She kept looking, and a tiny light struggled to reach her face. There was a lot churning inside her. Then she took a deep breath, as if the tightly wound straps of her life had loosened a bit, as if someone had taken down her soul from the burning cross and fanned it.

She lowered those bright, captivating eyes and wrote, 'I do not know what to do. All this is so sudden...' Then two heavy drops fell from her eyes and got fixed to the paper like stars. She hid her face in her dupatta, and I could see that she was now crying freely.

I didn't want to come in the way of this fortunate crying. At the same time, the peon with the deformed face brought and slammed down another pile of letters on the counter, and I thought that his face really did not seem so deformed at all. I got engrossed in my receipt book. Strange, when I had been crying the previous day she had got through the registered letters, and today...

When the letters were disposed off, I turned to her. She was already looking at me. Her gaze was soft, as if the sharp edges of her feelings had been rounded off. She did not move her gaze from my eyes for a long time, as if scared that were she to look away, she would once again be engulfed by killer whirlpools.

The colour of her eyes dissolved in my every pore. Every nerve of mine was tingling; music had entered my heart. Beyond the hedge, under the sunlit sky and beyond the whispering saffron fields, I thought I could see waterfalls. And my quick heartbeat brought the message of some rising tide.

'What's your name?' I asked. 'Please speak and tell me. This internal correspondence that you've started within the post office—I don't like it.'

She started at my speaking, as if speaking was something strange.

'Speak,' I said, 'I need to know your name.'

'Tripat,' she replied.

'What a beautiful name,' I said. 'And your voice...I told you that your lips spoke of sweetness.'

I saw that her forehead was flushed pink, flowers bloomed in her cheeks, a happy twinkle appeared in her eyes and she looked away.

'Tripat, I want to spend my life with you.'

Her response was a slightly questioning glance, as if she had not quite understood my meaning.

'If you ever give me the chance, I will win your confidence every morning, every evening. Tripat, I want to marry you.'

The pink flowers on her cheeks changed to lilac. Then those, too, vanished and were replaced by the paleness of cactus flowers.

'You...even after knowing everything...'

'Yes, Tripat,' I said. 'Can I be so fortunate?'

Gradually, a shy colour returned to her face, a virgin coyness touched with a child's innocence. My answer was in her eyes, and then they filled up, as if they wanted to rain tears again.

'No, Tripat,' I said. 'It's not good to give away life too much to tears. Look at the sunlit valleys of the future where countless smiles are yearning for the touch of your lips.'

The postmaster was standing behind us.

'How goes the work?' he asked.

'With the companion you have given me, I find the toughest jobs in life easy.'

'What?' he asked. I had clearly surprised him.

I said, 'We need your blessings to do everything together in life, besides these registered letters.'

He looked at Tripat, then at me, and understood everything.

'You are a true writer. Now I can believe in your stories. I will talk to Tripat's mother myself.'

Qazi da Kot

A little celebration was on at deep dusk around the Lamba well, a kilometre or so from Qazi da Kot. A few chickens had been roasted, and the bottles looted from the Arora wine shop were being emptied rapidly. On a fire of acacia stumps, a young calf was being cooked with rice in a large vessel.

The warriors of the newly formed Pakistan had looted Qazi da Kot that evening. The ones with horses had stuffed their saddlebags with the fresh loot, and had returned to their villages or were on the way. But most of the warriors were not so fortunate, having come on this looting campaign on foot, and had to return on foot carrying their loot with them. Seeing the approaching night, they had decided to sleep at the Lamba well.

Hashmat belonged to the Musali tribe. He took two sips from the bottle and turned his squint eye towards the Kashmiri labourer, Ghulam Sarwar, who, like his entire ilk, was colloquially referred to as Hatho.

'Oye Hatho, why are you slumped down like that?'

'Just look at him,' Jumma the oil presser added his bit, 'as if he has come to bury his mother.'

Ghulam Sarwar grit his teeth but didn't say anything.

'Tell me, Hatho,' Hashmat the Musali mocked, 'you couldn't

get your hands on anything in such a rich village?'

'He did, of course. He looted this lantern!' Jumma rubbed salt into the wound.

Jumma the oil presser was not lying. In the chaos of the last two or three hours, Ghulam Sarwar had not looted anything from this prosperous village except a lantern. The previous night he had tripped and broken the chimney of his own lantern and, to make up for that loss, he had unenthusiastically and hesitatingly picked up a lighted one from a looted house.

'I say, Jumma.' Hashmat pulled Jumma out of the hooch-induced comfort.

'Go on, Musali,' he responded.

'It isn't good that this Hatho didn't get a thing. He didn't get his hands wet even in a flowing river. Oye Hatho, we're with you. Why are you staring at the ground? Here, take a couple of swigs.'

Ghulam Sarwar turned away his face. He had never touched this prohibited thing. Even when they had been looting the Arora wine shop he had stood aside, watching the drama. He hadn't been interested in looting anything else in Qazi da Kot either. The purpose with which he had joined the mob had remained unfulfilled. Most of the women they had found in the houses were already dead, having swallowed poison when they heard the mob entering the village. Those who had hesitated or were caught unawares had been taken away by the strong Gondal Jat boys. Nobody had paid heed to Ghulam Sarwar's need, or the fact that he was now nearly forty and hadn't been close to a woman's shadow so far.

All of a sudden Ghulam Sarwar looked up. Then he stood up straight. He had an axe in one hand and a lantern in the other. When he started walking quickly towards Qazi da Kot, Karima the butcher called out, 'What's happened to him? Oye Hatho, there's nothing left there now.'

'Let him go,' the Musali said. 'I mean to say, was he paralysed at that time? And is he now going to sift the ash?'

'Some are habituated to it,' Karima remarked.

'What did you say?' the Musali asked.

'I said, some are habituated to it.'

'To what?'

'To sifting ash.'

'Exactly what I said.'

Ghulam Sarwar knew he was only going to sift through the ash. But sometimes one can find a pearl in ash.

Time was when his young heart had been full of desires. But as the years passed, his yearnings began to die. Now in his middle age, a longing had risen in his heart again, along with the birth of Pakistan, a longing that whirled inside him like some misguided bat.

He began to search each of the looted houses of the village. In that carnival of destruction all he saw were dead bodies. Disappointed, he turned to go when he saw a house whose door seemed bolted from the inside. The doors of the other looted houses were wide open.

Ghulam Sarwar knocked on the door. Then he shook it with all his might. But no one opened the door. Convinced that someone was hiding inside, he broke it down with a few strong blows of his axe.

An unconscious young woman clung to the body of a young Sikh in the long lobby of the house. She hadn't come to even with the noise of the door being broken with the axe.

Ghulam Sarwar raised the lantern and looked around. The lobby led to a large hall, and when he glanced into it he instantly realized that this wasn't a house but a gurdwara. He surmised that the body was of the granthi of the gurdwara, and his wife had lost consciousness as she mourned him. He hadn't been in the group that had killed the granthi. The mob had divided itself into four groups as it had entered the village, so as to block off the four directions and prevent any Hindu or Sikh from escaping.

Ghulam Sarwar lowered the lantern near the dead man's face. He could make out from the man's complexion and features that he was Kashmiri. He knew that when young Sikh men left Kashmir they didn't go to chop wood or carry loads; they became granthis in the gurdwaras of Punjab or cooks in prosperous homes.

The young man had not been over thirty, and his wife was a few years younger. He couldn't get his eyes off the beauty of that unconscious face. What luck, he thought. Truly God's mills grind slowly but surely: a young woman and that, too, beautiful as a fairy. The important thing was that she wasn't Punjabi but a Kashmiri. From his own land. Her body was made of the clay of Kashmir. Allah had reserved her for Ghulam Sarwar. No Gondal, no Cheema, no Varaich could lay claim to her. They were all Punjabis who deserved to be hated. If Allah had saved her from the eyes of those rogues then it was only for Ghulam Sarwar Kashmiri.

The lascivious stare seemed to awaken the girl. She raised her tear-stained face and looked at him. Sparks of hatred flashed in her eyes. It seemed to Ghulam Sarwar that those sparks would engulf him in a blaze. He averted his gaze from those burning eyes and said, 'I didn't do this. I didn't kill your Sardar. By the Holy Quran.'

The sparks didn't lessen.

'I'm speaking the truth. This is the handiwork of Punjabi Muslims. I am a Muslim, of course, but a Kashmiri Muslim, your countryman. I don't like bloodshed. I hate Punjabis. They are not human beings but butchers. They have burnt village after village. They have mown down Hindus and Sikhs like carrots and radishes.'

When he paused to catch his breath, he thought for a moment that he was having some effect on her, and the hatred flashing in her eyes had lessened.

He spoke with a little more daring now, 'If only I'd been here at that moment, no one would have dared to look towards your Sardar. I'd have cut them in pieces. I'd have given up my life but would have saved my brother from Kashmir.'

Despite his words, the eyes continued to emit sparks. Catching the direction of her look he said, 'This axe? I carry it around just like that. I swear on God that I have never killed a man with it, only chopped wood. And see, there is no axe wound on the Sardar's body. That deep wound on the temple is from a spear, and his insides have been dragged out with a sharp sickle. Believe me, I'm not one of those looters and killers.'

'Then what have you come here for?'

He started when she broke her silence suddenly.

'I've come to take you.' Ghulam Sarwar thought it wise to speak the truth.

Like a flash of lightning, the girl's hand flew to the dagger hanging from her black sash.

'Beware,' she shouted. 'Don't you dare touch me. Or there'll be not one but two bodies here. The second one will be mine or yours.'

Ghulam Sarwar realized that this battle wasn't going to be as easy as he'd thought. He would have to approach it sensibly. He shouldn't try to grab victory in one go but proceed in tiny careful steps.

'Get out from here, you monster!' the girl's voice was like the roar of a tigress.

Ghulam Sarwar was finding it difficult to understand the situation. He had never before seen the warrior form of a woman. Then a clever thought crossed his mind.

'I'll go,' he said in a low voice, 'but first...'

'First what?'

'Give me something to eat first. I'm dying of hunger. I swear by the Prophet that I haven't eaten anything since dawn.'

'I'll make you a roti. But swear that you will get out after eating it.'

'I swear.'

'Come in.' She crossed into the courtyard of the gurdwara. 'But remember, no tricks.' Her hand went again to the steel dagger at her side.

The courtyard of the gurdwara was long and wide. The side where the three doors of the hall opened into it was paved, but the rest was not and a thick crop of maize stood there. Ghulam Sarwar understood how the girl had managed to escape from the mob.

The girl kept a sharp eye on him as she lit the fire and made the roti.

'You hid in the maize?'

She nodded in assent.

'What's your name?'

She didn't reply.

'I'm asking your name.'

'What's my name to you?'

'Is it a crime to ask someone's name?'

'Anup. Anup Kaur.'

'You've come from Kashmir?'

'Yes.'

'Where from?'

'Tekri Shah Murad.'

'I'm from Rangpur. My maternal grandparents are in Tekri Shah Murad. Only ten kilometres separate Rangpur from Tekri Shah Murad.'

She didn't say anything. Silently she kept putting roti after roti on his plate.

As the roti and dal went into his hungry stomach, Ghulam Sarwar's wavering hopes began to rise again. This big-talking woman was actually very weak and vulnerable. Her husband had been killed by the mob and she was alone, surrounded by enemies, in a land which had suddenly become foreign. She had no option left but to surrender to him. She would flap her wings for a while but would fall into his hands ultimately. Little did she realize that the short dagger, with which she repeatedly threatened him, would hardly pierce Ghulam Sarwar's hard-working steely muscles. It would be good if she agreed gently; otherwise it would only take one blow of his hammer-like hand to subdue her.

If, after her husband's death, anyone had a right to this woman born in Tekri Shah Murad, then surely this right belonged to Ghulam Sarwar of Rangpur. They were both born of the soil of Kashmir. So what if her name was not Begma, Noora or Reshma but Anup? What difference did a name make? He resolved that he would take his right and would keep it safe from the rioters. He would not allow any Chimni, Gondal, Cheema or Varaich to as much as look towards her. Those Punjabi animals had taken away thousands of Hindu and Sikh women of the area, both married and unmarried. Only he had a right to this one born of Kashmir, and he would die for the sake of this right.

He had been very hungry, no doubt, but it was also true that he had made the food an excuse. Actually he was waiting for the night to deepen, so that everybody would be fast asleep. Only the Muslim mobs posed a danger to him, not Hindus or Sikhs. His intention was to go from Qazi da Kot to Gujranwala railway station after midnight, and catch the train to Rawalpindi at five in the morning. From Rawalpindi to Poochan was a six-hour ride by lorry. He had no doubt that he would succeed in his intentions. Though this woman didn't look like she would melt easily, he too had resolved that even if he had to use force and cruelty, he would not let go of this gift from Allah.

He was hardly a stranger to force and cruelty. After all, this world, this life had used all kinds of force and cruelty on him. He had been hardly ten when he'd had to leave his home, his homeland. He had spent six years of his innocent youth cleaning utensils at the shop of a baker, Kadir Bakhsh, in Rawalpindi. He was paid only an anna and given two meals. The smallest of mistakes would result in a sound beating and the forfeiture of the evening meal as well as the anna. He had slept countless hungry nights on the rough shelf in the shop, a worn-out blanket under him and his knees stuck to his stomach. Though Kadir Bakhsh's shop had a common wall with the Friday mosque, he had no fear of God. In fact, he was less a baker and more a butcher.

When Ghulam Sarwar was seventeen and his limbs became capable of hard physical labour, he took up work at a Sardar's timber yard across the Mission School. He was the only labourer in the huge yard. In the flush of youth he thought nothing of splitting fifteen maunds of acacia logs in a day. The Sardar was very happy with him and paid him five annas a day. Then someone said that Kashmiri labourers were paid more as one went from Rawalpindi towards Lahore. Ghulam Sarwar left the Sardar's employment and Rawalpindi and went to Jhelum, which had the largest market for construction timber in Punjab. He spent three years in the timber market there, pulling the saw and splitting the blocks of deodar. The fine dust of the wood would fill up his soul and each nerve, each muscle in his body would ache. Then he abandoned Jhelum and reached Gujranwala. He spent many years where new buildings were coming up, carrying brickloads or preparing lime and mud plaster for seven annas a day. One day he heard from another Kashmiri labourer that Choudhry Ali Ahmed of Bhatian in 'Pindi was building a new mansion, and was paying eight annas a day, besides two meals. So he moved from Gujranwala to Pindi Bhatian. After the birth of Pakistan, when the mobs of Muslim peasants of Pindi Bhatian had rushed to loot Hindu and Sikh villages, he too had picked up his axe and joined them.

All his life he had seen force and cruelty. The strong had destroyed his home and poisoned his childhood. The memory of the injustices of his childhood would hover in his soul like the hood of a serpent. The back-breaking labour for earning his livelihood had crushed that serpent's hood, but the bitter poison of that crushed hood was ever present in his mouth.

He had been treated like an animal for all his labour in foreign lands. He couldn't recall if he'd ever been called by his name after leaving Kashmir. Whoever called him and whenever they called him, addressed him only as 'Hatho'. The hidden contempt in that word had stung him all his life.

'Water,' he asked, after the last sip of dal. 'You didn't give me water with my food.'

She got up to pour water from the earthen pitcher that rested on its stand near the wall of the hall. As she glanced through the half-open door, she started and the glass fell from her hands. The Granth Sahib had not been put to its nightly rest yet. Like lightning she went into the room and took her place by the holy book.

Ghulam Sarwar saw red as the girl ran into the room. But he was surprised that she had left the door wide open. Picking up his axe, he followed her into the hall. As soon as he stepped in, he felt all his strength, all his energy draining into the ground. The axe fell from his hand and he crumpled on the cotton matting. The girl was sitting on the wooden platform and reading the holy book of the Sikhs in the light of the lantern. The ends of the thick muslin dupatta that covered her head were tucked behind her ears.

Suddenly a childhood memory, one that he had spent a lifetime trying to forget, forged its way into his mind. It seemed he wasn't in the gurdwara at Qazi da Kot but at home in Rangpur, and his mother was reading the word of God, bent over the Holy Quran. She had doubled her thick black muslin dupatta on her head and tucked its ends behind her ears. Her dupatta had a tear in the middle and it was for that reason that she used to double it up, so that her head would be fully covered, in respect for the Quran. That was his last memory of his mother, which he had hugged all his life even as he had tried to forget it. His mother had been reading the Quran and he, a ten-year-old boy, had been slurping kahwa from an earthen cup, when Jamadar Bikram Singh had leapt off his horse and come in. He recalled clearly the thick lips and brown gums of the jamadar as he barked out the command that his mother must go to Jagirdar Karamat Ali. Caressing his head and kissing him on his forehead, his mother left, compelled to go with Jamadar Bikram Singh. To deny his command would have invited disaster.

Earlier, the jamadar had similarly taken away his father, Fateh Din, the poorest farmer in Rangpur, in debt to the roots of his hair, to the moneylender. Every year Fateh Din would sow rice on his postage stamp of land, and would reap a harvest of tears. That year the rice crop had failed, and the farmers of Rangpur and Tekri Shah Murad had resolved not to give a third of their produce to the jagirdar. Then one of them had gone and squealed to the jagirdar, and named his father among those who had incited the rest. His mother, who was in the habit of visiting shrines for forty days in a row to pray for the well-being of her husband and son, had sat down with the Holy Quran to pray for her husband's return, when she too got called away to the jagirdar.

The vision of his mother wrapped up in her doubled black muslin dupatta reading the Holy Quran was etched forever on his soul, because after that he saw neither his mother nor his father again. In a while, news began to surface in Rangpur and Tekri Shah Murad. People said that the jagirdar had caned his father till he died. His body had been thrown into the ravine to feed the vultures and kites. Jamadar Bikram Singh had kept his mother in his camp for three nights. Early on the fourth day, she had run away and jumped into the river.

Then how was it that his mother, who had died thirty years ago, was sitting today on the wooden platform before him? The same age, the same complexion, the same features, the same black dupatta of thick muslin, the same ends tucked away behind the ears...

He saw, and his guilty soul trembled. The knowledge of the sin that he had contemplated scourged his consciousness. His life had been destroyed anyway, but by committing this sin he had been about to ruin his afterlife too. Though he had not laid a hand on that vision of purity, the seed of sin that had burst in his soul could not have been hidden from God. He had no doubt that worms would infest his grave and he would burn in the fires of hell.

Transfixed, he kept looking at her for a while. Then he could no longer bear the glow of that bright forehead. Picking up his axe, he struggled to his feet. His breath caught in his throat. Coming out of the hall, he filled a glass of water from the earthen pitcher and drained it. His eyes rested on the storeroom stuffed with acacia logs. He brought out some logs from the storeroom, and began to split them with his axe.

When Anup finished the service of putting the Granth Sahib to rest, she came into the courtyard and stared at him in surprise.

'For your Sardar's pyre,' explained Ghulam Sarwar, wiping the sweat off his forehead.

Together they arranged the pyre in the long entrance of the gurdwara. When Anup was reciting the last prayer, Ghulam Sarwar stood bent, hands on his knees, as if he was reciting the namaz.

When the flames of the pyre rose high, Anup saw a few tears fall from Ghulam Sarwar's eyes on to his wide chest.

His voice, too, was choked with tears when he said, 'I've heard that the Hindus and Sikhs of Gujranwala are collecting in the gurdwara near the pond. If I can take you there... After that, let it be God's will.'

Seeing her hesitate, he continued, 'Move now. I can think of nothing else, and why should we waste time?'

The shadows of suspicion had not yet vanished from the girl's eyes.

'I swear by the Holy Quran that you are my sister, you are my mother. If anyone casts an evil eye on you on the way, my axe will cut him to pieces.'

The wounded night was still sobbing, but the sobs could not be heard. The silence was so thick that it seemed as if the sky had clamped its hand on the night's mouth.

Anup walked in front. Her one hand held the holy book, wrapped in silken layers, on her head. The other held the lantern. Ghulam Sarwar did not need any lantern. A lamp had been lit in the darkness of his soul. Gathering the light of this lamp in his mind and heart, looking left and right like an alert guard, he followed a few steps behind Anup.

A Defender of Humanity

Today I thought of you again. I always remember you this way, all of a sudden. And I remember you often. Always when the sun is shining brightly on my life, chasing away the shadows. When the valley of my life is wreathed in smiles, when sunflowers are blooming, when my son comes back victorious from some debate competition, when my daughter makes a new design of Japanese ikebana, when my wife puts a plate of my favourite peas pulao in front of me, wipes her hands on the end of her sari and smiles at me, I remember you all of a sudden, with all my heart.

That was how it happened today too. My daughter was telling jokes and we were all doubling up with laughter. She's got an endless store of jokes. Doctor jokes, lawyer jokes, husband–wife jokes, priest jokes, truck-driver jokes. Today she was cracking truck-driver jokes when without warning my eyes filled up with tears and I left the lawn and withdrew to my room. I could hear my daughter's voice coming after me.

'I bet that Papa has gone to write a story.'

I hadn't gotten up from the lawn to write a story. But my daughter's words woke your story up inside me. Why not write your story today? The story that has been stoking your memory in my mind for these last thirty-six years.

That cloudy morning of September 1947 is fresh in my mind, the morning when all of us climbed into your lorry. You were in the driver's seat, intently looking into the mirror to straighten the Pathan turban that you had tied over the little black cap on your head.

Outside the lorry it was all mist and cloud. Inside there was utter terror. The passengers sat, huddled into themselves, their hearts in their mouths. Even in this atmosphere of fear I was transfixed by your fine features, your handsome face. The mingling of Pathani, Pothohari, Greek and Afghani beauty that had been taking place for centuries in northwestern India seemed to have reached its apogee in your face.

Suddenly someone exclaimed, 'Look, the earlier lorry has returned.'

We all turned to look. The lorry that had left at six in the morning from Rawalpindi for Srinagar had indeed returned. Its passengers were frozen with fear, unable to speak. But its Muslim driver was relating, with extravagant gestures, how the tribals had reached the road that ran from Rawalpindi to Srinagar, how they had fired upon the lorry near Ghorhagalli and tried to puncture its tyres, how he had not lost his nerve but had brought the passengers back to safety by driving the lorry in reverse gear for nearly six furlongs.

There was no joy on the faces of the passengers who had been rescued. They knew that the death they had escaped now awaited them here. All the routes for getting out of Rawalpindi to India had been cut off. Trainloads of passengers were being massacred even before they got to Jhelum or Wazirabad. In the last ten days not a single train had managed to pass Lahore and reach Amritsar safely, and now there were no trains running at all. There had been some hope of escaping by road towards Srinagar. Now this hope, too, had been strangled by the tribal raiders. The stabbing incidents in Rawalpindi itself were on the rise and one by one they would all be killed. They hadn't a shred of hope left.

At that moment you turned back and looked at your passengers, saw their distress, read the intense hopelessness in their eyes and took measure of the terror that gripped their souls. I saw a dark glint appear in your fearless eyes. Thumping your chest you said, 'I will take you to Srinagar, even if I have to stake my life on it. Are your ready to go?'

Such courage coming from a Muslim driver couldn't but touch the hearts of the Hindu and Sikh passengers. They were ready to go; in any case, they had no other choice.

The driver of the first lorry pleaded, 'Don't go, Hussain. Think of yourself: you have an old mother, an unwed sister.'

But you paid him no heed and put your foot down on the accelerator.

Nurpur, Kohmurree, Nathiagali, Ghorhagalli passed without incident. Kohalla was twenty-five miles from Ghorhagalli. At Kohalla there was a bridge across the Jhelum River. On this side of the bridge the new country of Pakistan ended, and on the other side the territory of Kashmir state began. It was downhill all the way from Ghorhagalli to Kohalla and the lorry had picked up speed. But the passengers were still afraid. Would they ever cross that bridge to breathe free in the India of Gandhi and Nehru, or would their bodies be picked to the bone by vultures on these rough hilly slopes under a merciless sky? Holding their breath, they watched each passing milestone. Now Kohalla was seventeen miles away.

Then suddenly we heard gunfire and saw blood spurting from your left arm. Behind me sat Pritam Singh Sodhi, a compounder who used to volunteer his services at the Rawalpindi Singh Sabha's charitable hospital. He jumped to his feet. Your wound wasn't deep. The bullet had gouged a gash through your muscle and gone out of the lorry's window. Pritam Singh Sodhi took out the first-aid kit from his suitcase and bandaged you. Even as he was ministering to you, you didn't let the lorry's speed slacken one bit. You had lost a lot of blood but your face was still flushed with determination and the black glint in your fearless eyes had not dimmed a whit.

We heard the sound of gunshots again when we were only twelve miles from Kohalla. We looked in all directions. Twenty yards behind us stood four young tribal men, their rifles aimed at the lorry's tyres.

'Is there a driver among you?' you asked, without taking your eyes off the road. 'If so, then he should come up here fast.'

Jodh Singh spoke up, 'I've been driving buses for the Nanda Bus Service from 'Pindi to Lahore. But I don't have any experience on hilly roads.'

'Hold the steering wheel,' you said. 'It's downhill all the way to Kohalla. Keep your foot on the brake. And for the sake of your Guru, don't stop the lorry this side of Kohalla.'

And you stepped up to Sardar Shamsher Singh and requested, 'Sardar ji, please give me your sword.'

Uncomprehending but without a minute's hesitation, Sardar Shamsher Singh handed you his three-foot-long sword. You unsheathed it and jumped off the moving lorry, saying, 'God be with you.' We saw you roll into the bushes and then swerve off into a bunch of trees. In your hand was the gleaming sword that Guru Gobind Singh had put into the hands of the Khalsa to protect the weak. It looked beautiful in your hand because it was the sword of humanity and you were the defender of humanity.

Three more bullets were fired but they didn't touch the tyres. Then the bullets stopped. We could see that your gleaming sword had caused pandemonium among those young tribals.

I don't know what happened to you. You were one against

four. And who knows how many more were hiding in the trees. And they had rifles.

When you jumped out of the moving lorry, I sent up a prayer, 'May Allah protect you, Hussain. May he grant you the remaining lifespan of cowards like me.'

I do not know if He heard my prayer or whether they finished you off. What happened to your mother, what became of your sister, that too I do not know.

But I remember you often, and always in the happy moments of my life. This life and its joys are your gift to me. That is why when your memory knocks at my door, a hundred prayers burst forth from my heart. I hope to God that you are still alive. But if you're not, I hope that Allah has given you a place in heaven. Wherever you may be, through this story today I send you my salutation, the salutation of my wife, son, daughter and of all humanity.